P. J. Allen

DEAD RECKONING IN FREDERICK

authorHOUSE®

AuthorHouse™
1663 Liberty Drive
Bloomington, IN 47403
www.authorhouse.com
Phone: 1 (800) 839-8640

Published by AuthorHouse 06/23/2017

ISBN: 978-1-5246-9551-4 (sc)
ISBN: 978-1-5246-9552-1 (hc)
ISBN: 978-1-5246-9553-8 (e)

Library of Congress Control Number: 2017908893

Print information available on the last page.

This book is printed on acid-free paper.

Disclaimer

This is a work of fiction. Some places in Frederick and the environs are real, such as restaurants, the National Museum of Civil War Medicine, Baker Park and Mt. Olivet Cemetery. Names of current characters (not historic individuals) and other buildings, places, events, and incidents are either the products of the author's imagination or used in a fictitious manner. Any other resemblance to actual persons, living or dead, or actual events is purely coincidental.

To the exploited

Acknowledgments

I would like to thank Diane Daugherty for her very helpful editing of the book and for her thoughtful comments and suggestions. It is a better story due to her insights.

I also would like to thank Monique Pasquale for the hospitality she offered me and my husband, Howard, for being so generous in introducing us to her wide network of friends and family in Frederick, and for helping to make us residents of this fine town.

Prologue

No lie is strong enough to kill
The roots that work below,
From your rich dust and slaughtered will
A tree with tongues shall grow.
—Countee Cullen

"Shhh. Stop whimpering. Move!" The young man tripped as he tried to comply with the order. "Believe me—you do not want to be caught."

"It's hard to see."

"Of course it is."

"Is everyone with us?" the gruff voice inquired to his partner bringing up the rear.

"Yeah, everyone except for Lucas."

"Oh, yeah? Well, he should have listened to me."

There was an immediate reaction to this statement, with the dozen or so men and women whispering among themselves. All were carrying their only belongings. Some had them tied in a large shirt or skirt. Some had found a knapsack of sorts. Some wore shoddy footwear; others were barefoot.

"It's so cold," someone murmured.

"Here, use my cloak."

"Shhh. I'm telling you, if we don't stay quiet, we won't be safe. Mind my words."

The group rounded a corner to see a downward grade along the muddy, slippery path into more darkness.

"How much longer?" a young woman asked, sounding fearful and tired.

"Not long."

"Will it be better than where we were?"

"About the same. Okay? Things will get better soon, though. I promise."

"Promises, promises."

"What did you say?"

"Nothin'."

"If you don't like the situation, go ahead and leave. But you won't last long out there, and *that* is a promise."

Aside from an occasional cough, silence ensued as the group continued to march on.

"Okay, hold on; the shelter is coming up."

The group stopped and stared ahead, noting the outline of a new abode.

"Looks like we're never goin' ta get a break," one man whispered.

"You got that right."

Chapter

1

As a rule, men worry more about what they can't see
than about what they can.
—Julius Caesar

"Don't go there. It's not time. We're not ready."

Kayla peered into the shadow-filled room. She didn't know if her heart was pounding because of the ascent up the stairs or due to anticipation. Her breathing halted momentarily due to the musty, damp odor that permeated the room. Her eyes widened as she strained to see what the room possessed. Windows on the opposite wall distorted her vision. The shadows danced, black on more black. Perhaps moving tree limbs were creating them, but it was unclear; it was too dark.

She heard a subtle schussing. *Could be tree limbs, but then again?* Though somewhat anxious and heart still pounding, Kayla was definitely intrigued, despite what her colleague, Henry, was whispering.

"I think it's okay. I *know* it's okay," Kayla whispered back with conviction.

She moved stealthily into the room and flashed successive photos, creating a strobe light effect for anyone watching from the street.

"That's it. Let's go," Kayla said, turning hastily to leave. But from the corner of her eye, she caught a movement. It passed in front of one of the windows. The movement was large enough that it obstructed even her minimal vision for a split-second.

"Did you see that?"

"What?"

Kayla glanced back to see if she could make anything out, but whatever it was, if there had been anything at all, it did not reappear.

———————•◦•———————

The motion detector light flicked on as Kayla pulled into her narrow driveway in the alley behind West Fourth Street. She jumped out of her car and headed quickly to her shed with her camera and other paraphernalia. In fact, it wasn't actually a shed. It had been a carriage house way back when. It had remained on the property in a rather dilapidated state, so she'd turned it into a darkroom after installing electricity and plumbing. The interior was primarily brick, though one wall was stone. Kayla had left the old wavy glass windows in but had strengthened their support by replacing some of the wood frames that had developed wood rot. A corner built-in wardrobe was the only furniture that had been in the building. She had built-in wardrobes in her house, too. The floor was also brick, so she'd added thick carpets for ambiance as well as winter warmth—a necessity given the twenty-foot ceiling. Locals reckoned it had been built in the late 1700s.

The carriage house was a bit spooky, too. Over the years, it had been a residence, with living quarters for the caretaker in the tiny upstairs with its tiny fireplace. Kayla often thought that even though people were shorter back then, compared to now, the caretaker must have walked around all hunched over when he went upstairs. She always did.

Kayla's house was old too, but not this old. The realtor had told her it was built in the 1860s. It stood about five hundred feet from the former carriage house. It also had the wavy glass windows. She'd been lucky enough to buy it after selling her house in Fairfax County, Virginia, where she'd worked as a commercial photographer: family photos, crying babies, uncooperative dogs, and argumentative weddings.

Working for a paranormal agency was quite a step up, Kayla figured, and after moving to Frederick, she felt like she owned a piece of history.

Now, finally, she could get to work. Being in her darkroom was one of Kayla's most satisfying times. Here, all of the hard work and intrigue came to fruition. Actually, that wasn't exactly right. It *might* come to fruition. That type of outcome, the fruition thing, was a rarity, but it was the possibility that drove her. Kayla entered the room with that usual feeling of anticipation and kicked on Frank Sinatra or *Ol' Blue Eyes* as his ardent fans called him.

Even the lingering acerbic smell of the chemicals from the last time she'd been here excited her. Being a photographer had been a dream since fifth grade. Mrs. Gleason, Kayla's teacher, became one of her favorite adults that wonderful school year. The way Mrs. Gleason taught American history was unique. For every historical event the syllabus required, if the textbook did not include a female who also played an impactful role, Mrs. Gleason found one. During the session about the Great Depression, Mrs. Gleason introduced the class to Dorothea Lange and her iconic photo *Human Erosion in California (Migrant Mother)*. Kayla cried when she saw it. Here was a pretty woman with two small, unkempt children clutching their mother as she held an infant. To Kayla, the deep lines of worry etched in the mother's face suggested utter hopelessness.

She was right. Mrs. Gleason explained that the woman photographed by Lange was thirty-two but looked at least ten years older. She, her husband, and seven children lived in a lean-to. They were sustained by frozen vegetables from the ground and birds that the children killed. Lange sent her captivating yet heartbreaking photos and written descriptions to a local newspaper, which sent them to the White House. Kayla smiled while thinking about what happened next: President Franklin D. Roosevelt had twenty thousand pounds of food sent to the migrant workers.

That was then, Kayla thought, *and now, eighty years later, an improvement in humanity is a certainty; isn't it?*

Kayla knew right then and there that she, too, wanted to be a photographer. She was going to make people's lives better through her photos, just as Lange had. The documentary photographer, along with Mrs. Gleason, were her role models and heroes.

She hadn't made it to that pinnacle yet. In fact, she'd been a regular commercial photographer, until that night at the bar when she'd met the Dulany Paranormal Team. But she couldn't think about that now. She had work to do.

Kayla set up her trays as she'd done so many times before and then held her negatives up to the light. She cross-referenced them with her digital photos, trying to detect any difference. Disappointed, she noted nothing of interest within the digital set.

She nonetheless persevered and examined the negatives, beginning with the one she wanted to enlarge first—the last photo she'd taken just an hour ago. Kayla turned on the light and then set the lens aperture and adjusted the focus. It was a black-and-white photo, and she wanted to make it as sharp as possible. She'd learned that black and white were more conducive to contrast compared to color photos, and given the nature of the pictures, contrast was imperative. Lange's photos were so impressive in part because they were black-and-white, a fact that added to Kayla's commitment to excellence.

Kayla developed her test strip and then examined the results. Of the six photos, one turned out to be especially crisp. It was the one she most wanted to develop.

As the image began to appear, Kayla held her breath. Once it formed, she turned on the bright lights, shook it, and hung it up to dry. Then she pulled out her magnifying glass. Slowly, slowly, she circled the glass around the photo, looking for anything out of the ordinary.

What was that? She could not get a good fix on something in the corner. *Too dark.*

She zoomed in to enlarge just that area of the negative. It took up the whole of the photo paper. Again, after pinning it up to dry, she looked closely with the magnifying glass.

Finally, it was dry. She removed it and set it on her desk, where she could get closer to it. Rolling her chair up to the table, Kayla examined it with her magnifying glass, scrutinizing it. There it was. Something shiny white was in that corner, about four or five feet up the wall, she figured, given that the ceilings were at least nine feet tall. But it was still indistinct. She remembered she'd bought some reading glasses. The glasses coupled with the magnifying glass should help.

Kayla searched for a couple of minutes and located the reading glasses in the back of the desk drawer. They still had the purchase tag on them. Now armed with five eyes, she rolled her chair up to the table and peered at the photo.

Gradually, the image began to make sense, but she still couldn't fully comprehend its meaning. Was that the white of an eye? Was that a face? Where was the mouth? Then, with hands to her own mouth, Kayla stifled a scream as she rolled back from the table, pedaling with the balls of her feet to escape the specter staring back from the shadows.

Chapter

2

Belief in ghosts is irrelevant, if they are really there.
—Oliver Kaufman

Kayla ran out of the darkroom, clutching her cell. She called Henry. "It's there! Something is there!" she cried breathlessly.

"What? What are you talking about?"

"There's something in that room, or there was something in it."

"You found something?"

"That's what I'm saying. Please, get over here."

"Be there in fifteen," he replied.

Kayla sat down on the curb, hugging her knees.

Henry arrived after ten minutes, rolling around the corner to her house in his Honda Civic. He extinguished his headlights as he pulled into the driveway and jumped out.

"What is it? What have you got?"

"Come in and tell me what you see," Kayla responded, somewhat calmer now.

A couple of minutes later, Henry was still examining the photo, trying to decipher if there was anything there. "I ... I guess what's troubling is this shiny white spot."

"Pull the magnifying glass back a bit."

Henry did as he was told.

"Oh. Ohhhh." His head whipped around to gaze at Kayla. "Wow. This is, well, it's disturbing, to say the least."

"What do you think?"

"I think we should've waited and done our homework. We have no idea who this entity might be, much less why he would show himself. But he's a gruesome fellow for sure. Looks like he's got a deformity. Maybe he's a hunchback, too?"

"Oh, God."

"Well, something's wrong."

"Henry, sometimes you're too much. It's too fuzzy to make it out clearly, except for the eye," Kayla muttered, knowing deep down that it did look like the apparition was deformed. Then she examined it again. "You know what? I think it's a child."

Henry grabbed the photo from her and scrutinized it. "Maybe," he said slowly. "Maybe."

The project that she and Henry were currently beginning was by far the most unusual. Usually, their clients were residents, normal people with an abnormal issue (or issues, in some cases). But now, the Frederick County Landmarks Foundation had asked them to investigate a two-hundred-year-old house called Beacon's Way. "Something was wrong," had been the only description when the team had been contacted. When asked to be more specific, they were told that the "something wrong" was that the building had taken on a personality. That was all the young man at the front desk could say. He gave Kayla a key to the house and told them that a woman by the name of Polly Rutledge would meet them there at noon tomorrow to describe in more detail what had been going on.

After a long day's work finishing a report for a family that had hired them to check out clacking noises emanating from their attic, Kayla had announced that she was going to pass by Beacon's Way on her way home and "just have a look." Henry had tried to talk her out of it, since they knew nothing about the problems with the house, but Kayla would have none of it, so he decided to follow her, just to be on the safe side.

"Okay, well, forget the deformity," Henry said. "The eye is clearly an eye. So *someone* was in the room with us. That's already far more than we usually get. Now we know the room's a hot spot. We'll find out more tomorrow."

"Do you know anything about the house?" Kayla asked; unlike her, Henry had lived in Frederick all of his life.

"Not really. It's always been a landmark, but that's about it."

"Okay," she said, sighing. "Thank you for coming over, Henry. I know it's late."

"Not a problem," he said, looking at his watch. "Are you feeling better? I mean, if I'd seen that image appear, it would have freaked me out too."

"Really?"

"Of course, it's unnerving," Henry said as he rose to leave. "But listen—don't lose any sleep over the photo."

Hmmm. Easy to say, Kayla thought.

Chapter

3

The belief in a supernatural source of evil is not
necessary.
Men alone are quite capable of every wickedness.
—Joseph Conrad

Kayla was wide awake. She checked her phone. It was now three ten. Sleep was not going to visit her again on this night. She couldn't get the image of the specter out of her mind. *My God,* she thought, *it was staring right at me. Why would it do that?* Then a chill ran down her back. *It wanted me to see it.* At this point, Kayla debated whether she should go to her darkroom to study the photo some more. She had to admit that it spooked her. So she just lay in bed, literally tossing and turning. Finally, she threw the covers off and got up. She decided she'd go for her run. Granted it was early, but by the time she'd had a cup of coffee, it could be close to five o'clock.

Should have looked outside first, Kayla thought as she started jogging through the fog. It was still not quite dawn, and the fog was thick, shrouding the entire surroundings. Across the large lighted lampposts lining the sidewalk, she could see tiny droplets from the fog swirling downward. She felt the cool dampness caress her cheeks. It was quite simply magical. She noticed that the ducks were sound asleep, curled up along the grassy shore by the creek, teal heads cushioned among their chocolate brown feathers.

Just then, the Baker Park clock tower bell sounded; it was 4:30 a.m. *Thank you, Mr. Baker, for your vision and your philanthropic soul,* Kayla thought. *Maybe I should double the route,* she thought happily, trying to shake off the specter.

She saw someone walking slowly along the street, but other than that, Kayla was alone. *I should do this more often. It's so liberating,* Kayla reflected as she ran under the weeping willows; their silhouettes dotted the park. About forty minutes later, she approached the red covered bridge for the second time. Daylight was now beginning to make its way through the fog. As she started across the bridge, Kayla looked through the open window at the creek below. A split-second later, she stopped dead in her tracks. She walked over to lean out of the opening, straining to discern the something that had caught her attention. Her heart began to race as reality sank in. Kayla rushed to the other side of the bridge and ran down the bank, slipping as she did so, sliding the rest of the way to land only inches from the body.

Kayla was still trembling an hour later as she sat in the back of the police van. The detective, Nick Nucci, had provided a flannel shirt for her, but it didn't address the internal cold from shock. She watched as they pulled the gurney out of the ambulance and placed the now-covered body on it.

"More coffee, Ms. Dunn?" the detective asked.

"Yes, please. Call me Kayla."

"Okay, Kayla."

He nodded to a colleague, who returned within minutes to provide another cup of steaming coffee for her.

"Thank you. What happened to her?" Kayla asked.

Nick was now sitting in the van as well. "We don't know. We won't know for a while. How much of her did you see?"

"Enough. I saw the lines around her neck. The handkerchief around her eyes. Dirty nails. Dark skin. I saw enough. Oh, God."

Nick wanted to put his arm around Kayla's shoulders to console her but didn't want to seem inappropriate.

"Do you have a friend you can call?" he asked.

Kayla shook her head. "What time is it?"

"Six o'clock."

"I don't know if anyone would be awake just yet." She was thinking of either Henry or her other colleague, Parker Troxell.

"Well, we'll be here for a quite a while. Are you sure you don't want someone from our medical team to check you out or perhaps go to the hospital?"

Kayla shook her head no, as she continued to stare at the ambulance driving off, silently. Tears ran down her face, and she started to sob all over again. This time, Detective Nucci thought, *The hell with protocol*, and protectively wrapped his arm around the disconcerted woman.

Chapter

4

> I freed a thousand slaves.
> I could have freed a thousand
> more if only they
> knew they were slaves.
> —Harriet Tubman

Kayla arrived at the office at nine o'clock. Henry and Parker were already there. The two were in the middle of a conversation when she entered. They immediately stopped talking to stare at her. Kayla realized that somehow, in some way, her experience with the tragedy must be apparent.

"Are you okay?" a concerned Parker asked.

Henry stood up to pull out a chair for her.

"I guess it shows," was all Kayla could say as she sat down.

"What happened?" Henry asked.

As she tried to hold back tears, Kayla explained the incident in its entirety. When she'd finished, Parker just shook his head. "That is truly awful. What a tragedy, and what a terrible experience for you."

"It's heartbreaking," Henry added.

Kayla nodded as she stared out the window, holding her coffee cup. "The victim was very young."

"Do you think it was an accident? I mean, could she have drowned?" Parker asked.

"No. It was murder. I am 100 percent sure," Kayla responded. "Someone did it to her. Someone killed her."

Henry got up to get more coffee. "Would you like more?" he asked them both. They both nodded.

"Are you going to hear anything more from the police?" Parker asked. "I mean, will they let you know what they find out?"

Kayla nodded. "Detective Nucci said he'd call me once they have some examination results." She reached in her pocket to feel his card.

"That's decent," Parker said. "You'll let us know too?"

"Of course."

"Well, I'll skip my meeting today and go with Henry to Beacon's Way. You will need some time off. I'm sure the encounter is taking a toll."

Kayla looked up when she heard this comment. "No, I don't want to take time off. That would be the last thing I'd like to do," she added adamantly.

Henry set the coffees down. "But, well, I hate to say it, Kayla, but you don't look so good."

"It's temporary. I don't want to be alone now. I want to be engaged. You both can understand that, can't you?" she asked, looking back and forth between the two of them.

Parker nodded. "Yes, it makes sense. I have never experienced anything like what you've just been through, but yes, it makes sense. Well, okay. It should be interesting, to say the least," he said, changing the subject. "Henry was describing the photo you took. I mean, this should be very, very interesting."

Kayla nodded. "I know. In fact," she added, looking at her watch, "let's get going, Henry. I'll drive."

"Yeah, okay. I'm ready."

"So, who's this lady we're supposed to be meeting?" Henry asked innocently as they headed to Beacon's Way.

Kayla sighed. Henry was a good technician, an architectural engineer, in fact, but he could never remember a name.

"Polly Rutledge. I looked her up. She's the VP for the foundation. So I gather it's a pretty important situation."

"Wow, VP? You're right."

"Yeah, I hope she's not the uppity sort. Usually happens when you have that VP attached to your name. Anyway, I guess that's her," Kayla said as they pulled up to Beacon's Way; a woman was getting out of a new SUV.

It was a massive brick home, sitting back on a rolling hill surrounded by Japanese maple trees dressed in beautiful, varying colors of red. A couple of weeping willows also dotted the terrain, creating an almost heart-aching feel, it was so aesthetically beautiful, all of which had been missed in the darkness of the night before.

Polly Rutledge walked briskly toward them, hand outstretched. "You must be Kayla and Henry," she said, looking at each of them and smiling effusively. "I'm Polly. It's so nice to meet y'all."

Kayla noticed that the woman seemed quite pleasant. She was about five feet tall with reddish-blonde hair cut in a bob and was wearing smart, athletically fashioned clothes. Her voice indicated a southern accent with a slight twang. She appeared to be about fifty.

"We're happy to meet you too," Kayla replied, noting the woman's light brown eyes as she got closer. "We're eager to hear about the house and what you've been experiencing."

"Yes, of course; come with me. Jason said he already gave you a key. Have you had a chance to check it out?" she asked as they entered the foyer, which opened into the grand living room.

"He did," Kayla said, glancing at Henry. "We stopped by last night for a quick run-through, but we wanted to hear from you before we begin our research."

Kayla would not be taking photos during this visit. It was too disruptive. As per every first visit, they just wanted the host or hostess to describe everything he or she could think of during the initial meeting. As Kayla looked around the house in the daylight, it was more magnificent than she could have imagined. Oil and watercolor paintings peppered the walls; a gorgeous hearth and fireplace were featured in the center of one wall, while a Fessler tall case clock stood opposite it. Plush imported rugs were aesthetically placed. Fine furniture, much of it carved, filled out the room. The lighting was perfect.

"By the way, Jason mentioned that the house seemed to have taken on a personality," Kayla added.

"He's right." Polly pointed to two wing-backed chairs for Kayla and Henry. "Have a seat, y'all. That's what we discussed at our staff meeting," she offered as she sat on a taffeta-covered antique loveseat. "I know it must sound strange."

"Well, probably to most folks," Henry commented, "but not to us."

Polly chuckled appreciatively. "Of course." And then she leaned forward in an almost conspiratorial manner. "To be quite frank," she started, looking around as though someone or something might hear her, "I think the house has become … depressed."

"Depressed?" Kayla and Henry said in unison. They had heard houses described as "possessed," "angry," "rabid," and of course "haunted," but never, ever "depressed."

Polly nodded, eyes wide.

"Why do you think this has happened?" Kayla asked.

"Don't know, sweetie. Why do people get depressed? A loss, a change of lifestyle, something doesn't go right? Whatever; something has changed." Then she shook her head. "Now, where should I begin?"

"Um. Just tell us what and when," Kayla suggested, still trying to digest Polly's comment.

"Yes, that's a good idea. Well, first, let me give you a little background about the history of the home and why it's considered one of Frederick's finest landmarks." Kayla and Henry nodded. "It was built in 1820 by a wealthy farmer named Gustav Abel. He had migrated with his parents from Germany when he was a child and grew up in town, where his father started a watch repair shop. It was Gustav's fondness for animals and being outdoors that piqued his interest in ranching. He started out by offering to work on ranches throughout the area, and when he'd earned enough money, he bought a tract of land. He had a knack for breeding cattle, and over time, he kept expanding the land he owned by buying up neighboring tracts. And it did not hurt that he fell in love and married a nearby rancher's daughter, Chloe Watson. The two built Beacon's Way. They wanted to show people that if they worked hard, they could have a good life. It was their shining example for Frederick. They loved it here. They had four children, two boys and two girls, all of whom were successful in their own right."

"So it always remained in the Abel family?" Kayla wanted to know.

"Yes, up until the crash in 1929. Then, somehow, no one knows how, who, or why it was all lost. Perhaps too much invested in the wrong places. It was quite devastating for the two remaining Abel children. Two brothers."

"What happened to them?" Kayla wondered.

"They left town, tails between their legs, never to be heard from again."

"No one ever found out where they went or searched for them?" Henry asked.

Polly sighed. "I know it seems a bit unfair that no one in Frederick might have reached out to find them, but you have to remember what it was like back then. You could get lost in a matter of days if you wanted to. You could literally disappear. Communication wasn't what it is today."

"So … who purchased it?" Henry asked.

"Well, it's belonged to different families over the years, changing hands here and there. Eventually, the land was parceled out. This is what's left," Polly said, widening her hands as if they could envelop the whole of what was now Beacon's Way.

"Seems like a sad story," Kayla added.

"It is, especially given the house's name. But it was not the Abels' fault. A lot of people lost a lot during that depression. And the foundation does not dwell on that aspect of the house's history. The tour is for people to learn about the architecture and history of change over the decades, including furniture, artwork, Frederick's Fessler clocks, you name it," Polly said, smiling. "Can't look at the negative. Never good," she added, smiling even more. "So to provide a history of Beacon's Way for those interested, we, the Frederick County Landmarks Foundation, open her up to the public in the summer time. It's a large house, as you can see, with a couple of acres of grounds. It would cost a lot to maintain if we kept it open year round. We just closed it at the end of August. A little after the closing, we started noticing some strange things."

"Who's we?" Henry asked.

"We have a maintenance person, someone who goes around to see if there are any problems with the house itself, and a cleaning service. Both come on alternating weeks, so the house gets at least one visit every week." Polly looked back and forth at the two and then continued. "So a few days after the building was closed, the maintenance person, Seth Gibson, reported that the ceiling paint was peeling."

All three looked up. Sure enough, some strips were starting to hang. Kayla looked down to notice that a few paint chips lay around here and there, as well.

"Why didn't you fix it?" Kayla asked innocently enough.

"We tried," Polly said, appearing uneasy. "We tried and tried. We've had it repainted twice now. It just starts all over again."

Henry and Kayla looked at each other. This was new.

"Who keeps the keys?" Kayla asked.

"They're always returned to a lock box in my office. I have them."

"Oh."

"So yeah, it's not from inside meddling. Anyway, it's too hard to conceive of. The ceilings are twelve feet high. Someone would have to go to a lot of work to make this happen."

"Yeah. Agreed," Henry said, nodding.

"And look at this," she said, jumping up and walking over to the heavy maroon drapes enveloping the huge windows.

She examined the material and shook her head. The two walked over to join her. Kayla reached out to touch the fabric. In contrast to much of the other items in the room, it was not old. There was no immediate explanation for the fraying, runs, and holes that she observed.

"We have been keeping this house up ever since we were established in 1975," Polly said. "And yet, over the past two months … well, let me show you something."

Henry and Kayla followed her as she started up the stairs, the same stairs that Kayla and Henry had taken to get to the top room the night before.

"I would have thought the paint and the torn curtains were enough," Henry whispered to Kayla.

Kayla nodded. After reaching the landing, Polly turned to the right, opened the door, and entered the first room in the long hallway.

"This is the master bedroom," she said.

The large room was covered in a bold, masculine black and green striped wallpaper. There was a mahogany dresser, a four-poster bed with two nightstands of the same mahogany, a bookshelf crammed with books and knickknacks, and two overstuffed pale green upholstered chairs with a small table and lamp between them. The floor was hardwood with no carpet or rug. White sheers held by laced tie-backs surrounded the two six-foot windows, allowing for direct morning sunlight to stream across the space.

While it was all quite magnificent, Kayla and Henry could not help but notice that standing in the middle of the room was a rather massive armoire. Neither mentioned it, however. It was always best during the pre-investigation to let the person explaining the situation provide the description, with as little interruption as possible.

"This is where the last owner of the house lived and … died. That was in the late '60s," Polly continued. "By the time the foundation came into being, the house was a bit beaten down, but not bad. Easy enough to rectify, from what I've been told. And until recently, it was easy to maintain. But … well, no one knows who moved this armoire. We don't even know when it took place, to be exact. You can see where it was against the far wall because the sun has bleached the paper a bit," she added.

Kayla and Henry looked over to confirm that, indeed, the furniture had blocked the sun's rays for apparently some time.

Polly continued, "Then Seth checked on the house three days ago, as scheduled. So we know this armoire was moved between the cleaning and when Seth came. However, no one could move this monstrosity single-handedly. It weighs well over six hundred pounds. And there are no scrapes on the floor indicating where perhaps two or three people might have dragged it." She looked at the two of them for answers.

"Did you contact the police?" Henry asked.

"No … no reason. Nothin' was taken. Is this the kind of thing y'all have seen before?" she plaintively asked.

"Yes, most certainly," Henry answered. "Entities have a way of making themselves known, and displacing items is not uncommon, although," he continued as he walked over and tried to rock the armoire, with no success, "although I personally have not seen anything quite this large."

"How did the man die?" Kayla inquired.

"Who? Oh, the last owner? It was a hunting accident," Polly replied.

"What was his name?" Kayla asked.

"Earnest Birdwell," Polly replied.

Kayla pulled out a small notebook and jotted it down, while Henry noted it in his iPhone.

"Any children?" Henry wondered.

"No. He'd donated the house to Frederick in his will. Fortunately, we came along not long thereafter." Polly looked back and forth at the two investigators. "Shall we continue?" she asked.

"Yes. Of course," Kayla said.

"Good. Let's go to the cupola."

Cupola, oh yeah, that's what that room is called. Kayla could never remember what that stunted tower on an old house was named, even though this was where she'd ended up taking her photos.

They followed Polly up two more flights of stairs. As Polly swung open the door for them to enter, Kayla immediately recognized the now-familiar musty odor. She stared at the far corner, trying to see if there was anything there resembling an apparition. Nothing. Just as a precaution, as though circling the room, she walked over to the corner. No difference in temperature. The entire room was empty, just as it had been the night before, or so they had thought. Kayla still couldn't explain why last night she had climbed the stairs so eagerly, with Henry following behind, to shoot photos of this room. It had just been intuition. They had left immediately afterwards, not even glancing around at the rest of the house.

"What's that?" Henry asked, walking over to the opposite corner from where the specter had appeared. "Up in the corner of the ceiling?"

"Uh huh. That's the problem up here," Polly acknowledged. "You might consider it a water leak."

"It is a water leak," Henry replied, standing directly under a large discolored circle in the ceiling.

So that's what was causing the odor, Kayla thought.

"Yes, it's a water leak. But we've had the entire roof examined, and there is no leak. Another mystery," Polly added.

"Well, the source of leaks is often hard to identify," Henry stated matter-of-factly.

"Yes, we know that too. That's why we've had three different companies come out here to examine the roof. All three indicated that there is nothing wrong with the roof. One of them even used some kind of x-ray device that was quite expensive, I might add."

Kayla and Henry shared a surreptitious look between them. Henry even chanced raising an eyebrow. Electricity was a huge conductor of ions, which in turn attracted spirits. This was not just hearsay; it was fact.

"Can we have a look at their reports?" Henry asked.

"Honey, I will give y'all every report we have regarding all of the goin's-on. Not to worry." Kayla and Henry nodded. But Polly was not one to dawdle. "There unfortunately is more. Follow me. Now we need to go out back."

The three traipsed back down the stairs, through the kitchen, and out French doors to a brick patio. However, Polly did not stop there. She kept walking far into the well-manicured backyard. Kayla and Henry followed. Then Polly turned to face the back of the house.

"Notice anything?" Kayla surveyed the scene.

"There is no other way to describe what this house is becoming, except morose," Polly stated.

Indeed. The house was sagging, especially on each side. The gutters were starting to droop, and the shutters hung loosely, askew. Tiles that had slipped from the gray slate roof created gaping pockets of void. The tiles themselves lay in pieces on the ground. It appeared that the bricks were chipping away as well, giving it a ragged appearance. All in all, the house emanated a sense of gloom, of malaise, a house not just in disrepair, but in its death throes.

"I didn't notice the front looking like this," Henry commented.

"It's starting to," Polly responded, shaking her head pessimistically. "Something is definitely very wrong, wouldn't you agree?"

"Yes," Kayla and Henry said, again in unison. There was that phrase again: "Something was wrong."

"What about the basement?" Kayla asked.

"What about it?" Polly asked, surprised.

"Have you noticed anything down there?"

"Oh, honey, I've never been down there, so I won't know if anything is changed. We can get Seth to comment on it. I'm sure he checks it out regularly."

"Well, let's just go take a peek. We need to know how to access it, at the very least."

"Okay, let's go," Polly agreed, being the trooper she appeared to be. "It's through the kitchen. I'll show you the door."

When they reached the kitchen, Polly pointed to a door half the size of a normal one. Its hinges were flat and black and looked handmade, indicating that they were probably the original ones. Kayla pulled on the handle, but it was locked. She looked quizzically at Polly.

"I don't know. I don't have a key. Honestly, I didn't think about the basement."

"Try the one we used to get in the front door," Henry suggested.

"That's not going to work," Kayla said. "Look at the keyhole. We need a skeleton key."

They all began to search around the kitchen, opening drawers and reaching to feel on top of the cabinets. Kayla even opened the refrigerator.

"Who drinks Flying Dog?" she asked.

"What?" Polly asked, incredulous.

"Yeah, there are a couple of bottles of ..." Kayla paused to read the name: "Secret Stash Harvest Ale." Flying Dog was a local Frederick brewery.

Polly started laughing. "Well, that's not allowed. I'll have to figure out who left this."

"Found the key," Henry said excitedly, ignoring the beer debate. Kayla and Polly quit talking and turned to look. "Yep, this is it," he said as the door reluctantly swung open to expose absolutely nothing.

It was pitch black. Henry reached for the light switch and gave it a flip. Still nothing.

"Light must be out." He pulled out his flashlight. "It's a long flight down," he said to the two ladies. "Let me go first. There's a handrail. It's okay. The steps are in good shape, but they're not very deep. Come on down."

Polly went first so Kayla could shine her flashlight from behind for her. Henry did the same from below. Kayla followed.

"Is there a light down here?"

"That's what I'm looking for," Henry replied, shining his own light around the room.

"I can't believe I never thought to come down here," Polly commented, looking around at the vastness of the space, the dark alcoves, and an entrance to another room.

"Here's a light switch," Kayla noted. She flipped it, but it too did not work.

Henry shined his flashlight onto the ceiling. "Well, that's why: There's no light bulb in the socket."

"We can get one later to see more clearly. For now, let's just walk around and look for anything strange," Kayla suggested.

They moved slowly across the cement floor, shining their flashlights across the brick walls and wood-beamed ceiling. Plumbing pipes and air conditioning ducts ran along the latter.

"What are those?" Henry asked, pointing to hardware secured in the wall.

"Looks like a bunch of hooks. Probably used for hanging tools back in the day," Polly suggested. "Often, just like today, these basements, cellars as they were more often referred to, provided space for making furniture or other items."

Henry stepped up to them looking closely. "Maybe, but these are not old."

"Really?" Polly seemed genuinely surprised. "Well, maybe someone replaced the old ones to demonstrate what used to be," she suggested.

"Could be," Henry agreed.

The three moved on to the next room. The plumbing pipes were here as well, along with cobwebs and some abruptly disturbed spiders that skittered here and there.

"Definitely not part of the tour," Kayla muttered.

Once again, they observed hooks on the wall. Henry inspected these too and determined that they were not old. Finally, they moved on to the third and final room. As soon as they entered it, the three immediately smelled a foul odor.

"Wow, what is that?" Polly asked, pinching her nose with her forefinger and thumb.

"Not sure. Not pleasant, smells faintly like body odor, which is pretty much out of the question," Henry said, swinging his light around.

"Yeah, not possible," Polly concurred.

There were hooks here also, which Henry concluded were the same as the others.

"I never knew there was a washer and dryer down here," Polly exclaimed. "Of course, I've never been down here, as I mentioned, but, but ... these are almost brand new."

Kayla went over to check them out. She pulled the lint holder out and shined her light at it. Lint was definitely present. "Looks like they might have been used recently," she commented.

Henry and Polly joined her.

"I wonder where the vent is?" Henry asked. "We'll look for it outside."

"Maybe whoever uses it likes to drink beer while the clothes are being washed," Kayla quipped.

Polly frowned, shaking her head. "I need to find out who all has been in here," she muttered.

"Oh, look here," Kayla exclaimed, having moved on. She was pointing her flashlight at the floor. "Looks like some kind of door."

She knelt down to examine a faint outline in the cement. She got as close as possible and carefully rubbed the palm of her hand across the entire surface.

Henry squatted next to her and tapped on it with his flashlight. "Made of steel. But there's no handle."

"Hmmm. I guess you're right," Kayla agreed, standing up. "Probably closed a long, long time ago."

"Let's get out of here. It's oppressive," Polly said, rubbing her upper arms in a hug. They all turned and left. After they were back in the kitchen, they sat around the table. "So what's next?"

Henry started, in a very professional manner, "Well, first, thanks for the key. We'll need to come and go freely, so that's very helpful. From this point forward, we'll bring our team in here and do a run-through, similar to what we've done with you, but we'll examine the entire house. Kayla will take photos along the way. If we have any questions, we'll get back to you with those. Then, we do a more in-depth examination of any potential hot spots that we identify."

"Hot spots?"

"Yes, places where there seems to be paranormal activity. For example, the living room, with the chipping paint and torn curtains, and the master bedroom. Both of those places already exhibit some kind of abnormal behavior, as does the cupola."

Polly nodded and said, "I see. Okay."

"We'll stay in close touch, always reporting our findings, which will be confidential. We will do everything we can to help understand why this activity is occurring and to resolve it."

"Well, at least we have time. The house doesn't open again until next April. What are the chances that it will be resolved, based on what y'all have seen?"

"Polly, I've been in this business for ten years. We have very few unsolved cases. The outcome may not be what is expected or even desired, but there is almost always an explanation. I'm confident we'll find out and stop the 'depression,' as you refer to it," Henry concluded.

Kayla added, "We will document everything. We'll have digital as well as 35 mm photos for you to examine, tape recordings, and anything else that is physical in nature. Basically, it's supporting evidence along with the reports."

Polly looked back and forth at the two of them and sighed. "I'm sure glad I contacted you. Some of the staff at the foundation are skeptical about your ability to help us, but I'm not."

"Do you believe?" Kayla asked, regretting immediately that she had spoken out so abruptly. But the question did not seem to faze the woman.

"Um, yesss, to a certain degree," Polly said, smiling. "Oh," she said, starting to jump up, "I think I forgot to close the master bedroom door. It helps to conserve the energy."

"I'll go," Kayla offered as she headed toward the living room and stairs.

"Thanks," Polly said, sitting back down.

Kayla looked at her watch and realized they'd been here over two hours. Now, there was so much work to be done examining Beacon's Way that she felt rushed. She took the stairs two at a time up to the master bedroom. As she reached in to pull the door shut, she felt her heart leap into her throat.

The armoire was back against the wall.

Chapter

5

As Kayla and Henry observed a much-shaken Polly Rutledge drive off, Kayla shook her head. "Poor woman; she's never going to be the same.

Henry looked at Kayla in a concerned way but decided not to say anything about her experience in the park. "Well, I hope she gets over it. But this house … this is another story altogether. I gotta say, Beacon's Way must have received some bad juju. You don't get that kind of action from just any ol' spirit. Something really serious is going on here."

Not this again, Kayla thought.

Henry hailed from Ghana; well not directly. His parents had moved to the States in the late 1960s, prior to his birth. His grandmother still lived in West Africa. When Kayla had first gotten to know Henry, he kept talking about his Grandma Mercy: Grandma Mercy was a shaman and helped to get rid of juju spells; Grandma Mercy was a mid-wife; Grandma Mercy wanted him to visit, and on and on.

"What's juju?" Kayla had asked.

"Well, it's a spell of sorts," Henry had explained. "It can be good juju or bad juju."

Kayla still hadn't believed him. But then, last Christmas, he'd said he was going to go visit his Grandma Mercy in Ghana. When he returned, he had a slew of photos. Kayla had been dumbfounded.

She hadn't known that Mercy was a common English-speaking West African name for girls, but the photos didn't lie. Henry was there with his grandma. Kayla was glad she never told him how much she'd doubted him, though she most certainly did not (nor would she ever) believe in juju.

"Well, bad juju or not, let's call Parker to debrief. I guarantee you he's going to want to lead this investigation."

"Yep," Henry nodded, cellphone to his ear. As he spoke into his phone, Kayla overheard him describing in detail what they had already seen at Beacon's Way, starting first with the armoire and ending with the armoire. "Yeah, no kidding … okay, okay," she heard Henry saying before he clicked off. "You're right. Parker's very, very interested. We'll start the walk-through first thing tomorrow morning, eight o'clock sharp, if you're up to it," he added. Kayla shot him a glance. "Those are Parker's words, not mine."

She smiled and said, "Okay. I'm okay. I'll be ready."

"Hey, are you going to Angie's party tonight?" Henry asked.

"Oh, shoot, I totally forgot. But yes, I told her I would come. Actually, I'm happy to. I was already thinking that I didn't want to just sit home tonight."

"Well, let's go. If you don't mind, can you drop me off at Spin the Bottle? I told her I'd bring a bottle of wine. I can walk to get my car." Spin the Bottle wasn't far from East Street, where their office was located.

"Sure," Kayla responded, remembering she'd better bring something too.

As she pulled up curbside, Henry got out and then leaned back into the car. "That house is cursed with juju," he said, as he backed up and shut the door.

Always has to get the last word in, Kayla thought, driving off to find parking. It wasn't always easy to do so. The downtown streets of Frederick were often quite busy, as was the case today.

Nevertheless, Kayla loved Frederick. It was situated near the Catoctin Mountains, the first foothills of the Appalachians. The town looked like a Norman Rockwell painting. It was founded as Fredericktown in 1745, with many of the downtown buildings dating back to that century. No one knew for sure who it was named after, but most sources believe it was Frederick Calvert, 6th Baron Baltimore. It was also known as the City of Clustered Spires, due to all of the church towers peppered throughout it. In fact, an ordinance had been enacted that prevented any buildings taller than seven stories from being constructing, which allowed the many unique spires to be admired and helped to ensure that the quaintness of the town would remain, *unlike some other towns in Maryland that were being ruined by greed*, Kayla thought.

Additionally, there were multiple restaurants, clothing stores, and antique shops. Many of the sidewalks and some streets were still brick. And beautiful Baker Park housed the largest musical instrument in Maryland: the Joseph Dill Baker Carillon, though that park now had a dark side, Kayla reflected grimly. As a bona fide paranormal photographer and investigator, the characteristic she liked the best was that Frederick was considered one of the most haunted cities in the country.

After she dropped Henry, Kayla made her way to En Masse, a flower shop on Market Street, and bought a bouquet. She figured Angie would really appreciate it after a busy day getting ready for the party. Her friend loved to entertain, and she was very good at it, so her parties were always a hit. As Kayla drove home, she reflected once again on the murdered girl in the park. She figured she'd never really get over it. The poor girl's parents were going to be distraught, Kayla knew. She felt terrible and started to cry again. So sad, she thought, so senseless.

Once home, Kayla went directly to her darkroom to organize her photography equipment for tomorrow. She wanted to be active so she would not continue to dwell on the dead girl's image. *Will I ever get it out of my head?*

Then she remembered she wanted to look up the last owner of Beacon's Way, Earnest Birdwell. She Googled him coupled with Frederick, Maryland, and Beacon's Way. Bingo! The man's photograph was included with several articles about his social life. *Hmm, quite the playboy way back when, a veritable Gatsby.*

She added "hunting accident" to the Google search box, and a number of articles popped up, starting with "Tragedy, Horrific Accident" and the like. *Aha!* Yes, he was shot in a hunting accident. His best friend and business partner, Arlo Vaughn, "had mistaken him for an animal, thinking that Ernie was behind him, not in front of him." And, yes he had shot him in the face, *Cheney style. Wonder if his friend said he was sorry? Uh-oh, his friend was charged with manslaughter ... but never served time. Of course not.*

In another article, she read that they had brought Birdwell back to his house, where he had died in his bed. *Yep, that's what Polly had said too.*

So who was the specter in the photo? In the safety of daylight, Kayla pulled it out to examine it again. This time, she was calmer and could inspect it from a more academic perspective. She peered at it again through the magnifying glass with her reading glasses on. Yes, it was unequivocally an eye within a face, or partial face. The rest of the body was just too fuzzy to make out anything like clothes. She was sure, though, that it was not a full-grown adult. There was something about it.

Kayla pulled out her negatives one more time to see if she'd missed anything. She zoomed in on one that showed the specter from a different angle, sans eye. That's when she noticed something gleaming. It was very tiny but did not seem to be part of the form. It was more as though it was being worn. *Jewelry? Perhaps the specter was female?* She once again went to her enlarger. She focused on the spot so she could fully develop it. After drying the paper, she went back to her magnifying glass. *Well, it could be something,* was all she could conclude. She looked at her watch and decided she needed to get to the party. But now she had something else to show Henry and Parker. She set the photos on top of her equipment case and left with the flowers.

<hr />

Polly Rutledge was still shaking like a leaf when she drove off from

Beacon's Way. She'd pulled off the road because she didn't feel she could drive properly.

What or who did that? she wondered. *What was going on at the house?*

In all honesty, she had been a skeptic, although she did not want to admit it to Kayla and Henry, so she'd told a small white lie when they had asked if she believed. On the other hand, she had agreed that hiring someone to look into the activity at the house was the right thing to do, but "this business with the armoire. "I mean, we didn't hear a peep," she muttered to herself.

Granted, they had been outside or in the basement, where it would be difficult to hear much, but something that heavy might have at least created a shudder or something. She looked at her hands. They were still shaking. She glanced at herself in the mirror. She was as white as a ghost herself. She took a deep breath. She'd go to the office, clear some things off her desk, and then go home to rest.

What a day, she thought as she began driving again. After pulling into the Schifferstadt House from Rosemont Avenue, where the foundation's office was located, she made her way to her office and sat at her desk, still very much disturbed. Jerry Tower, the foundation's accountant, poked his head in to say hi.

"You look like you've seen a ghost," he said, laughing. Then he frowned. "You're not well, are you? What's wrong?"

"Honey, I had a bit of a fright, I guess," she responded, brushing back her hair and dabbing a tissue at the corners of her watery eyes. She then proceeded to tell him what happened with the armoire.

Jerry was speechless. Finally, the only thing he said was, "Are you sure?"

This made Polly laugh a little. And it was intended to do so; Jerry was that kind of guy. "I still can't get over it, though. I mean …"

"You know, Polly, I must admit that I do believe in those things. I mean, I always have." Jerry attended all staff meetings and was well aware of the issues with Beacon's Way.

"Really?"

"Yeah. This will be resolved. It doesn't sound like it's an angry spirit. It seems like it's bent on messing up the house is all."

"Yeah, you're right. I'll get over it. But I don't know if I can go in there again."

"Wait and see. You don't have to. They have the key, right?"

"Yes," she said, her lips trembling slightly.

"Okay. Why don't you just call it day?" he suggested.

"I will. I just have to go through this mail," she said, pointing to several envelopes. "Then I'm leaving."

"Good idea. Take it easy," he said as he exited her office.

Once Polly became absorbed reading the mail, she started to feel better. Letters sent to her were usually positive in nature. They were both official and personal. One described a home the sender thought should be labeled an endangered site. Polly had a pile for this issue, since there was a committee to address just that. Another thanked her and the foundation for helping apply for and receive a historic plaque.

As the pile decreased in size, she started to feel so much better that she poured herself a cup of coffee, checked her emails, and then returned to finish the mail. The next envelope was addressed specifically to her. She would say later that she noticed it had no stamp and no return address but did not think twice about it.

She opened it up to find one sheet of paper enclosed with a typed message:

Back off from Beacon's Way.

Chapter

**In the end, there was nothing else to do but wait for
the stairs to creak.**
—Hugh McLeod

Detective Nick Nucci was driving to the coroner's office. Dr. Theresa
Wild, the coroner, had informed him by phone that the girl's death
was indeed a homicide. God, he really hated this part of his job. The
only thing worse was informing family members. Fortunately, it was
rare. In fact, there had been no murders in Frederick in 2004 and 2005.
The highest number in the last decade was five in 2007. This was the
first one this year, and he hoped it would be the last.

He was ushered into the morgue by Chester Tomlin. The two had
known each other for several years. "Dr. Wild wanted to show you some
things," he said somberly.

"Thanks, Chet."

"Hi, Nick."

"Hi, Theresa. Sorry to see you under such terrible circumstances. It
seems like just yesterday we were enjoying the fireworks on the Fourth
of July."

"I know. I wish we were there now instead," she said, sighing.

Dr. Wild was around forty-five years old; Nick knew her husband

and two teenage daughters as well. *This must have been especially hard for her,* he thought, as he glanced over at the covered body.

"So what have you found?"

"Well, she appears to be sixteen or seventeen years old. She was sexually abused, over a period of time, I might add, and appears to be malnourished. Cause of death was strangulation. She didn't drown, in other words. She was dumped in Carroll Creek."

"Do you know when?"

Theresa nodded. "She died at approximately three o'clock this morning. So it was between then and when the jogger discovered her, which was ...?"

"We got the call at five fifty," Nick said.

"So yeah, there's your window."

"We were able to lift some shoe prints, but of course since it has not rained in several days, they are not too reliable."

"Nothing else was found at the crime scene?"

Nick shook his head no.

"There is more, however," Dr. Wild said.

"Oh?"

Theresa walked over to the table and raised the sheet to expose an arm. "It's her wrists. There are faint ligatures on them. Same with her ankles," she said raising the sheet to expose a foot.

"What from?"

"I have no idea. It was quite a while ago."

"I've also taken samples of the material under her nails and expect those results, as well as her stomach contents, the day after tomorrow."

"Okay. Thanks. By the way, do you know her ethnicity?"

"I think Indian or Nepalese."

"What? Why?"

"Believe me—I'm no ethnicity scholar," Dr. Wild said as she turned over the wrist to show the name "Kamala" tattooed on it. "It's Hindu."

Nucci just stared. "This is quite hard to grasp," he said.

"I know. Any missing person calls yet?"

"No. Could be too soon, but still, you would think."

"You would think," the doctor said, nodding in agreement. "By the way, who found her?"

"Her name's Kayla Dunn. I told her I'd let her know the outcome."

"Yeah, it's best to do that. She'll need closure. But just knowing won't necessarily help."

Nick nodded. "Okay, well, thank you."

"You're welcome. It's too bad."

Detective Nucci decided to walk down to the crime scene and re-examine it again, alone. It was growing dark, and he wanted to inspect the area from the perspective of the killer, or at least the person who had dumped the body. He nodded to the guard on duty and showed him his badge.

The guard lifted the yellow tape for him. "It's a shame," the man said, "what happened, I mean."

Nick agreed. "Let's hope we can get to the bottom of it," he added.

The detective felt confident that his team had conducted a thorough investigation, but he wanted to look again, all the same. He squatted curbside and peered into the foliage adjacent to the creek, where Kayla had discovered the body. Definitely no struggle; there did not appear to be any disruption of the grass. Next, he shined his light on the ground and looked once again for any signs of prints or turned-up dirt. Nada. The ones they had already made prints of were still there. Probably nothing as well.

The street was Nick's next target. He looked up and down Carroll Parkway, not really knowing what he hoped to see or discover. It was an upscale neighborhood. He decided to personally query the neighbors, in case anyone was an insomniac and happened to notice something out of the ordinary in the wee hours.

Nick then decided to look again at the crime scene from the bridge, from where Kayla had first seen the body. He started towards it and then stopped. Squatting, he surveyed the planks on the covered bridge's floor. *What kind of tracks were those?* Since the bridge had been roped off as part of the crime scene, no one had been on it today. He waved his flashlight across the entire bridge. The tracks had come from the opposite direction. It looked like they belonged to one of the service vehicles that maintained the park. He pulled out his pocket knife and a small collection bag to take a sample from them. Then, careful to avoid walking on them, he followed the tracks to College Street, where the vehicle had either entered or exited the park, or perhaps both.

He hoped his team had photographed the bridge as well. Maybe they too had seen the tracks. Just in case, however, Nick returned to the bridge and snapped photos, zooming in as close as he could to the tracks in order to capture the width and tread pattern. There was a slim chance any of this would lead to anything, he surmised, but he had to try anything and everything. Someone had murdered a young girl, and he was going to get to the bottom of it, one way or another.

Chapter

7

> **It is true that we cannot be free from sin,**
> **but at least let our sins not be always the same.**
> —Saint Teresa of Avila

"Hey, girlie girl," Hunter Crowley half-whispered as he came up behind Kayla, drink in hand.

She turned to see who it was. *Ugh.* This man was not one of her favorite people. She'd seen his Beemer with his signature license tag: "Jobs 4U", parked in front of Angie's house. Somehow, or for some reason, he always sought her out. A lot of people felt that way about him. He was just a bit odd. Not a bad-looking guy, but not handsome. On the tallish side, with a barrel chest, he had a ruddy face, featuring an aquiline nose and broad lips. Deep brown eyes were always flitting around, lizard-like, as though he might miss out on something.

It was strange that Angie would even invite him, but then it seemed everyone felt compelled to invite Hunter to Frederick events, *probably because he had money*, Kayla thought cynically. And he was ensconced in the Frederick social groups such as the Red Cross, Chamber of Commerce, Rotary Club, and the like. What was even stranger is that no one knew where he came from. He'd just shown up a few years ago.

Hunter was always vague about his past. In fact, he reminded Kayla of Jack Nicholson in *The Witches of Eastwick*, forever a stranger.

"Find any ghosts lately?" he asked with a rhetorical tone, grinning.

Oh yeah, and he always made fun of her profession, which she always tried to ignore.

"Hey, Hunter."

"Pretty nice party, don't you think?" he asked, leaning in a little too close for her comfort.

"Yes, of course," Kayla said, looking around at the decorative candles, the water fountain, and the pretty white lights strung throughout the bushes and trees.

Music could be heard from multiple speakers. People were milling around, snacking and laughing, drinking of course, and just having a good time.

"Angie always puts on a nice party, which reminds me, I need to get these flowers in a vase," Kayla said, holding up her flowers. "See you later," she added as she headed for the back door, leaving Hunter alone with his drink.

The back door entered into the kitchen, whose condition indicated that it had suffered a lot in the effort to get the party together. *Oh well, Angie would get it in shape in no time.* Kayla looked around for a vase and found one in the next room. She put the flowers on the coffee table and exited back through the kitchen. She still hadn't seen Angie. Oh, there she was, chatting away while filling wine glasses.

Uh-oh, now the very cerebral (*not*) Gloria Marshall was headed toward Kayla, looking down while shaking her head. Her wide hips swished as she approached. Her cropped hair was dyed bright red. At best, Kayla hoped for a parallel conversation.

As Gloria got close, she shook her forefinger in Kayla's face. "You've been really bad for not getting in touch with me."

Yep, it had already started, she thought. "Get in touch about what?" Kayla asked aloud.

"Oh, don't play coy. Found any ghosts lately?" Gloria asked, raising an eyebrow. "I read that a lot of parents don't want to take their children to the Halloween activities in Baker Park this year because they think it's too scary."

Jeez, she's already talking about Halloween when it's still September, Kayla thought. *Yeah, par for the course.* "Well, I didn't have anything to do with that."

"The Schifferstadt Architectural Museum is haunted, you know."

"I don't know …"

"That's where the Frederick County Landmarks Foundation has its office."

"Well, that's true, but …"

"I thought it would be a lot warmer tonight, which is why I wore this tee shirt," she said, continuing to interrupt and pointing to her purple top.

"Oh, jeez, Gloria, I'm sorry to run, but I've got to help Angie open some wine bottles," Kayla said. "I'll catch up with you later, okay?"

"Yes, but I'm still mad."

Kayla looked around. She needed a drink and headed toward the bar, where a small crowd had congregated. The music was louder here, which made people talk over it, but there was definitely an argument occurring. Kayla couldn't believe that both Eleanor and Buzz had been invited to the same party, especially since Angie knew Buzz was now with Sally. Eleanor and Buzz had been the Camelot couple of Frederick some ten years ago. She was a tall, beautiful brunette with striking blue eyes. She owned a successful real estate company, albeit a small one. Buzz was a high school quarterback and had become the school's coach himself after finishing college.

But not unlike Camelot, the marriage had apparently begun to suffer, and eventually Buzz had met Sally. *Why would Eleanor come? Was she a masochist?* Then Kayla realized what everyone else was realizing: Eleanor had come to crash the party.

"You're a terrible woman to steel my husband away," she was saying. "You should be in jail. She's not worth it, Buzz."

"Eleanor, please," Buzz entreated. "It's over, it's been over. I'm sorry. Please, you've had too much to drink. It's time to go home."

She started sobbing and started to leave, zigzagging across the lawn. "Shouldn't someone drive her home?" a young man asked, concerned.

"She lives around the block."

"Oh."

Buzz and Sally decided they would leave then too, so it seemed that Eleanor had succeeded, in part. Just then, Henry walked up with a nice-looking woman. Henry always had a different date.

"Hey Kayla," he said and then introduced her to Tina. "Have you heard from Parker?"

"No, why? Should I have?"

"He received a call from Polly Rutledge."

"And?"

Henry grinned. "The saga continues."

"Don't joke, Henry. What did he say?"

Henry lost his smile. "He said Polly received a threatening note about Beacon's Way."

"What did it say?"

"Don't know. Just said it was threatening."

"Oh, no. The poor woman. She was already so shaken. Who would have done that?"

"He wants to discuss it tomorrow."

"Yeah, okay; it's getting late, so I'm going to head home. Nice to meet you, Tina. See you tomorrow, Henry."

And with that, Kayla turned to leave. As she did so, she saw Hunter talking up a young woman. Nonetheless, he winked at her surreptitiously as she walked away. *Creep? TBD.*

Kayla thought about the crowd at Angie's as she walked home. They were all decent people, but sometimes things got out of hand. True, people were drinking, but it seemed that a darkness had descended on them lately. This wasn't the first time Eleanor had blown up. She'd heard that it had happened in one of the new superstores when she just happened to run into Sally. She wasn't drunk then. It was too bad. And now, to hear that Polly had received a threatening note.

What was going on?

Chapter

8

Hunter Crowley had just returned from Angie's party and now sat at his spacious oak desk, drinking a scotch on the rocks. As he scanned his encrypted emails, he patted his Labrador golden retriever named Second Chance. Hunter explained to folks that he'd name him that because he was a rescue. Impulsively, Hunter punched the button under his desk, and a well-camouflaged door across the room seamlessly slid opened. Hunter got up and walked into the adjoining room. He checked his tapes and rewound one of them to watch; he observed the people in it carefully as he listened to the recording. Hunter almost laughed at one point but then just shook his head when the people exited the room. He sighed as he turned off the tape player and left the hidden room. Returning to his desk, he closed the door just as he'd opened it. Hunter checked his watch and compared it mentally to the time in Russia. His contact should still be awake. He reread the email he'd written earlier. *Yes. It was clear. No need for edits*, Hunter thought as he hit Send.

Sighing, he leaned back in the leather office chair, intertwining his fingers behind his head. It was time to move again; the plan was solid, as it always was. Hunter's assistant, Tommy Mitka, was already organizing the various teams, and their supplies had been gathered. As he swished the ice cube with his tongue between his cheeks, Hunter felt pleased. Yes, all beneficiaries should be quite satisfied, he noted. Then he thought back to the evening at Angie's. What a crew. Hunter chuckled slightly as he remembered the petty fight between Eleanor and Sally, with Buzz in the middle. *What would you expect?* he wondered. But he loved Frederick and its environs. He enjoyed contributing to its betterment, and he especially appreciated its history and all that came with it. Now, with the newest exercise about to be initiated, Hunter called up his bank accounts. Two were local, but the rest were offshore tax havens, the ones that mattered. The balances reflected Hunter's large success. He smiled slyly, quite pleased with himself.

He abruptly tossed the rest of the drink down his throat and stood up, calling out, "Come on, boy; time to go for that walk."

Chapter

**These are a few of the open-air spirits;
the more domestic of their tribe gather within doors,
plentiful as swallows under southern eaves.**
—William Butler Yeats

Kayla arrived at Beacon's Way a couple of minutes ahead of the eight o'clock meeting time. Parker was there, but Henry hadn't arrived yet. "Hey, Parker," she called.

The windbreaker accentuated his beefy physique. "Hi, Kayla. Did you bring coffee?"

"Thought you would."

"Uh-oh. Lucky I had at least one cup," Parker said, grinning. Then his expression turned to one of concern. "How are you doing? How was your evening?"

"Good. I'm going to be okay. I'm doing well. Honestly. Thank you for asking."

Just then, Henry pulled up. He hopped out of his car, holding three cups of coffee in a tray. "Coffee, anyone?"

"Saved," was all Kayla said.

She unlocked the massive door, and the three entered the house.

Kayla led them directly back to the kitchen. After laying down the equipment, they sat at the table with their coffee.

Parker began, "So Kayla, let's see the photo you took in the cupola."

"Actually, I have that one and now another one," Kayla responded, pulling them out of her case. Henry looked quizzical, not having known about a new discovery. She set the photos down and handed Parker the magnifying glass along with her pink reading glasses.

"What are these for?"

"I bought them to get even closer. They work."

Parker looked skeptical but donned them nonetheless.

Henry laughed out loud, saying, "They don't do much for you."

Parker just shook his head and picked up the magnifying glass. "What am I looking for?"

"Just tell us what you see," Kayla insisted.

He circled the image and then stopped near the top of the page. "What the ...? Is that what I think it is?"

"Which is ...?"

"An eye?" Parker responded hesitantly, looking up. "It's an eye, for sure."

"And a strange body," Henry added.

"It could be a child."

"We think that too," Kayla confirmed.

"It's looking right at the camera," Parker commented. "It wants you to see it. It's not unusual that an apparition is caught by camera, but in this case, he ... it ... positioned himself just so ..." His voice trailed off.

"I know. I realized that the first time I saw the photo. I think that's what spooked me more than anything," Kayla commented.

Parker nodded thoughtfully.

"Now look at this other photo I developed," she added, passing it to Parker and Henry, who moved his seat over closer so he could see it too. "See anything?"

Again, Parker perused the photo with the magnifying glass, retaining the pink reading glasses.

"It's something shiny."

Kayla nodded. Henry took the photo to peer at it up close with the magnifying glass.

"It looks like something external to the apparition. Could it be a reflection of something?" Henry wondered.

"I thought of that, but there was nothing in the room. Remember? It was dark, very dark, with just a bit of diffused light from the outside." Henry nodded in agreement. "So if we were to conjecture, what do you all think it might be?"

"Jewelry?" Parker asked.

"It could be a belt buckle," Henry suggested. "It's near the middle of the form."

Kayla sighed, nodding. "Yeah, it's not clear, but it's something.

"Well, let's look more closely at the location when we get up there. Oh, by the way, Kayla, did Henry mention to you that Polly received a note?" Parker inquired.

She nodded.

"It's pretty straightforward, no enigma or anything," Parker said as he pulled a file folder from his black satchel. He opened it on the table, exposing the sheet of paper and envelope.

Henry and Kayla just stared.

"Who even knows that the foundation hired us?" Kayla asked.

"My thoughts exactly," Parker said, nodding somberly.

"What was the exchange with Polly like?"

"Yeah, I was wondering the same thing," Henry said. He no longer seemed in the mood to make jokes about it.

"She's understandably upset. She was thinking of doing exactly what the message demands, until I talked her out of it. I told her to at least let us proceed with the preliminary walk-through and see what we discover. Maybe there will be no significant findings, and indeed we can let it go. That seemed to appease her." He sighed.

"Well, I doubt there will be no significant findings," Kayla commented. "There's a lot going on here."

"I know. It was a delay tactic, as much as anything. So the armoire just moved on its own volition?" Parker asked, changing the subject.

"We all saw it in the middle of the room," Henry said, nodding. "I tried to move it myself, and it wouldn't budge."

"Okay then. Let's start with the cupola and work our way down. But on the way up, I want to look in that room to see the armoire."

And so they did. Kayla opened the door with trepidation. It was just as it was when they left it yesterday. The armoire was against the wall. Everything else was the same as well. She closed the door when they left, just to make sure they complied with the energy issue. When they reached the cupola, they looked up at the water stain. Polly had been right. It had changed in shape ever so slightly from the day before, as in growing larger, though there had been no precipitation over the past twenty-four hours. Kayla immediately started taking photos, three quickly with the digital camera and others with her 35 mm.

"Polly said they've had it checked out?" Parker asked.

"Right. She said they've had three different companies examine it, but none of them could find the leak. One even used a portable x-ray."

"Oh, great," Parker responded, for the same reason that Kayla and Henry had noted. Spirits thrived more where there was energy.

Parker began speaking into his recorder. He would turn his notations over to the team members who handled equipment setup, analysis, and the like. These folks worked on an ad hoc basis, mostly because they liked being involved in paranormal activities, but all held other jobs. "Cupola: Examine spot on ceiling and take sample to determine composition of liquid; establish video camera pointed to said spot." Then Parker walked around as he always did, feeling the walls. "It's cold here," he said.

Kayla's heart beat faster. That's where the specter had been. She walked over and felt it too: a slightly lower temperature and a moistness.

"It did not feel that way yesterday," she remarked.

Parker nodded, adding into his tape recorder, "Place another video camera on the northeast corner; line and powder the floor." Then he walked to the rear of the room and stared thoughtfully out the back window down at the lawn below. Finally he turned and said, "Okay, let's go."

They proceeded through the rest of the house. Since there was paranormal movement occurring, it was decided that they would use standard procedure; they'd place a video camera and cover the floor with powder in the master bedroom, using a black plastic liner. They'd do the same in the living room, due to the peeling paint and deteriorating drapes. They'd also add a recorder to catch any electronic voice phenomenon (EVP). EVP recorders were one of the paranormal search tools that Kayla had really been impressed with. Some of the EVPs she'd heard had really surprised her; others frightened her no end. The EVP recorder could capture voices that you did not hear in real time. You could be present and have the recorder on and never hear a peep, but then when the recording was played back, voices might be heard, suggesting that there were others present you did not see or detect.

The one experience that still gave her chills was when they were investigating why a two-year-old child was suddenly having hysterical outbursts. Before the Gammons had moved into their house, which was built in the 1930s, their little girl was sweet and happy, but shortly after they moved in, Janie began to behave in a very uncharacteristic manner, screaming and throwing things, becoming dour, and spending time in the corner of her bedroom, talking to herself. The team set up an EVP and captured the threatening, guttural voice of a man claiming that Janie belonged to him, while they were all eating dinner and talking among themselves.

After researching the house, they discovered that the original owners had lost their little girl to yellow fever when she was two. A photo of her revealed an uncanny similarity to Janie. Once the Gammons heard the recorded voice, coupled with the history, they literally bundled up their little girl, packed up their car, and fled from Frederick. *Yes,* Kayla thought, *if there were spirits moving around in the Beacon's Way living room, perhaps they would capture their comments over time and any foot traffic, as well, even while the team was present.*

"So we've got the basement and the backyard left, correct?" Parker asked, looking at his watch.

"Yes," Kayla replied. "Let's go outside, it's this way."

Just like yesterday, they walked a good distance out so they could get the view of the back of the house in its entirety. The dilapidated profile did not disappoint.

"Jeez," Parker commented, crossing his arms across his broad chest and shaking his head. "If I didn't know better, I'd think it had been neglected for years."

"I can't be sure, but I think more tiles have fallen from the roof," Kayla responded, snapping photos, again first with the digital and then with the 35 mm, zooming in on places here and there.

"I agree. Let's hope there's not a face in one of those windows when you develop those," Henry kidded.

"What about eleven faces," Kayla joked, noting the number of windows on that side of the house.

Parker just continued to shake his head. "Place two cameras in backyard, each covering half of the house," he noted in the mic. "Okay, let's hit the basement."

Kayla glanced at Henry, but he didn't return the look. Something was up with Parker.

"Hold on," Henry said suddenly. "I want to look for the dryer vent." He loped over to where it most likely would be located and then met up with Parker and Kayla as they were about to re-enter the house. "It's new. Just like the washer and dryer."

Kayla raised an eyebrow. She explained to Parker what they were talking about and then added, "It's strange that Polly doesn't know anything about those appliances. You'd think it would be an expense that would have to be approved, especially for budgetary purposes."

"Maybe it's not her department," was all Henry could offer. "I'll go first," he said after entering the kitchen. He pulled a light bulb out of his jacket pocket when they got to the basement stairs. Kayla had to laugh; she'd already forgotten. "Okay, flip the switch," he called up. Parker did so, but nothing happened.

"Did you check the bulb?" Parker asked.

"Yeah, of course. It was in a working lamp when I unscrewed it. Burned myself," came the muffled reply from below.

"Well, we'll use our flashlights then," Parker said, sighing.

Kayla detected frustration, which was uncharacteristic of the normally cool and calm Parker. But she had to admit, things were more than just abnormal; it seemed like the day was presenting more problems than answers. Right before she began her descent, Kayla quickly opened the refrigerator to see if there were any additional beers. Nope. Everything was the same as before. Once the three were together, they made the tour again, with Henry leading. He pointed out the newly embedded wall hooks.

"They look like they were selected because they look old," Parker commented, agreeing with Polly's assertion.

Henry shrugged and replied, "Yeah, maybe, but why not recreate other elements from the past as well?"

"Don't know."

Kayla took photos of every inch of the room, zooming in on the hooks. Everything seemed the same as it had been yesterday. When they reached the third and last room, the odor still lingered.

"Do you smell anything?" Kayla asked.

"Yeah, I smell something, and it's foul. Body odor?" Parker asked.

"That's what I think," Henry replied. "I think it's a bit less potent than yesterday, however. What do you think, Kayla?"

"I think Polly would still be pinching her nose, but yeah, it's not as strong. There's something more interesting than the smell, though, or at least I think so," Kayla continued. "There's a hatch door here that doesn't have a handle."

"It's been welded shut," Henry added.

Parker lowered his large frame to get a look. He traced the door, just as Kayla had done yesterday.

"What do you think?" she asked.

As Parker stood, he searched the room again with roving eyes. "There's something wrong down here," he stated abruptly.

The statement and tone created goosebumps on Kayla's upper arms. She rubbed them unconsciously.

"What do you mean?" Henry asked, looking around nervously.

"I mean," Parker said sternly, "there's something malevolent occurring."

Parker was a licensed electrical engineer by training, but he had the gift of intuition. He had a knack for sensing things, specifically paranormal things, which is why he'd hung up his wire strippers and followed his heart, or rather his intuition, to set up this business. He'd told Kayla he'd never looked back.

"Place a video recorder in each room in the basement, powder on the entire floor in all three rooms down here," Parker barked into his mic. Then he added, "And let's get a welder down here," as he headed up the stairs with Henry on his heels. Kayla finished taking photos as fast as possible so she would not be left behind alone.

Chapter

10

Kayla felt unnerved when she entered her darkroom to develop the multitude of photos that she had taken at Beacon's Way. Normally, she couldn't wait to get started, but after their visit, she'd found herself procrastinating. Finally, just around dusk, she mustered up the courage to get going. Once she had entered her darkroom and turned on her lights and music and began her work, she was actually much happier than she had been while putting it off.

What would Dorothea do? she asked herself, shaking her head. She started with the photos from the cupola, to see if her "friend" was still there. *Nah, no such luck.* She closely examined the presumed water spot. It had a strange outline to it. Rather, the demarcation between the spot and the ceiling was not as one would imagine. It was a fuzzy white, almost like foam. She zoomed in and redeveloped it. It looked three-dimensional. Maybe it was mold. Next, Kayla proceeded to the master bedroom. She'd taken several photos of the armoire as well as the bed, since the last owner of the house had died in it.

Kayla was swishing a close-up photo of the armoire in the rinse bin when she first heard a scraping at the window. Then the motion detector light came on. She froze. There was nothing out there except for her car. So had someone been watching her? Even though Kayla decided that she should not be afraid and should not get spooked, she could feel her heart racing with fear. She liked her job and the people working with her too much to start to be ineffective; *this was the nature of the profession, for goodness sake,* Kayla reminded herself as she located a flashlight, opened the door, and swung the beam around in front of her. Nothing but trees. She cautiously headed around the corner to where the noise had occurred.

As the motion detector light flashed on again, she was startled to see that a large cat, a tabby, was sitting on the hood of her car. Ah ha, it had not been a scratching on the window, after all. It must have been the cat's paws landing on the metal. Poor thing, it was probably cold and needed a place to warm up, thinking the car might provide it. Kayla doubted any heat emanated from the engine after being parked so long, but perhaps it was a habit the cat had.

As she got closer, Kayla realized how beautiful it was, in a beastly way. The cat looked up at her with diamond-shaped, emerald eyes. As if on cue, it elicited a long, mournful meow. When she reached out to it, the cat rolled over on its back and waited submissively, perhaps for a belly rub. Kayla didn't know why, but for some reason it made her laugh out loud. It could also have been due to relief.

"Hey kitty," Kayla said soothingly as she rubbed its belly while keeping an eye on its claws. It remained still, waiting. "How did you get here? Where's your home? What's your name?" she continued, as she searched for a collar. Nothing. "Come on with me," Kayla cajoled.

But the cat wouldn't move. Kayla decided she would get some milk to see if that would help. Once she set the bowl on the hood, the cat slowly stood up and strolled over to it. She sniffed it and then went back to the other side of the hood. *You've got to be kidding me,* she thought.

She continued to talk to the cat as she picked it and the milk up and carried it into her darkroom. The animal was heavy, maybe twenty pounds or more. It seemed well-cared for. Kayla wondered why it had come here. She just couldn't leave it outside. Tonight was supposed to be a bit chilly. She decided to call the animal shelter tomorrow and put some signs up around the neighborhood, in case someone lost their cat.

The cat still ignored the milk but seemed keen on getting comfortable on Kayla's coat, which she had tossed on the desk chair upon entering earlier. Kayla observed it for a couple of minutes, thinking it might not be bad to have a pet, but she didn't want to get attached to this one. She was sure someone would be looking for it.

Kayla went back to hang her photo up. Even though it was still wet, the armoire looked normal. Nevertheless, she picked up the magnifying glass and perused it more carefully while it dried. Nothing out of the ordinary. She went to the photo of the bed and began to swish it around in the bin with her tongs. While she did so, the cat jumped off the chair and continuously wrapped itself around her lower legs and ankles. She had to admit she liked the company.

When the photo finally materialized, she was astonished to note that the bed did not appear as it had in the room. There was a minuscule difference; the blanket was slightly indented, as though someone had been lying on it. *Could that be right?* She once again went to her enlarger and made another close-up, closer still. With the magnifying glass, she could see that she was right. There was an indentation. She knew the bed had not looked like that. The cover had been taut, pulled under the mattress on all three sides. She figured the foundation wanted it that way. *Another specter? Something for sure.*

She almost talked herself out of developing the photos of the back of the house, but she persevered. Nothing showed up except what had already been present. She examined all eleven of the windows just to make sure no one was staring back. No one was. Now the cat decided it was time to jump up on her working table. *Uh-oh.* "No!" she shouted. The cat stared at her and blinked slowly. "Get down."

It did a cat stretch and curled up under the lamp, still staring.

"I guess as long as you stay put, you're okay there."

Kayla decided to develop the photos from the basement next. In the end, she had nothing to fear. There were no anomalies. The photos reflected the reality on the ground. *Nothing unusual here.* She sighed. The bedroom had delivered something very unusual that would need further investigation, similar to the cupola, but there was no real cohesion between the specter in the cupola and the specter taking a nap. Had she really thought that? She chuckled to herself. Looking at her watch, she decided it was time to head to bed. She looked over at the fat cat.

"You want to come with me or stay here?" It seemed to understand because it jumped off the table and walked over to stand by the door. "Okay, but you're not going to sleep with me. I don't even know if you're safe to be around."

The next morning when the alarm went off, Kayla opened her eyes to find a fat tabby staring at her, only inches away.

━━━◆━━━

It had been two days since Kayla had discovered the body in Carroll Creek. She didn't jog yesterday, but during the night when she couldn't sleep, she chose a new jogging route. She switched to the Mt. Olivet Cemetery. It was a bit of a hike, not as close as Baker Park, but ... well, it was peaceful here, she reflected as she ran by the row of buried Confederate soldiers. She'd seen a couple of other joggers and one bicyclist, but that was all. She knew from visiting the grounds that she could get in a good eight-mile run if she followed all of the roads and paths. It was huge in terms of the buried, as well. The population matched that of Annapolis. And there were famous people here. Francis Scott Key was undoubtedly the most famous. All in all, not a bad substitute for her other route, Kayla decided after finishing a good run.

Chapter

11

While Kayla was exploring her new jogging route, Hunter Crowley was contacting one of the many people beholden to him.

"No one is going to be available, do you understand me? The welders of Frederick are all tied up for the foreseeable near future."

"Yeah, but that's not going to stop them. They'll do it themselves."

"Not if the foundation demands that it's done by a licensed welder, which it will. Am I right?"

"Yeah, of course."

"Then get on it. Let me know the status by tomorrow. I don't like to be kept waiting."

"Yeah, yeah."

Hunter could hear the man stifling a yawn. "You sound like you're disrespecting me."

"I always sound like this. No disrespect intended, sir."

Hunter hung up the phone with a slam. Guy Hardy was a nuisance but a necessary one.

In many ways, Guy wished he'd never met Hunter. His life had been hard enough these past couple of years without having to be at this man's beck and call. After he'd been fired for tax fraud a few years ago and had served time for the felony, he'd lost everything. Now he was poor. And the United States of America did not like poor people. If you were poor, you were fair game for exploitation, which is what Hunter was doing to him in a covert, nasty kind of way. Guy had made his way to Frederick by chance and had hung out at various locales, trying to find a job. He had about a thousand dollars left to his name when he'd come across a position advertised at the Frederick County Landmarks Foundation. The people had been extremely nice to him and liked how he'd interviewed. They especially liked that he seemed entirely at ease with maintenance jargon and appeared to be very comfortable with the finance end of contracting. Guy had a job.

It wasn't long before Guy had run into Hunter, a man bigger than life. It was casual at first, but then Hunter seemed to show up wherever Guy was working. One late afternoon, just as Guy was leaving the office, he saw the man in his three-piece suit leaning against Guy's beat-up old car.

"How's it going, my man?" he had asked.

"Fine, Hunter. How are you?" Guy thought back, remembering that he'd just wanted to get to his apartment and pop a beer.

"Listen—I was thinking of putting in a good word for you," Hunter had commented. "I think you deserve a raise, a big raise."

Guy had been quite surprised. Boy, he could use more money. It wasn't easy living paycheck to paycheck. And he hated the cheap watery beer he was forced to buy. "Why?" he'd asked.

"Because I'll need some help from you from time to time. Help with the foundation's work." Guy's antennae had gone up immediately. "I'm sure you'll be amenable to it. It's either the raise or the truth. The truth about your past," Hunter had threatened.

Guy's spirits had sunk when he heard Hunter say this. He knew his work with the foundation would be over once they got hold of his felonious history. How the hell had the man found out? Guy had never told a soul in Frederick. Hunter was creepy, no doubt about it. But there wasn't anything Guy could say. So he'd sighed, sucked it up, and agreed. And Hunter was true to his promise. The next week, Guy had received a substantial raise, something very rare in this day and age. So far, Hunter's requests had been pretty benign, as far as he could tell. They sometimes took a little finagling with the fine folks at the foundation, but he had a good rapport with everyone there, so things had always worked out.

Now, however, he needed to figure out if there was some rule that said only licensed welders could work on the heritage homes and buildings. If not, well, anyway, he'd just have to make it so.

Chapter

12

**If you believe in reincarnation, each of us has each
been a ghost thirty times over; if you don't believe
in reincarnation, there are a hundred billion ghosts
among us.**
—Cici Coons

Kayla drove to Beacon's Way full of anticipation. Results from the surveillance equipment would be available. They would examine every room, and she needed to be there to take photos, especially of the rooms with the powder on the floor, a kind of pre- and post- review. Kayla couldn't wait to mention the photo of the human indentation in the bed, but that would come later. Parker must have picked Henry up in the van, since she didn't see his car.

"Are you ready?" Parker asked, as she came running up.

They always entered a building together during this stage of the investigation. It was a precaution Parker had explained when she'd first started working with the team, in case something really abnormal had occurred due to their interference. Parker didn't want anyone to be alone.

"Sure, let's go," she said, taking a deep breath and glancing at Henry.

He seemed especially quiet this morning. Kayla opened the door, and they entered, with Henry bringing up the rear. In the grand living room, there were no footprints on the powder, but a lot more paint chips. Kayla snapped several photos.

"The peeling paint appears to be accelerating," she noted, snapping away at the ceiling as well.

Parker and Henry nodded.

"I'll get the camera when we return," Parker stated. "Let's go up to the cupola."

After reaching the top and catching their breath, they entered the room.

"Oh, man," Henry exclaimed.

Kayla put her hand to her mouth, eyes wide. She started snapping away again. The leak had spread over almost the entirety of the ceiling. Kayla then focused on the floor.

"It looks like multiple footprints," she commented.

"I don't think so," Parker replied, squatting to get closer to them. "I think they indicate that someone, something, was pacing."

"Pacing? What makes an apparition pace?" Henry asked.

"Whatever is bothering him, or her," Kayla guessed.

Henry almost laughed, but while it was funny, it was probably also true.

While Henry squatted next to Parker, Kayla zoomed in on the prints with her lens. "You're right, Parker," Henry concluded as he rose, stopping midway up. "It's the same print. Just all over the place. What's that, there in the corner, or who?"

Kayla slowly turned to see what he was referring to. She couldn't believe she hadn't seen it before. She started walking toward it.

"Stop!" Parker ordered. "Don't go near it. We don't know what that material is."

Kayla halted. He was right of course, but it was mesmerizing. *Was it a shadow from someplace else, outside, reflecting against the wall? Had someone drawn it?* In the same corner where Kayla unknowingly snapped the photo of the specter, an image appeared. Within it, a large brown eye stared back at them.

"Just take photos of it. I'll have someone with protective gear examine it later," Parker said as he gingerly made his way to retrieve the tapes and videos, carefully avoiding the footprints. He dropped them in his large satchel and then turned. "Let's go see the master bedroom."

On the way down the stairs, Kayla described the apparent human indentation she'd found in her photo. Parker nodded.

"Cool," Henry said.

After they'd reached the master bedroom, Parker swung the door open. There were no footprints, but the armoire was back in the middle of the room.

"I don't believe this," Henry said as he collected the cameras. "Let's not tell Polly about this."

"Let's not tell Polly about any of this, not until we figure things out," Parker replied.

Kayla wondered how long that was going to be. At this rate, they were just discovering more weirdness. Resolutions did not seem to be part of the trajectory. She took photos and concentrated on the bedding as well, which now appeared taut. *Seriously, what was going on here?*

"Did you get the electricity to work last night?" Henry asked, turning to Parker.

"Nada."

"How long did you work on it?"

"Until I realized I couldn't get it to work. There's nothing in my fifteen-plus years as an electrical engineer that has baffled me so much. I put lanterns in the kitchen, one for each of us. Let's go."

When they reached the kitchen, the three descended the steep, narrow stairs with their lanterns, which created a strange spectacle of shadows against the old rock wall, almost as though they were living in a previous century, sans electricity. Parker halted before he stepped off the last step, virtually creating a jam-up.

"No footprints," he said as he continued. "Let's go check the other two rooms."

Similar to the first room, the middle room was untouched.

Nonetheless, Kayla took photos in both rooms. The three headed to the third and last room.

"Uh-oh," Parker said as he swung his lantern into the room.

Henry and Kayla immediately squeezed into the doorway to see. Through the shadows and swinging light, multitudes of footprints could be detected.

"This time, they are all different sizes," Henry observed. "Look, some are really small, some larger. Some barefoot, some with shoes. Maybe dancing?"

"Not dancing," Kayla said, snapping her photos. "There would be more smudges in the powder than we're seeing. These all look pretty distinct. Almost, by contrast, as if standing, moving now and again, but not by much."

Henry took some more time to observe. "You're right," he agreed.

"Kayla, you get the videos and tapes; you're smaller," Parker suggested, alluding to the congestion on the floor.

She tiptoed into the room and collected the material, avoiding the footprints.

"Okay, guys, let's go back up," Parker said, looking around a final time.

Kayla did the same. This room gave her the creeps.

"Let's talk," Parker said as he sat down at the table. Kayla glanced over at Henry. He looked very somber. She supposed she did too. She set her equipment and satchel down.

Parker started, saying, "I have never seen anything like this, have you?"

"What do you mean?" Kayla asked.

"This house doesn't have a history of being haunted. It hasn't been occupied for years. Now, literally out of the blue, she's starting to change, deteriorate, if you will. And we know there is at least one specter present. And your most recent photo of the bed suggests possibly another one, footprints suggest there are others, a huge piece of furniture keeps moving, and I can't get a simple electrical connection to function."

"Why would ghosts turn on their own abode?" Henry asked. "It doesn't make sense."

Kayla spoke thoughtfully. "It does if there's something they don't like about it."

"But what's not to like?"

"Maybe a better question is, What has changed?" Kayla suggested.

Just then, Parker's phone rang. "Yeah, go ahead. Are you sure? You're sure. Okay, thanks," he said before snapping his phone shut. "The analysis from the leak on the cupola's ceiling came back. It's salt water."

Chapter
13

Still mulling over the findings from the day spent at Beacon's Way, Kayla made her way to town. Along with just about everyone else she knew, she was going to celebrate the last "Alive at Five" for the year. It took place on Carroll Creek, on the opposite side of town from Baker Park. A live band started playing at five. Admission was $5, and food, wine, and beer could be purchased. The weather had cooperated; it was going to be a lovely evening. She saw her friend Della from a distance and waved. Della had brought her dog. Lots of people brought their dogs. It made Kayla think about the cat that had taken up residence in her house. She was as big as some of these little dogs, even bigger. Kayla still wasn't used to the oversized furry animal, but it did like being with her in her darkroom, which was nice, even comforting. She had decided that she wanted to keep this tabby. She had put up dozen of signs about the lost cat after contacting the animal shelter a couple of days ago, but so far, no one had claimed her. When she thought about losing her, Kayla felt a stabbing pain in her heart.

"Hey, Kayla, good to see you," Joe said, interrupting her thoughts.

"Hi, Joe, what have you been up to?" Joe Welter was one of the many artists living and working in Frederick. He was really good.

"Painting," he said, laughing and sitting down next to her on the stone bleachers built into the grassy hill.

"Other than painting," she said, smiling as she sipped her wine.

"Not much. Trying to stay abreast of all of the gossip is actually quite difficult. Did you hear about Eleanor?"

"No. What did she do now?"

"She's getting married."

"Married! To whom?"

"Person named Irakli Guramishivili. He's Georgian, as in the Republic of Georgia. She met him on the Internet. He's flying in from Tbilisi to tie the knot."

Kayla was shocked. "That sounds crazy."

"Yeah, it does sound crazy. But Eleanor's not necessarily always 100 percent balanced, so it kind of fits."

Kayla decided there was some truth in that, so she just nodded, thinking.

"Are they going to live here?"

"Dunno."

"What's Buzz say?"

"Dunno that either. But I bet he's relieved. Okay, I'm going to get more wine, you want anything?"

Kayla shook her head no. *Well, good for her, I hope*, Kayla thought. Just then, she noticed Gloria Marshall across the way. It looked like she'd cornered Angie. She made a mental note to try to avoid her at all costs.

"Hey, girlfriend." She turned to see Hunter Crowley standing behind her with Second Chance on a fancy leash. "How ya doin'?"

"Hunter, please don't call me that," she snapped. "Don't call me 'girl-anything.' Not girlie girl, not girlfriend. It annoys me." She didn't care how much money or political influence the man had. She was sick of his sexist comments.

"Wow. Touchy, touchy. What, no ghosts this week?"

"Plenty of ghosts this week." Oops. She wished she hadn't said that.

"Oh, over at Beacon's Way?"

Kayla was surprised and knew that it showed.

"I saw the van over there. I figured … old house, something's up. What is it?"

"Nothing. The foundation thought there was a problem, but it was a false alarm," she lied.

"But I thought you said plenty of ghosts."

"I was just trying to defend our work."

"You don't have to do that. I believe in ghosts."

"Really? You don't seem the type."

"What's type is that?"

"Never mind. Just didn't think of you as that type of person." *Because you always mock the work*, Kayla thought but bit her tongue.

"Well, I do. I'm going for a drink. You want anything, Kayla?"

"No, thanks, I'm fine." *What a jerk*, she thought as he sauntered off.

Suddenly, Polly Rutledge was in her face.

"Kayla, I'm afraid," she said.

Kayla looked around to make sure they were out of earshot, but it didn't matter. The band was loud, people were drinking and talking, some were dancing down near the stage, and one lone woman was hula hooping. Nonetheless, she put her arm around Polly's shoulders and walked away from the crowd.

"Polly, Parker showed us the note you received. I think it must be a prank," she began, which wasn't exactly true.

The woman was visibly shaken. "It's not just that, darlin'," she said as she dabbed a tissue to her nose. "The National Museum of Civil War Medicine is starting to have new problems, too, same thing."

"What do you mean?" Kayla asked, alarmed.

"Just like Beacon's Way. It's got damage on the third floor."

"Did you call Parker?"

"Yes, of course I did. He's a sweet man," she added, sniffling. "He said y'all have to review your findings from Beacon's Way tomorrow, but you'll get to it as soon as possible. What's happening is downright frightening."

Kayla nodded, wondering what was going on.

"Any furniture moving?" she asked, to lighten the conversation, but it didn't work.

"Lord only knows. I'm not goin' there. You can ask the proprietor to let you up to that floor. You know it's off limits to the public."

"No, I didn't know that. I'm sure there's a logical explanation for both of these ...," and here, Kayla paused to find the right phrase, "changing conditions."

Polly didn't look convinced.

"Come on, Polly, let me buy you a glass of wine."

"Nooo, honey, I'm not in the mood anymore. I'm goin' home.

"Are you sure?"

But the woman had already turned and was headed in the opposite direction. Kayla couldn't believe it. *Another building?*

She went to get another glass of wine, but Polly had changed that desire. Then Kayla noticed that it was getting dark. It was fall time at last, she realized, feeling kind of sad about the end of summer, the last Alive at Five, the end of Daylight Savings Time, the inevitable graying skies. Kayla decided to head home too. But as she was leaving, her phone rang. She didn't recognize the number.

"Hello?"

"Kayla, this is Detective Nucci. Nick."

"Oh, hello."

"Hi. How have you been doing?"

"Good. I'm good," she said, trying to sound upbeat. But just hearing the detective's voice brought tears to her eyes. "I'm trying to stay busy," she added.

"I'm sure that's helpful," he replied and then paused. "Kayla, I don't want to have you relive the entire episode from Baker Park, but I do have additional information from the coroner now, and I told you I'd contact you. If you don't want to hear it, that is certainly understandable."

Kayla wondered herself if she wanted to hear it but then thought that she couldn't not know more. "No, I mean, yes. I do want to know. What have you found?"

"Well, I'm just getting off work, and I was wondering if you are free.

We could meet at, say, Firestones. It might be better than discussing it over the phone."

Kayla glanced up and realized she was not far from the restaurant. "I think that would be fine. I'm leaving Alive at Five, so I could meet you there shortly."

"That's great. I'll be there in a few minutes."

Kayla walked around a bit downtown, window shopping, and then she made her way to Firestones.

The downstairs bar area was busy. Kayla told the hostess she was waiting to meet someone. "The detective? He's upstairs," the hostess replied, motioning.

"Thanks." Kayla headed up the stairs and saw Detective Nucci by the window. A drink sat on the small table.

The detective stood when she approached. "Hi. Glad you could make it," he added after they shook hands.

She realized she had not really observed him earlier. He appeared athletic, six feet or more, maybe mid- to late thirties.

"Thanks again, Detective," Kayla responded as she sat down.

He motioned for the waitress. "I'm glad you decided to come," he started, "and please call me Nick."

"I must say I know I need to hear what happened, but it's hard. As I mentioned, I've been keeping busy just to avoid thinking about it."

"That's probably a good tactic. How are you feeling now?"

"I sometimes begin to dwell on it … her. I have not forgotten in the least what I saw and how I felt."

Just then, the waitress approached. Kayla ordered a glass of wine.

"These things, these types of incidents can be extremely disturbing."

"No kidding," Kayla said, looking out the window at the pedestrians rushing here and there, dashing between the evening traffic. It all seemed so civilized. But someone had been murdered in Frederick. A very rare event.

"As I mentioned, I met with the coroner. According to her," Nick continued, "she was sexually abused but died from strangulation, as you may have suspected."

Kayla frowned. "So someone killed her by the creek?"

"It doesn't appear that there was a struggle there, so maybe not. I mean, our investigative team was only able to pick up a single pair of footprints. Of course, we're going to continue to search the area for more evidence, but as of now, it seems that she was probably brought there."

"You mean dumped there."

"Perhaps that's a better description," Nick agreed, remembering that that was how Dr. Wild had described it.

"I just don't know how anyone could do something like that."

"I know." After the waitress delivered Kayla's wine, she asked if they wanted anything to eat. Neither had looked at the menus. "Not right now," the detective replied as Kayla shook her head no.

"How long had she been there?"

"Well, it seems you arrived relatively close to the time she might have been … dumped there. The coroner said she was killed around 3 a.m.

"Oh, my God. So it could have happened while I was in the park."

"Yes, that's right. I also had some vehicular tracks on the bridge analyzed. I thought they belonged to the park and recreation vehicles, but apparently, they belong to a golf cart."

"A golf cart? What's that tell you?"

"I don't know. They apparently belong to a very expensive golf cart. It could have been the way the killer brought the body there."

Kayla shook her head as if to say, *What next?* "I have to say I don't usually run that early. I couldn't sleep."

Nick nodded.

"What more can you tell me?" she asked.

Nick proceeded to relay everything he knew. Kayla was surprised when he explained that the victim was most likely Nepali. "How many Nepalese live in Frederick?" she asked rhetorically. "Her parents must be going nuts. Have they been contacted?"

Nick shook his head. "Right now, unfortunately, she's a Jane Doe. There was no identification on her, except for the tattoo. We're still waiting, hoping for someone to report her missing. We do have someone identifying all Nepali inhabitants of Frederick, including checking out all of the schools, but it could be that she was adopted, which might mean an Anglo name, or even just visiting."

Kayla nodded.

"I'm sorry you had to find her, but at the same time, we're grateful she was found so soon after she was murdered."

Kayla nodded again, thinking. "I wonder why she was killed?"

"Yeah, motive is always difficult in cases like this. That's why it's so important to find her parents, to better understand her, know where she might have been, who she hung out with, what school she attended, and any other pertinent details."

There was silence for a few minutes. Now both Nick and Kayla were staring out the window.

"My biggest desire is for you to find out who did this and bring that person to justice," she finally said. "Will you let me know what else you find?"

"Of course. And if you think of anything that might be important, please call me. I know you said you only saw one other person that morning and that he was walking on the other side of the park."

"He had a cane."

I know. It might not have been that man, though we are searching for him as well, to see whether he saw or heard anything. For example, did you hear any cars start up?"

Kayla thought for a moment. "No. In fact, I was marveling at how peaceful everything was. I would have remembered hearing that."

"Understood. But again, if anything pops into your head about your jog, anything, just let me know."

"Okay." Kayla looked at her watch. "I've got to get up early tomorrow, so I'd better get going."

Nick nodded. "By the way, what do you do, if you don't mind my asking?"

"Not at all. I work for the Dulany Team."

"The paranormal investigators?"

"One and the same," she said, surprised he knew about them.

"Well, that must be interesting."

"It is," Kayla replied smiling. "Incredibly so."

"Good for you."

Chapter
❖ 14 ❖

The next morning, Kayla got up early in order to take her cat to the veterinarian. Henry had suggested his cousin, Gabriel Kotei. Dr. Kotei was located on the outskirts of town, on the way to Middletown. Kayla could not find it at first but then realized the office was in a building located a good distance behind what used to be a barn, which was now in disrepair and collapsing. Numerous buildings surrounded the barn, but there appeared to be no activity within them. The small parking lot in front of the clinic was empty. Kayla figured she was the first customer of the day.

"Well, Ms. Dunn ..."

"Please, call me Kayla."

"Kayla, you have a fine feline specimen here. She's in great shape, no worms or fleas," the kind doctor explained after examining the cat. "She has a good, strong heartbeat, and her teeth are very good as well. I'd say she's around three years old. Someone took really good care of her."

The cat stared at Kayla during the entire checkup.

"So how did ... or rather why ... or what is she doing here?" Kayla sputtered. She had spoken to Dr. Kotei when she made the appointment and told him how she had come to have the cat.

"I don't know. But I would suspect someone dropped her off near your house."

"You mean intentionally?"

"In a way. Someone may have had some bad luck, maybe a foreclosure, maybe had to move and just couldn't take her. You've done everything you can," he continued. "I don't think anyone will claim her. I'd take down the signs."

Kayla's heart jumped when she heard this. "Really?"

"Yeah, she's so fine, someone would have come for her by now," Dr. Kotei concluded, admiring the cat, who was just sitting on the examining table, continuing to stare at Kayla, emerald eyes gleaming.

Kayla's happiness soared when she heard his words. "Okay, well, what do I need to do now?"

"I recommend we provide a microchip." Kayla nodded her agreement. "I'll give you a copy of the report with the number on it, in case she gets lost. You simply call the Humane Society and let them know what it is. It will help them identify her if she's been turned in. I will also give her the necessary shots, and finally, you need to give her a name."

"A name?" Kayla was taken aback. She had never even thought about naming her.

"Give her something fitting; maybe a reflection of her character. Just don't name her Lucky. That name will invariably forsake you. Think about it. Don't be hasty. You need to like it. And anyway, you haven't done it yet, so …"

"Fritchie."

"I beg your pardon?"

"I'll name her Fritchie."

Dr. Kotei hesitated for a minute and then burst out laughing.

"That's a good one," he agreed shaking his head. "That's a good one."

Kayla couldn't agree more. Barbara Fritchie was a famous local heroine. She'd lived in Frederick for almost a century, through both the Revolutionary and Civil Wars, and was described as a brazen, stubborn Unionist. A poem, written by John Greenleaf Whittier, was titled after the good woman, and depicted an elderly lady waving the American flag at Stonewall Jackson and his troops in September 1862 as they'd marched through town:

"Shoot, if you must, this old gray head,
But spare your country's flag," she said.
A shade of sadness, a blush of shame,
Over the face of the leader came;
The nobler nature within him stirred
To life at that woman's deed and word:
"Who touches a hair of yon gray head
Dies like a dog! March on!" he said.

"You know, Winston Churchill recited the entire poem to FDR when he visited Frederick on their way back from Camp David," Dr. Kotei commented.

"Really? I didn't know." Somehow, that made the name even more significant.

"Yeah, she's Fritchie all right," he agreed as he administered the shots.

Fritchie didn't seem to mind, however. She never took her eyes off Kayla.

Chapter

15

Hunter Crowley was lonely. He wanted to find a wife. At the age of forty-two, he decided the time was finally right. He wasn't that bad looking, but even if he wasn't great, he had a lot of money. That should definitely be a plus to any prospective mate. He'd hoped to find someone in Frederick, but so far, there didn't seem to be too many likely prospects. He liked that girl Kayla Dunn. She was pretty enough, in a tomboyish way. But somehow, he'd rubbed her the wrong way. *Go figure.* "Ah hell, boy," he said to Second Chance as he mixed Kahlua in his morning coffee. "We'll have to start over. I may need to go south, see what's up in Bethesda or even DC."

As he started to put the leash on Second Chance, his phone rang. He could tell it was his private line, given the ring tone. He looked at his watch. It was around 3 p.m. in Moscow.

"Yes?"

"Package will be sent through Canadian Port A. Challenges taken care of in advance. Border crossing arranged. Frederick arrival on the 12th." Click.

"Sorry, boy," Hunter said. "We're going to have to postpone that walk. I need to check some things."

He sat down at his computer and called up Port Inventory. Ah ha, Port A was Port of Toronto. *So that's how he was able to do it so fast.*

Wonder how he got the border cleared, but these days, anyone could be bought, so it probably had not been that hard. He picked up his phone, the one he'd just been on, and called Tommy Mitka. He repeated the message, just as he'd heard it.

"I'll be there to facilitate it," was all Mitka said, before hanging up.

Hunter smiled. "Well, Second Chance, everything is going as planned, and I mean, really well. Ready to go for that walk now?"

As Mitka started to pack for the trip, his wife began grousing. "Why are you always leaving me?" Lily cried. "You're off without a minute's notice, and you never tell me where you're going or when you're coming back. You could be dead along a freeway, and I wouldn't know to start looking for you for weeks, until you were unrecognizable due to the elements."

"Enough with the drama queen act," Johnny snapped.

"It's not an act," she pouted.

God, she was beautiful, Tommy thought. *Vapid, but beautiful.* He changed his tactic in order to appease her. "Nothing's going to happen to me," he said as he sat down on the bed and pulled her onto his lap. "Nothing. I promise you."

"But why can't you at least call me?" she implored. "Just call to let me know that you are okay when you get to wherever you're going."

"It's not that kind of job. I need to remain invisible."

"But sweetie," she cooed. "I'm lonely and worried when you're gone. Please, please call me. Just say something short, like, 'I'm here,' or, or, even just one word: 'Arrived.' I just want to hear your voice. Please do it for me?"

"Okay. I'll do it. But be prepared for it to be a very fast phone call."

"Thank you so much. I love you, Tommy."

Tommy's heart thumped an extra beat whenever he heard those words.

Chapter
16

To be haunted is to receive an unwelcome secret.
—Michael Burris

After dropping Fritchie off at her house, Kayla drove directly to the Dulany Team office on East Street.

"Sorry I'm late," she said a bit breathlessly as she entered the viewing room.

Parker handed her a coffee. "Don't sweat it. We just arrived too. How was your evening? You holding up okay?"

Kayla nodded. "I met with Detective Nucci."

"Oh? What have they found?" Parker asked, with a worried look on his face.

"It's not good," Kayla replied, shaking her head. She proceeded to tell Parker and Henry what Detective Nucci had told her.

"It's too grisly," Henry commented. "I mean, it's hard to believe something like that occurred here, in Frederick."

"It's rare, thankfully," Parker said. "But yeah, it's terrible. He'll continue to let you know how it's progressing?"

"Yeah. I sure hope they find that monster," Kayla said.

There was silence for a couple of minutes, and then Parker spoke: "Right before you came in, I was telling Henry about Polly's telephone call. She told me there's some strange paranormal activity at the National Museum of Civil War Medicine. She was pretty upset."

Kayla nodded.

"I told her we'd get to it as soon as we could, but we needed to at least finish collecting and synthesizing information from Beacon's Way, even if we can't resolve it immediately," Parker continued.

"But everyone knows that the museum is haunted," Henry commented.

"Polly said the museum director told her the activities that are occurring are new," Parker replied.

"I wonder if there's any connection?" Kayla asked. "I mean between Beacon's Way and the museum."

"We'll find out. Right now, we have a bunch of videos to review," Parker said, turning to look at the white screen while leaning back in his chair, clasping his hands behind his head. "Let's start at the top with the cupola and work our way down."

After a couple of hours, the three of them were totally exasperated. Absolutely nothing had been revealed from the videos.

"You would have thought with all of those footprints, something would have shown up," Kayla proclaimed.

"Yeah, but you know it's not always that straightforward," Parker reminded her.

"I hear you. I'm going to look through the negatives I took."

Parker nodded. "Let's start over with the recording tapes. Maybe the spirits are more talkative than visible. This one is from the cupola." At the beginning of each of the tape recordings, they always asked, "What is the reason for your presence here?"

The cupola tape provided nothing but silence, until almost the very end. In fact, it seemed as though there really was nothing, but then Kayla heard something, or thought she did. "Back it up. Just a minute or so." Parker reversed it a little. "There. Did you hear that?"

Henry nodded. "A slight tinkling."

"Exactly."

"I wonder what it is; keys, perhaps?"

"Maybe," Parker agreed. "But there are a number of possibilities. It's just something we'll have to keep trying to discover."

Kayla was becoming frustrated. "Why don't the ghosts just come out and tell us what they want us to know?"

Henry and Parker laughed. Of course, Kayla knew why they didn't. Specifically, entities were composed of energy. They simply did not always behave the way a human would want or expect them to behave. *Perhaps they were doing the best they could*, she concluded to herself.

"Let's see if there are any more signs in the other rooms," Henry suggested.

Parker nodded and flipped the next tape into the recorder. The master bedroom was next. The tape was almost finished when a huge *thud* occurred, making the three of them jump.

"The armoire," Henry stated matter-of-factly. Parker and Kayla nodded, imagining the armoire as it sat in the middle of the room. "I wonder if it will continue to move it around. I mean, what's the point?"

Kayla shrugged. "Just for us to not forget that someone has the power to do it."

Henry frowned but didn't say anything else. The grand living room proved to be soundless.

"The cellar's next," Parker said as he reached for the tape. "I can't wait."

Kayla couldn't tell if he was kidding or being serious. She for one could easily wait. There was a strange feeling down there, especially in the third room. And Parker had said as much.

"Did Polly ever get back to us about the welder?" Parker asked, as he looked at his watch.

"She said they were fully booked for some time," Henry responded, leaning back in his chair.

Parker frowned. Kayla laughed and said, "All welders booked... what's going on in Frederick that we have no welders available?"

"We'll just have to do it ourselves," Parker stated.

"I mentioned that to her, but she said there's a rule on the books that says only welders contracted through the foundation can be used. And they're all booked."

"That's ridiculous," Parker commented, visibly annoyed.

"You mean the rule or that fact that they're all booked?" Kayla asked.

"Both." He hit the Play button. There immediately began an eerie silence, in that a sound of soft static could be heard.

"It sounds like it's the tape recorder," Kayla noted.

Parker shook his head. "Not possible. The machine is top of the line in order to avoid such an occurrence."

"Shhh. What's that?" Henry asked.

"It sounds like scraping," Kayla replied.

"Not scraping, shuffling," Parker added. "It's on the floor. I've heard it two other times in old buildings here in Frederick. Remember the Spite House?" he asked Henry.

Henry nodded. The Spite House was so named because the owner had built it when he heard that the city planned to place a road through his empty parcel of land next to his existing house on Church Street. An ordinance indicated that if one had started construction of a building, a road could not be initiated, so Dr. Tyler built the house to spite the planners, though he never lived in it. The Spite House was also reputed to be haunted.

The shuffling began again and continued for another two minutes or so. Then back to just the static hum. Then silence. The three strained to hear more. Nothing. Then … suddenly whispering, among multiple voices:

"Watch out."

"Don't let him see that."

"Where are we?"

"Same place. Don't you recognize it?"

"Where's Lucas?"

"Dead."

"We're all dead."

The whispering stopped as suddenly as it started. Then a young girl began crying, followed by another voice: "Shut up!"

Kayla jumped. Henry dropped his pen. The tape came to an abrupt end. The three sat, stupefied.

"Have either of you ever heard anything like that?" Kayla asked, realizing that she was whispering now too.

Parker and Henry shook their heads.

"That's a first," Parker finally said. "I was right, unfortunately. We've got something evil occurring here. Not good. I don't want any of us to go there alone. I mean that."

"Don't worry," Henry agreed.

Kayla nodded in total agreement.

Chapter

17

The team decided to call it a night after listening to the last recording a second time. They would reconvene at the office tomorrow. In the meantime, even though it had been a full day and nothing had shown up on the videos, Kayla still wanted to develop the photos, as she'd mentioned to Parker and Henry.

"Fritchie, Fritchie," Kayla called for the cat as she entered her house and turned on a lamp from the wall light switch. Quickly she scanned the room. "Fritchie, Fritchie," she called again. "Fritchie, Fritchie, where are you? Come kitty, kitty, kitty."

Kayla wasn't accustomed to calling for cats (or any animals, for that matter). She tried a higher pitched tone. Nothing. Of course, the cat had just been given the name this morning, so chances she knew it were nil. Nonetheless, *where could she be?* Kayla thought, her heart beginning to race. She continued calling out to Fritchie as she searched the kitchen and then raced upstairs, checking in the two bedrooms, under the bed, and then in the bathroom. She even checked behind the shower curtain. Now she was biting her lower lip, a habit she constantly tried to break, but which came roaring back whenever she was upset. She ran down two floors to check out the family room. That's when she halted. Her back door was ajar. *How?* But rather than be alarmed about the opened door, Kayla fretted about Fritchie. *Oh Fritchie, please come back.* "Kitty, kitty,

kitty," she called out on the porch, clapping her hands. But nothing. No tabby came sauntering up.

She returned to the kitchen and wrapped her arms around her torso as she paced. Then she stopped and opened the refrigerator. She reached for the milk and poured some into a bowl. When she returned the carton, she spotted leftover pizza and grabbed it. Kayla went back downstairs and placed the bowl of milk just inside the door and left the door partially open, just as she found it. "Please come back, Fritchie, please." She went back upstairs, took the pizza, and exited through the front door, making sure it was tightly shut. She got her gear from her car and unlocked the door to the darkroom, switching on the light as she entered.

"Fritchie!" she cried. "How did you get in here? Oh Fritchie, I'm so glad you're here. How did you get in here?" Kayla kept switching back and forth from being upset to relief.

The cat was simply sitting on the desk, staring at the door as though waiting for Kayla, who was now picking Fritchie up and hugging her as she danced around the room with her in her arms. Finally, she stopped and put the cat back on the desk. Then she walked around the entire room, trying to see how the cat might have entered. One window was unlocked, which surprised her, but it was not open. She looked around outside as she locked it. Then she had a really creepy feeling. Maybe she'd put Fritchie in here in the morning, after she'd come back from Dr. Kotei's clinic. Kayla tried to recall her actions but honestly could not. She had been in such a hurry to get to the office that maybe she truly had deposited Fritchie in the darkroom. Still, why was her back door opened? *Well, that could have just been carelessness.* She looked over at the tabby. Yep, she was watching Kayla as she checked the windows. *Oh well ... She's okay.* Kayla sat down at the desk and munched on her pizza, sizing the cat up once again. She was just gorgeous.

"Okay, Fritchie," Kayla started, finishing her pizza. "I've got some work to do."

Thirty minutes later, Kayla began to develop one of her more promising negatives taken from the cupola, one of the photos of the shadow painting in the corner; she must have clicked a dozen or more. "Oh, my," she said out loud as the image started to emerge. She hung it up to dry while she observed it. The picture with the brown eye did not look the same as it had appeared in real time. In the photo, it looked three dimensional. After it dried, she set it on her easel to observe it. Something looked familiar about it, but she couldn't place it. Then Kayla began circling it. The eye followed her, the figure turned three-quarters. That was it, she realized. It was a trompe l'oeil, a French term that literally meant "that which deceives the eye."

Kayla still remembered the day she had discovered the trompe l'oeils peppering Frederick's urban landscape. She had just walked across the Community Bridge at Carroll Creek when she saw the mural. It was mesmerizing. She'd taken a zillion photos. While there was a description on the mural itself of how it came to be, she'd needed to know more, wanted to know more. After some reading, Kayla had learned that there were over thirty such paintings and murals in Frederick, but the Community Bridge mural was the largest. The designer's name was William M. Cochran.

As the story was recounted, Cochran had come across teenagers at the potential mural site and asked them, "What object represents the spirit of community to you?"

One teen responded saying, "Two hands, one black, one white, one helping the other over the wall; doesn't matter which one."

Apparently, Cochran had asked a number of friends and acquaintances the same question but not strangers. He'd discovered then and there, following the response from the boy, that he wanted input from everyone. So he had reached out to people everywhere to ask the question. People from Frederick, the country, and all over the world began submitting images that reflected a combination of core common values. Cochran then proceeded to incorporate many of the images onto the mural.

Kayla hadn't stopped there, however. She'd wanted to know more about the trompe l'oeil technique itself. She quickly discovered that the trompe l'oeil had been invented around 400 BC and was quite the rage in both Greek and Roman societies. The example cited was that of real horses neighing at a mural of trompe l'oeil horses; the real horses were obviously reacting to the drawing. Another story told of a contest between two renowned artists. When the two artists came together to display their masterpieces, the first artist revealed a trompe l'oeil that was so realistic it was reported that birds tried to peck the grapes he'd painted. But the second artist knew he'd won when he was asked to unveil his painting by pulling back the curtains; the curtains were part of the painting.

Now Kayla returned her focus to the situation at hand. What or who had been able to create such an image in the cupola? How was it that it appeared so differently from the camera's perspective? But then she remembered that maybe it wasn't different. The team hadn't taken the time to walk back and forth looking at the figure. There were the footprints to avoid and the need to stay away before they could determine what had been used to create the image. Similarly, the video camera was static. She recalled that when she took photos of the murals in Frederick, they had reflected the artist's troupe l'oeil. So most likely, the shadow in the corner of the cupola was indeed the real thing: a trompe l'oeil. She would talk to Parker about going back tomorrow to make sure. *But more importantly, what did it mean?* Who drew it, how, and why? Her frustration was mounting.

Nonetheless, Kayla pressed on to the other negatives; first, the master bedroom. Nothing in particular appeared. Similarly, there was nothing to be found in the grand living room. She looked at her watch. It was time to look at the cellar. She looked over at Fritchie. The cat was purring loudly, watching her. She even appeared to wink. Kayla wished she could be so calm. The cellar at Beacon's Way scared her. *All those feet.* She was sure that they represented many people, many souls. She went to her mini refrigerator and pulled out a bottle of white wine. She uncorked it, reached for the wine glass on the shelf above, and poured herself a generous amount, which she sipped while pacing around the room, procrastinating. She couldn't get the "Shut up" out of her head from the recording they had listened to earlier, but the girl's sobbing was almost too much to bear.

Finally, with renewed commitment and now a little numbness to the trepidation, Kayla decided to develop the eight negatives from the cellar. As they started to dry, she squinted to examine them. Then she pulled out the magnifying glass. What was she looking for? Jeez, the footprints. Now she could zoom in on them. After she did so, Kayla counted a total of six different prints. Six different entities? What made them gather there? She was so absorbed with the prints that she failed to notice the shadows on the cellar's walls. It was like looking out your window at the trees bordering your yard and not noticing that a huge spider had built a web on the opposite side of the glass and was staring right you. When Kayla finally caught a glimpse of what she'd been overlooking, she got goosebumps. The crowd had suddenly come to life. They were not present, and yet they were. Their silhouettes indicated action, as in walking together. Where to was unknown. All eight negatives showed similar shots of them. *Were they ghosts from another era? Why were they there, together? Were they on some kind of mission?*

Kayla decided to re-examine them, slowly. She did not want to miss a thing. The shadows were interesting, to say the least. She could almost make out the clothing or at least imagined she could. In most cases, Kayla could tell that the garments did not fit properly, usually too big. She also noticed that some clothes were fraying. The larger footprints indicated shoes; the smaller footprints were bare feet. Kayla pulled her magnifying glass back in order to look at the scene in its entirety, hoping to gather contextual information. She almost jumped out of her skin when she caught the other image: a young man, crouching behind the washing machine. Very much alive.

Chapter
18

"Is that as big as you can blow it up?" Parker asked again.

"Yes. Any more and we'll lose all definition," Kayla explained.

"But I can't make out any distinctive features," a frustrated Parker complained.

"I know, Parker. It's the best I can do. We're not going to be able to determine who this person is," Kayla continued, referring to her discovery the night before of the live human being in the cellar at Beacon's Way. The photo was now reflecting back from the large screen they had pulled down to view it. "The point is someone was there. We don't know why or how often he has been in the house, but we do have this."

"Should we tell Polly?" Henry wondered.

"Yes, but we're not going to," Parker replied as he paced back and forth in the conference room.

"Then maybe we should show this to the police," Henry continued.

"What for? We can't make out the face, so neither can they," Parker responded.

Kayla said, "We may be getting all worked up for nothing. This could be someone down on their luck who just happened to be spending the night there. It could explain the beers in the refrigerator."

"I don't buy that for a second," Parker said. "First of all, if you're down on your luck, you're not going to be buying locally brewed craft beer. Second, but more importantly, this person is aware of the video camera. Why else would he be crouching? Hiding?"

"Well, maybe. Maybe he is hiding for another reason?" Henry suggested.

"Ugh," Parker said, sliding his fingers through his hair. He pivoted quickly. "We've just focused on his face. Can you zoom in on his feet?"

"I already tried that," Kayla acknowledged. "The photo didn't include them. It's really only a head and torso shot. One thing I think I'm noticing, though," she said as she approached the image on the screen, "is that this person appears to be on the younger side. I thought he was in his twenties last night, but not now. Do you see that? He's very slight, as though not fully matured."

"I thought that too," Henry said. "Yeah, it's a younger person."

Parker just shook his head. "Another clue, but really just another loose end."

Kayla disagreed. "I think it's important to know that this is occurring, or at least happened. I did check the other areas of the house, but there are no other instances of this."

"It's definitely creepy," Henry commented. "I mean, here is this person present at the same time or around the same time as the video captured all of those spirits nearby."

Kayla felt a chill. She and Parker looked at him. Neither of them had thought of that. They nodded.

"So now what?" Henry asked.

"We'll wait to see where this character fits into our investigation," Parker said. "It's all we can do."

"There's something else," Kayla said.

"There's more?" Parker asked.

Henry also looked surprised.

"Yes. About the feet in the cellar."

"What about them?"

Kayla spoke as she switched photos to show the area where the footprints were located. "The shadows of the owners of the feet are all over the walls ... six entities in all."

"Really?" Parker perked up with this news. "What are they doing?" he asked as he stepped closer to the screen.

"Same as we discussed. They seem to be perpetually walking. But they are different sizes. Some female. You can even make out their clothes, a bit."

Henry got close too. "Why are they there?"

"I think it's a meeting, or maybe a forced gathering," Kayla replied. "Look at their stooped shoulders. They're not happy players. Depressed ghosts in a depressed house. I hate to unload on you, but I made one more discovery with the photos."

Parker was shaking his head, and Henry laughed. Well, it was more like a snort.

"You know the image? The one in the corner of the cupola?"

"Yes," Parker replied. "We're still waiting to find out what it's made from."

"Well, it's a trompe l'oeil."

"A what?" Parker asked.

"To deceive the eye," Kayla said as she brought up the photo. "Similar to the ones at the Community Bridge."

"Oh. Is that what they're called?" Henry commented rather than asked.

"Yes. I really need to go check it out. See if it's one in real time."

"No, Kayla. Not yet. End of discussion," Parker stated adamantly.

Not going to stop me, Kayla thought as she was already trying to think of an excuse if she got caught. After all, she had the key.

Chapter

❦ 19 ❦

Hunter Crowley jumped from bed when he heard the buzzer. He quickly picked up the phone and listened, trying to ignore his throbbing hangover headache at the same time.

"I'm fine," he overheard.

"But where are you, baby? I miss you."

"I told you I can't tell you."

"Can I guess?"

"No. Stop it, Lily. I've got to go."

"Are you in the US?"

"No."

"Mexico," she persisted.

"No."

"I knew it. You're in Canada. Canada where? Big city, I bet. Ummm…Toronto, right?" Lily heard a sigh. She only knew of two cities in Canada, Toronto and Vancouver. By the sigh, she knew she'd guess right. "It's Toronto right sweetie?"

"Yes. Good-bye Lily."

Hunter had heard enough. He clicked off, punched in a number, and started dictating: "Abort! Abort! Abort! Abort operation! Repeat: Abort operation! Protocol broken. Protocol broken. Cease and desist.

Discontinue delivery of package immediately. Cease any knowledge of said ship. She is dead to us. Leave the country!"

"Damn! Damn you, Tommy!" Hunter now had to acknowledge that he'd just lost a small fortune.

Chapter

20

The murdered do haunt their murderers, I believe.
I know that ghosts have wandered on earth.
Be with me always -- take any form -- drive me mad!
Only do not leave me in this abyss, where I cannot
find you!
—Emily Bronte

Tommy Mitka had arrived at the designated Port A early in the morning. It was still dark, dark and foggy, and it was going to remain so for a good while, given the forecast. *Good.* The more cover, the better. His nonskid boat shoes barely made a sound as he began to reconnoiter the area looking for any conceivable trap or weakness in the delivery and facilitation plans. It was cold. He pulled up his dark hoodie to shield himself against the dampness. Everything seemed to be on the up-and-up. It appeared that business was minimal at this port. Only two of the docks seemed to be in use. Nonetheless, he surveyed Port A in its entirety. It was comprised of twelve docks in all. Dock A was where the package was to be delivered. He walked along this dock, noting the outdoor cargo storage area as well as the small warehouse building. Furthermore, there was a crane and two forklifts. A large ship was docked. In the distance, he heard the mournful wail of a ship's horn.

Everything was immobile, as though sitting on a movie set. The sound of water lapping against the seawall was ever-present. There were no people. Tommy remained within the shadows of the crane and smoked a cigarette.

All in all, this work was a good gig for him, he reflected while he waited. He'd received his transportation engineering degree from Penn State. It was a four-year program and had cost him dearly. He owed over a $100,000 when he'd finally graduated, only to find out that the jobs had dried up. Over and over again, he'd been told that the United States wasn't interested in repairing its crumbling infrastructure. That had not been the case when he'd started college in 1998. Since then, he'd been forced to take part-time jobs that paid poorly and offered no benefits. Over a decade later, he owed more than he'd started with because he could not always make the loan payments, which added late fees, and on top of that, the interest kept going up. He was about to go overseas to look for work when he'd received a very strange phone call. Would he be interested in working in the shipping business, on the receiving end? The man on the other end had told Tommy he would be paid well and quickly for the facilitation of the packages, with one-third always provided to him in advance. He would never know who the other operators were in the business, and he would never meet the person who contacted him or who arranged the delivery. No one would know Tommy either. "It was best that way," they said. And most importantly, Tommy himself would never know what was in the packages. He would be called on an ad hoc basis and must be ready to move at the drop of a hat. The only rule on Tommy's side was to never, ever talk with anyone about what he did and where he did it. And, most importantly, never make contact while on the job. He could quit whenever he wanted to.

"Why me?" Tommy had asked.

The answer was threefold:

People who knew him said he could be trusted. He knew what to look for at transportation sites, given his degree and experience, and he was broke and in debt. Tommy had laughed at that one, not really thinking about how anyone would know these things about him.

Of course he'd said yes. Why not give it a try? It just sounded so good. That was three years ago.

Tommy placed another cigarette to his lips and, shielding the lighter with his left hand, lit it. He inhaled deeply and blew the smoke out in rings. Then he looked at his watch. While it wasn't going to be a sunny day by any means, dawn would be here shortly. Something should be happening by now. Suddenly, he saw (or thought he saw) a person in black, walking on the adjacent dock. He frowned. Where had he come from? The figure quickly disappeared into the shadows. Tommy flicked his cigarette into the water and rubbed his eyes. Then he looked over his shoulder at the ship. He presumed the package would be coming from there. Anything? He decided to check out the warehouse. He walked from beneath the crane to the building. There was a padlock on the door, but it was unlocked. *Strange.* He unlatched it and held it in his hand as he entered the building. It was empty.

Sometimes, humans are unaware of their surroundings and therefore of latent danger. This was not the case. Tommy's antennae were up immediately, but still not soon enough. His last living thoughts were: *This is an ambush. Ah, Lily.* In the blink of an eye, he felt the wire around his neck. Death came quickly.

———————•———————

Fortunately, Lily Mitka was spared the knowledge that her beloved Tommy was no longer among the living. As she drove to work at dusk, a dump truck came out of nowhere and sideswiped her in a blatant hit-and-run. Her car spun out of control and collided with a tree at the curve. No one could have survived the impact.

Chapter

Nick Nucci quickly answered his cell. "Hi, Theresa, you know it's Saturday, I hope?" It was Theresa Wild, the coroner.

"People die every day of the week, my friend."

"We have another murder?" Nick grew alarmed, thinking he should be aware of another murder before the coroner.

"No. I'm referring to the Nepali Jane Doe. Conclusive evidence can arrive any day too. I thought I should meet with you to go over what the lab found. Doesn't seem imperative, but I think everybody deserves a chance at having their murderer identified, and I know time is always of the essence."

"It is. Are you at your office now?"

"I am."

Nick looked at his watch. It was noon. "Anything I can bring? Lunch?"

"No, I'm fine. Thanks."

"I'll be there shortly," he said and got ready to leave.

When Nick arrived, Theresa was sitting at her desk, typing on her computer. "Hey Nick," she said as she stood, shaking his hand. "Would you like some coffee or a soft drink?"

"Nah, I'm good. What are you working on?"

"Just putting the finishing touches on the report on Jane Doe. So I gather no one's reported her missing?"

"Not yet. You'd think ... a young girl, so vulnerable, and just no one. It's actually both alarming and disgusting. I checked with residents in the vicinity of the murder site, but no one heard anything. No one had ever seen anyone fitting Jane Doe's description, either. It's a first for me."

"Same here. Well, let me tell you what the lab discovered," Theresa said, changing the subject. "It's going to add to the mystery, I'm afraid," she continued as she retrieved papers from the printer. "Here, have a seat.

"The first anomaly is the contents of her stomach, which were paltry and which matches my observation that she was malnourished. Anyway, there were traces of beef. Most likely, she is or was born a Hindu ..."

"And Hindus don't eat beef," Nick said, finishing the sentence for her.

"Exactly. Probably not the strangest thing, but it is confusing. I mean, the cow is sacred."

"Yeah. Agreed."

"The next issue is the samples taken from her fingernails."

Nick raised an eyebrow. "Skin tissue?"

"Yes, but that's not a peculiar finding, given that she was sexually abused. What is peculiar is that there were minuscule fibers mixed with formaldehyde."

"Uh. I don't know what any of that means."

"I didn't either. Formaldehyde, of course, is a major element in embalming fluid, so there's that. But the fibers stumped me," Theresa added. "I couldn't for the life of me figure out what they were doing there ... where they had come from. I mean, they were too tiny to be part of a piece of clothing that she might have ripped in a struggle. Plus they were comingled with the formaldehyde. Then, well, it dawned on me in the middle of the night. The material is just that: material. The threads and formaldehyde are consistent with a resin that's found in clothing, the newer the cloth, the more concentrated. The resin releases the formaldehyde. I had to look that part up," Theresa said, smiling slightly. "It takes a lot of contact to get it under your nails. It appears that our girl worked around new clothes, or new fabric."

"Wow, Theresa. Did you ever consider working for the police department? Better yet, the FBI or CIA. That is some damn good investigative research."

"Thanks."

"But could we back up a minute?"

"Of course."

"Why is formaldehyde used in fabric?"

"All kinds of reasons, like to keep clothes from wrinkling, stop perspiration, to make cloth color-proof. It's not good for us, if you're wondering."

"Okay. Another grim piece of information. Thanks," Nick said, smiling. "So what are you thinking? I mean, where was she working?"

"Formaldehyde application and use is unregulated in the US. Therefore, we have to assume she may have worked at any department store ranging from very upscale to moderately upscale to a dollar store, you name it."

Nick immediately felt defeated. "Well, the only thing I guess I'm grateful for is that Frederick is relatively small. This is really helpful, Theresa, though it's also disturbing."

"I know. I told you it would probably complicate matters, but these are important clues, so I wanted you to have them sooner than later."

"Very much appreciated."

<hr />

After he returned home, Nick called Kayla and told her the new news.

"What does that mean?" she asked. "Was she working somewhere where she couldn't eat the right food and had to eat something against her religion?"

"Yeah, it sounds that way. It's obvious I've got my work cut out for me. I'll keep you posted."

"Thanks Detective ... Nick."

"Yep. You bet."

Chapter
22

We who are beyond the mortal world see many things from the edges; we hear subtle shifts of rhythm in the beat of a blackening heart.
—Emmanuelle du Maupassant

Kayla got up the next morning, fed Fritchie, and went for her early jog … in the Mount Olivet Cemetery. She still hadn't been able to return to Baker Park. *This was okay for now, or from now on*, she thought. She had easily rationalized going to Beacon's Way against Parker's order. *What? The image was made of uranium?* There was nothing about the image that frightened her. She just wanted to confirm that if she walked around it, it would follow her, so to speak. In other words, that it was a true trompe l'oeil. If so, it could be an important message. And indeed, as she returned to her house, Kayla believed it was going to be such an image.

She headed to her car after showering and changing clothes when she suddenly stopped. Kayla turned, went back into the house, and picked up the cat. "You like the darkroom, Fritchie?" she asked. The cat purred loudly. "Why don't you stay there today? Enjoy yourself. I'll be back later." The cat was more like a dog than a cat, she thought.

Kayla reflected on the fact that when she did let Fritchie out, she didn't hang out too long before she returned to the back door. *Maybe she just didn't like the outdoors, or maybe she'd been traumatized by the elements*, Kayla thought. Regardless, she was glad Fritchie didn't like to roam. And as it had turned out, regardless of where Kayla placed the cat at night, in Fritchie's own bed next to her on the overstuffed chair in her bedroom or on her dresser, Fritchie invariably made her way to Kayla's bed. Fritchie was so heavy that she often would wake Kayla up due to her sheer size. The bed would practically shudder when Fritchie landed on it, Kayla thought, smiling. She liked the tabby a lot and was glad she'd shown up. They were buds.

On her way to Beacon's Way, Kayla thought about her plan. She would simply unlock the front door, walk in, and lock it behind her. She'd been there many times, so it should not look suspicious to any of the neighbors. And besides, those houses were quite a distance away from Beacon's Way, due to the large swath of land the house sat on. Kayla parked a block before the house and walked along the sidewalk until she reached the walkway up to Beacon's Way. Though the chances were nil, she wouldn't want Henry or Parker to see her car in front of the place.

Once in the house, she decided to see if there were any beers in the refrigerator. She always had to check. When she entered the kitchen, Kayla noticed immediately that one of the back door's window panes was broken. Glass was everywhere. *Had someone else been in the house? Was someone there now?* She reached into her backpack for her phone to call Parker, but then decided that would be unwise, very unwise. Kayla would check it out herself instead. She opened the door to see if someone had tried to break in before breaking the window, but it did not look like it had been tampered with. She re-entered the kitchen and looked around. Nothing. Though she still didn't mind checking out the cupola, she was not going into the basement. For one thing, she had no light. If someone was down there, she'd be defenseless. Kayla proceeded to the grand living room. It was as they had left it.

Next, she went up the stairs, bypassed the master bedroom all together, and continued to the cupola. Kayla stopped at the doorway and glanced in. Everything looked the same. She took off her backpack and pulled out a small camera. Then she entered the room. Whoa! It was freezing. The minute she crossed the threshold, she noticed a 20 or 30 degree drop in the temperature. That wasn't all. As she perused the room, Kayla saw that the ceiling had tiny icicles hanging from it. She glanced over at the painted figure. It looked the same, except that an icicle dripped from the eye. Kayla stepped around the footprints. It *was* three-dimensional. She was truly frightened. What was going on? She started toward it, again avoiding the footprints. She wouldn't get too close. As she traversed the space, Kayla confirmed that it was indeed a trompe l'oeil image. *Well done.* She started snapping new photos.

Suddenly, an arm reached out toward her, fingers grasping. Kayla screamed. It was fleeting. Its moist essence passed through her and returned to its original position. She grabbed her backpack, raced out of the room, and dashed down the stairs. She stopped at the bottom. Her heart was pounding, and she could feel her entire body shaking. She sat down on the last step and hugged herself. Had that really happened? It had. Kayla knew it had. She'd felt it. She had seen it, for God's sake. As she started to calm down, Kayla began to analyze the situation. Had the entity meant her harm? She didn't think so. It was more a gesture, a beseeching. It was pleading. It wanted to tell her something. What it wanted to convey, Kayla didn't have the faintest idea. She thought about going back up, but the idea frightened her too much. She couldn't. She should, but she couldn't. Uh-oh. Had she messed up the floor? She was sure she had when she ran out. Damn.

As Kayla sat thinking, more paint fell from the ceiling onto her body. She unconsciously brushed it away. Then it dawned on her: She could practically feel the place breathing. Time to go.

"Henry?"

"Hi, Kayla. What's up? You okay?"

"Henry, I'm scared. I'm in more trouble." Then she proceeded to tell him what had happened. When she finished, the man said nothing. Silence ensued.

"Henry, what? I know. I messed up. What? Say something."

"Kayla, this is way cool," Henry practically whispered. "We've never had anything like this happen. You're sure?"

"Of course I'm sure," Kayla retorted, angry that he doubted her.

"Tell me again what it felt like."

"Moist, clammy."

"Tell me again how long it grabbed you."

"It didn't; it went right through me. But I could see its fingertips reaching out, as though it wanted to hold me."

"We've heard and read about such occurrences, but never ..."

"Henry, stop."

"You're right. We can discuss it later. Where are you now?"

"Sitting in my car. Staring at Beacon's Way. Still shaking."

"Let's meet at the office. We can talk to Parker there."

"He'll be furious."

"Believe me—when he hears what happened, he'll get over it. I mean, you have news, and you lived to tell it."

Henry was always the card, Kayla thought. But she knew he would never have done what she did. He wouldn't have gone against the rules. She could have jeopardized all of them, compromised them too. She felt terrible.

Chapter
23

We're all ghosts.
We all carry, inside us, people who came before us.
—Liam Callanan

"**T**hat was dangerous," Parker barked. "What were you thinking?"

"I know, Parker, but the photos were so incredible that I had to confirm the reality. I didn't want anything to happen to the image before I got a chance to check it out."

"Why? What does it matter if they're 'trump' whatever?"

"Because."

"Because?" he echoed.

"Because … it must mean something. It's too unusual. There's a message there."

"I think Kayla's right," Henry agreed, nodding.

Parker sat thoughtfully. "Tomorrow, we'll *all* go back to Beacon's Way. The three of us. Let's plan on meeting there at noon. In the meantime, I'll get someone to put some plywood over the window. Don't want to invite intruders."

"Sounds like a plan," Henry added in agreement as he followed Kayla out of the office.

On her way home, Kayla decided to stop at Paws in the City for some cat food for Fritchie. *That girl could eat,* she reflected. When she got home, Kayla decided to prepare dinner for Fritchie first and then go check on her in the darkroom and develop her photos. As usual, the mail was all over the floor when she opened the door. The mail slot in the door helped when you were away, but the mail always just fell indiscriminately, making a mess. She picked up the envelopes and headed to the kitchen, tossing the items on the counter. Then she noticed that one looked like an invitation. She quickly opened it.

Halloween Masquerade Party
Friday October 31

You are a special invited guest to what will become an annual Halloween Masquerade Party at the home of yours truly, Hunter Crowley. You won't want to miss it. Everyone who is anyone will be there. Come in your most innovative costume and see if you can fool the crowd.

Be there or be square.
RSVP 240-555-4567
Hunter@aol.com

Ugh. Kayla tossed the invite across the room onto the kitchen table.

Who talks like that, much less writes like that? she wondered. She knew she would go, though. She couldn't say no, unless she had a really good excuse, and at this moment, she didn't. She sighed. Now she had to come up with a costume by when? Next Friday. Oh well. She opened the cat food and started to fill Fritchie's bowl.

"Meow."

Kayla froze, spoon in air. Slowly, she turned. Fritchie sat on the back of the couch, staring at her. Her heart skipped a beat. How did that damn cat get in the house? She had to admit that while it was unnerving, it wasn't as bad as the first time the cat had shown up in a different place than expected. She slowly stirred the food and set the bowl down. "You must be hungry, Fritchie."

The cat stood up, stretched as only cats do, jumped off the couch, and sauntered over to the food. At the same time, Kayla began to check the windows and doors again. All were snugly locked. *It's as though a dog door existed. The kind with the flap. Yeah, cats could be trained to use those too.* Suddenly she had a thought: Maybe there was an exit down in the basement. But she didn't know if she could go down there right now. It seemed silly. It was her basement, nothing to be afraid of, but ... not tonight. *I'll go check it out another time,* Kayla promised herself.

After Fritchie had gobbled down her dinner, Kayla let her out and started to the darkroom, grabbing her backpack and cameras from the car. Even though it was still Daylight Savings Time, the night was unusually dark. *Storm must be coming.* "Come on, kitty. Come on, Fritchie." The cat followed obediently. *It seems as if we were meant for each other,* Kayla thought, smiling.

As was her custom, after reviewing all of her negatives, Kayla picked those that showed potential and began to develop them. The storm started to kick in just as they were coming to fruition. Suddenly, the lights flickered and then failed. She shook her head. *Not good. Now, where did I leave that lantern? Oh yeah, on the bookshelf near the window.* Frequent lightning and the resounding thunder kept making her jump as she headed toward it. When she reached for the lantern, she realized that Fritchie was now sitting on the wide window sill, gazing outward.

Strange, she never sat there before, Kayla thought, following the cat's gaze. Wait a second, what had she just seen?

Kayla waited for the next lightning strike. When it came, she saw it again. There was a huddle of people making their way across her backyard near her car, rather furtively. Some were quite small. *Were they children?* Kayla wondered. She became alarmed at this point, thinking she should call the police. But she needed to be sure. Pressing her face against the cold window pane, Kayla waited for another strike. Crack! She strained to view the passel again. But now, no one was there. Another lightning strike. Nothing. Nada. Then another boom. Refusing to believe that it had been her imagination, she debated whether she should go out to see where they were headed but decided the lightning might get her, if not a falling branch.

Then just as suddenly as the lights had gone off, they were back on. Kayla had to laugh at herself when she reflected on how she had behaved in the dark; everything seemed so normal now. At this point, Kayla had to admit that what she thought she saw must have been her imagination. What with the wavy glass, the shadows from the tree branches dancing around the yard, and the flashes of lightning, she thought she had seen something but then shook her head.

Just then, she noticed that Fritchie had not moved from the sill, eyes still staring outward. "Fritchie, hey kitty," she called.

The cat looked at the woman and then looked out the window again and then back at her. Finally, she arched her back, jumped off the sill, and went back to where she had been curled up on the desk. Kayla smiled as she returned to her task. Two hours later, she had to admit that sadly, nothing of interest showed up in any of her photos. The figure was a trompe l'oeil. But there was nothing new to discover. She poured herself a glass of wine and sat thinking. The activity at Beacon's Way was new. The house had never demonstrated any sign of being haunted before. The last owner had wanted it to go to the foundation, for heaven's sake. As she finished her wine, Kayla shook her head. It made no sense, she thought, sighing. Time to go to bed. She headed back to her house, Fritchie in tow.

The next morning, after her jog, Kayla was deep in thought as she headed to her car; she tripped and almost fell. Something had caught her foot. She went back to examine what had caused it. She looked around the sodden grass but didn't see anything, at first. *Oh, there it is. But what is it?* She pulled it up. A chain? Not just any chain, a heavy chain. It had become tangled on a tree root, creating a loop. Her toe must have just caught it. Strange. Kayla shook it, tossed it into the back of the car seat, and headed out.

Chapter

24

Kayla pulled up behind Parker and Henry, who were just getting out of the team's van. The two were laughing. "What's so funny?" she asked, wanting in on the joke.

"We're just talking about Hunter's masquerade party. Did you get an invite?" Henry asked, winking.

"Of course I got an invite," Kayla responded defensively. *Why do I care?* she wondered. *Sounds like a popularity contest.* "Well, what's so funny?"

"No, we were just thinking of different costumes to wear," Parker explained. He was divorced and had no children, so he was really like a kid himself when it came to parties, Kayla had observed.

"And thinking of what would suit certain people," Henry added. Then they both burst out laughing again.

"I guess you had to be there," Kayla said, sounding snarky. She wondered if she was included in their little imagination game.

"Yeah," Henry replied, dropping the conversation.

"Okay, you have the key?" Parker asked. "Let's get to it. By the way, how did your photos turn out?"

"I found nothing, literally," she replied as she opened the door. "Absolutely nothing."

The three headed to the kitchen. Henry went over and opened the back door. Sure enough, glass was scattered everywhere.

"You know Kayla, ever since you told us about this, there's something that's been bothering me," he started.

"What?"

"Why wouldn't whoever did this just open the door? Why break a window to get out, as you suggest?"

"I did think about that. An entity ... its energy ... could have done it. How was the armoire moved? I mean, I don't know the motive, but that's how it could have happened. Maybe it's another clue. Or maybe that kid who was hiding behind the washing machine didn't know how to unlock it. Maybe he was in a panic and couldn't get out."

Parker agreed. "Possible. Take some photos before we leave," he suggested to Kayla. "Now let's go check out the cupola. By the way, and I should have mentioned this sooner, the material, the paint, is your garden variety paint, house paint, that is."

Figured, Kayla thought.

The three traipsed to the top of the house. The room was as Kayla had left it. "I'll be," Henry whispered, noting the icicles hanging from the ceiling. Parker was obviously impressed as well.

"It's truly freezing in here," Parker noted. "Salt water freezes at a lower temperature than fresh water, so it's even colder than normal. I must admit, I've never seen anything like this," he added, shaking his head. Kayla's rapid exit from the day before had indeed messed up the powder on the floor around the drawing of the figure in the corner. "No harm done," he said as he surveyed the area. "We already have the photos and video of the feet, anyway. Let's take a look at this trump ... whatever."

The three of them walked back and forth, examining the three-dimensional image.

"That drip from the eye is really, really outstanding," Henry said. "Looks like a glass tear."

"No kidding," Kayla said, sighing. Sometimes it took an abnormal amount of effort to get these guys to believe her.

"Yeah, so what's the message?" Henry asked, now being the one sounding defensive.

"That's the $64 billion question, isn't it?" Kayla replied. "The only connection I can make, which isn't much, is that the water is salty, and tears contain salt. But that doesn't move us forward in terms of a message. More like a dead end."

Henry smiled. "You're right. There's nothing to see here, except there is."

Kayla smiled back. "Yep." The tenseness that started with the masquerade party discussion had dissipated. She figured they were all a bit stressed.

"Okay, are we ready to tackle the cellar together?" Parker asked. "We'll have to use lanterns again. Still no electricity."

Once again prior to descending the stairs, Kayla checked the refrigerator for beer. *Nope, no new beer bottles. Two still remained.*

They passed through the first two rooms relatively quickly, swinging their lanterns left and right. There was no sign of change. As they entered the third chamber, Parker commented, "So the images are on the walls ..." Then he stopped. "Holy cow. What the hell happened here?"

The three stood perfectly still, speechless.

The footprints were gone. The powder had been shuffled through multiple times.

Henry finally said, "I guess they had someplace to be."

Kayla immediately began snapping photos with her manual camera. "There's something else," she said.

"What?" Parker asked, ready for anything at this point.

"The images are gone. All we've got are my photos from before."

"Well, the images belonged to the feet, right?" Henry asked.

"Yeah, I suppose so.

"Okay, I'm going to call Polly and demand that we get that damn hatch door open. I will do it myself. She'll have to say yes," Parker added, staring at it. "Are you finished, Kayla?"

"Yes. I'll just take some shots of the glass when we leave."

"Okay, let's get out of here."

Chapter

"Hey, Guy, how ya doin'?"

"Super, Hunter. Just super."

The two were now standing outside the Schifferstadt House, Hunter leaning casually on his BMW, waiting for Guy. It was becoming downright cold. Guy had a windbreaker on, but it wasn't enough. He had knocked off early and wanted to get home. He noticed Hunter must be quite comfortable in his hounds-tooth coat, expensive scarf, and leather gloves. *Bully for him.*

"What's with the sarcasm? I haven't even given you your next assignment."

"Well, I don't want it. I can't get over the last one. I've had nightmares ever since."

"Oh, quit your whining. She was a nobody."

"She wasn't a nobody to somebody."

"Yes, in fact, she was. Only one feeble old lady, I think her great-aunt, showed up at her funeral."

"You went? Why?"

"Why do you think? Trust *and* verify ... Can't say it enough. Ol' Ronald Reagan got that one right: trust and verify."

"You're sick." *And one SOB.*

"Hey, who do you think you're talking to? Keep it up, and you're done."

"Yeah, yeah."

"I mean it."

"Yes, sir."

"I'm going to give you your next assignment, but I want to be clear: I don't want this man killed," Hunter said, chuckling.

"Good Lord. *You're* warning me not to kill him? That's rich, coming from you."

"I thought that might help you lighten up a bit," Hunter said. Then he proceeded to tell Guy what, where, and when.

Once home, Guy put his shoeless feet up on his coffee table and took a long swig from his import. The TV was on, but he wasn't paying any attention. He looked around. The place was nice. He'd found an affordable condo downtown on All Saints Street. From there, he'd joined the Talley Recreation Center around the corner at Baker Park for a nominal fee and had started working out; he also junked his clunker. He walked or took public transportation. He preferred it that way, anyway. At six feet two and two hundred pounds, Guy was in the best shape ever. This was the most comfortable life he'd had in at least the last three years, maybe more. His neighbors were nice, and he liked being close to downtown. It was great. He knew he wouldn't have been able to afford it without the raise that Hunter had facilitated. But … was it worth it? Now he was in possession of a walkie-talkie and told to conduct a stakeout. More orders would follow. Jeeeez.

Chapter

26

arker decided to visit Polly at her office rather than phone her. He figured he could be more persuasive in person. It was in her interest that they find out what was under the trapdoor in the cellar at Beacon's Way.

"Hi, Polly. How have you been?" he asked as they shook hands.

The woman seemed better. She was smartly dressed, as usual, and seemed to be engaged in a project. Photos, reports, and papers were strewn all over her large desk. He figured it was good that she was focused on another activity and not dwelling on their Beacon's Way investigation. At least he hoped that was the case, since the team didn't have anything conclusive yet.

"I'm fine. How is your ... uh ... investigation going? Do y'all know what's causing the destruction yet?"

Parker replied, "Well, we do know that there's a great deal of abnormal activity, but you already suspected that."

Polly nodded. "Well, don't forget about the museum."

"Believe me—we haven't. But there's one last issue that needs to be addressed, before we can move on," Parker said. "It's that steel hatch door in the cellar. I need to get it open. Henry mentioned that the foundation wants to use only welders they hire. Polly, I am quite capable of using a blowtorch. You don't have to worry. We need to see if there's anything untoward under it. I'll weld it back when I'm finished. You won't know anything was disturbed."

"Well … I suppose …"

Just then, a young man entered her office and handed her an envelope. Even from a distance, Parker could see the "URGENT" banner running across it.

"Please excuse me, Parker," Polly said as she ripped open the cardboard. She pulled out the contents. "Oh, no!" she exclaimed, holding the sheet of paper up for him to read:

LAST CHANCE:

BACK OFF FROM BEACON'S WAY

"Parker, please give me the key to Beacon's Way," she said. "I'm not going to risk something happening to someone, namely me, anymore."

He had to think fast. "I don't blame you one iota, Polly, but I don't have the key; Kayla does. I'll call her right now." He flipped open his phone and then left a voice message to a dial tone. He needed time. "I'll get the key to you as soon as I can find out where Kayla is. I promise."

"Okay, but don't delay. I don't want anyone else from your team entering that house. Do you hear me?"

"Yes, of course. I'm sorry you keep receiving these threats. This person should be ashamed of himself or herself."

"Yes, well, honey," Polly said, softening just a bit, "there are all kinds in this world, and we should tolerate them all, but not cruel people. They should be helped."

Parker just nodded. *What a philosophy. Quite an empathetic person.*

"You're right, Polly," he said, looking at his watch. "It's 3:30. If I can't locate Kayla today, I promise I'll have the key on your desk tomorrow."

"Thank you, Parker. I am sorry about the door in the cellar, but as I recall, it looks like it's been permanently sealed. I doubt it would provide any lead at all."

"Again, you're right, Polly," he said, deciding to be conciliatory. "And please don't worry."

"It's hard not to," she said, sounding teary.

————— • —————

"Do as I say, not as I do," Parker muttered to himself as he drove to Beacon's Way. It was just after midnight. The sky was dark: no moon, no stars. Streetlights were the only bother, but he hoped everyone was asleep. He parked across the street but adjacent to the side of the house. He then opened his trunk, pulled out the crowbar and the duffle bag with the blowtorch and lantern, and made a quick dash to the back. He was so preoccupied with not being seen that he failed to notice that another car was parked nearby as well: an unusual occurrence, given the location. With lightning speed, Parker pulled down the plywood, reached inside, and let himself in.

Upon entering the kitchen, Parker put his gear down and set the crowbar on the counter. As he started to remove his jacket, he heard a shuffling behind him. He froze. *What in the name ...?* He slowly turned and was immediately blinded by a flash of light. As his eyes adjusted, he was able to make out a tall man dressed in black, standing in the corner. A hoodie helped to shield his face, but so did the stocking mask.

"If you know what's good for you," he said, "you'll turn around right now and leave."

Parker didn't move. He was wondering if he could reach for the crowbar fast enough before the man could get to him. Then, when he heard the click of the gun, he knew it was all over.

"Leave!"

As calmly as he could, Parker turned, picked up his duffle bag and crowbar, and exited. He walked to his car, threw everything in the back seat, got behind the wheel, and sped off. *Who? How?*

Chapter

27

Kayla and Henry showed up at the office just as Parker was hanging up the phone. "We've just lost Polly," he said.

"What do you mean?" Kayla asked.

"She's taken an indefinite leave of absence." Then he proceeded to tell the two about the second note that showed up while he was speaking with her. "She wanted the key to Beacon's Way, Kayla, but I pretended I couldn't reach you and left a message instead."

"Who's going to replace her?" Henry asked. "I mean, who's going to be in charge of the activity now?"

"She said it will be a colleague named Helga Dorschner. I haven't contacted her yet."

"I wonder how much Polly told her? I mean, if she didn't say anything about the key, we should be able to hang onto it until we finish our investigation, whenever that's going to happen," Kayla suggested.

Parker nodded thoughtfully. "Maybe." He had decided during the night, after the frightening encounter, that he needed to confess his transgression to Henry and Kayla.

"Uh, there is something else," he began. "Something else that has happened." It was then that Kayla noticed how sheepish Parker looked. "Uh," he started again, "I breached my own command ..." and then he proceeded to tell them what had occurred less than twenty-four hours earlier.

"Ha!" Kayla blurted, almost with satisfaction, but not exactly. "You could have really been hurt."

"Tell me about it," Parker agreed.

"Do you have any idea who it was or how he got in?" Henry asked, still incredulous.

"No. There was no way I could recognize him, even if I knew who he was," Parker said.

"And you say you had to break in, so how did *he* get in?" Kayla asked, following up on Henry's question.

"I don't know. Could've broken in someplace else, I suppose."

"Maybe it's good that Polly's taking a leave of absence," Henry suggested.

Kayla and Parker nodded in agreement.

"Whoever doesn't want us to continue our investigation must have something pretty big to hide," Kayla remarked. "But what could someone want with a house closing in on itself, a house with ghostly apparitions, a house with a whole lot of paranormal activity?"

"I don't know how the two are related, but we've got to find out," was all Parker said.

"Maybe we should hire armed guards to stake the place out, inside, I mean. Each of them could hang out there for eight hours," Henry suggested.

Kayla and Parker simply stared.

"I don't want anything to do with armed anybody," Kayla said. "We could get ourselves in whole lot of trouble if something went wrong. I mean, we deal with the already deceased, not the soon-to-be-deceased."

Henry laughed. "Well, when you put it that way, I see your point."

"I agree," Parker said, smiling. "It's too risky. Let's drop the idea."

"Frankly speaking," Kayla said thoughtfully, "the point is we need more information, but I don't think it's going to come from this house."

Chapter

28

When Kayla got home, she went straight to the darkroom. "Fritchie? You in here," she called out, "or did you perform another Houdini?"

But no, this time, Fritchie had stayed put. She jumped off the desk and wrapped herself around Kayla's ankles. Kayla picked her up and hugged her tightly. The cat purred loudly.

"I bet you've gained at least a pound," Kayla said, a little worried. "I'll get your dinner in a minute," she added, noting that it was close to six o'clock. The phone rang just as Kayla deposited her backpack on her desk. It was Parker.

"Hi, Kayla. How are you doing?"

"Well enough. What's up?"

"Henry and I were just talking. We think it's time to find out what's going on at the museum." He was referring to the National Museum of Civil War Medicine, the museum that Polly had mentioned to Kayla during Alive at Five.

"Okay. Why now?"

"It's just as you suggested. We've seen a lot now at Beacon's Way. A lot is still unresolved; we know that. So it might help us to see what's up with the other disturbance, the one at the museum, and whether there's any connection."

"Yeah. Agreed. The timing is good."

"Can you be there in the morning? Nine o'clock. The director has agreed to meet us then."

"Yeah. Okay. Thanks, Parker." Kayla sighed after hanging up. *What a day.* For the first time in a long while, she decided to not work this evening. She picked Fritchie up and headed toward the house. She decided to order a pizza and watch a movie. She wanted escape."

Chapter

Hunter Crowley sat behind his large spacious desk, reviewing his plans for the next transaction. This time, the package would be picked up properly, and a seamless transfer would be made. He had made sure of that. He smiled. Irakli Guramishivili was the man he bet on, and he'd scored gold. Of course, the man had come highly recommended, but Hunter's intuition had told him to go for it. Now, he was going to be a local in Frederick, since he'd married Eleanor Bennett.

Again, Hunter smiled. It had been so easy to hook him up with Eleanor. He'd pretended to run into her at Olives on Market Street, but in fact he'd followed her there. She was sitting alone, having a glass of wine. They'd chatted for a while. She had loosened up after another glass and confided that she was still hurt, even after the divorce from Buzz had been finalized. Hunter had sympathized and suggested online dating. She was reluctant at first, but he said he'd tried it before, and it had been a very good thing to do. Eleanor didn't have to find anyone for life; it was just for fun. She finally agreed, and he'd written down the website and offered to help her set up her profile.

"You're a beautiful, interesting, and fun woman. You will be too modest, I just know it," Hunter had said convincingly.

The two had fun describing her interests, namely enjoying social activities and events, playing tennis, and going to movies. Hunter had immediately transferred the information to Irakli, so his interests would coincide. Just like that, the two were talking every night, emailing constantly. Eleanor had flown to Tbilisi, Georgia, at Irakli's expense, to meet him and his family. They were in love. Now Irakli had moved to Frederick.

Hunter looked at his watch. In fact, he was going to be late to his meeting with Irakli if he didn't hurry. "Okay, I'll be back soon, Second Chance," Hunter commented on his way out.

The two were meeting in Hagerstown, at an out-of-the-way restaurant called Freedom in Flight, just to be on the safe side. It would be very unfortunate if anyone found out they knew each other and even worse if someone realized they worked together.

"How goes it?" Hunter asked Irakli when he sat down at the booth.

"Not bad. Yourself?" Irakli had just a twinge of an accent. Hunter figured it worked in his favor, especially with the ladies.

"Okay. Pretty chipper, if I do say so myself." A waitress came and dropped off water and two menus, which were ignored.

"The package arrives next week," Irakli said, ending the chit-chat.

"Yes. Good. You continue to have everything under control?"

"Of course."

"Well, it's your first."

"Not my first. First here. I have been in this business since I was a teenager. I know it like the back of my head."

Hunter almost laughed but didn't. The man often got idioms twisted. "Well, when it arrives, make sure ..."

"I know what I am doing," the hulk retorted.

"Okay, okay." Hunter pushed the duffle bag lying under the table over to Irakli's side of the booth with his foot, while he stared at the man.

Irakli was laden in gold: humongous gold necklace, earrings, huge bracelet, and a huge watch, all genuine, he figured. Ugh. Hunter hoped he didn't go to work like that; the man with his thick dark hair looked like a pirate, for God's sake.

Now the waitress returned to see what they would like. Both men ordered a beer.

"How is your love life?" Hunter asked after she left.

"Okay. It is a tough way to go, but I realize I need the green card."

"Oh, come on. She's a great gal," Hunter chided him.

Irakli did not respond. Hunter sometimes felt a little intimidated by the man. He was physically large and decisive.

"So did you all find a house yet?" Hunter asked, changing the subject.

"Eleanor is working on it. She wants it to be downtown; to be close to where the action is, her words," Irakli added.

"It's a good idea to live downtown. Is your family okay with losing you to a Yank?" Hunter asked with a wink.

"My family is my business," the man replied in a low, almost menacing tone. "Do not tread there, ever."

Hunter was taken aback but tried not to show any reaction. He didn't know if he should be mad or scared, but he could feel himself trembling a bit. He finished his beer.

"Okay. I will talk with you via my phone tomorrow," he said as he stood up and tossed down a ten dollar bill.

Irakli nodded. On his way back to Frederick, Hunter thought about the man. Irakli would not mess up like Tommy had, but now, well now … he was beginning to wonder if he could trust him in other ways. Irakli certainly wasn't the person Hunter thought he was. That was now abundantly clear. He was wondering if he'd made a mistake. The man was more intimidating than Hunter was comfortable with. He didn't like that one bit.

<hr />

Irakli ordered another beer while he watched Hunter Crowley get into his BMW and drive off. *What a stupid man*, he thought to himself.

Irakli had been working in this industry for over two decades, and he didn't need a pompous blowhard instructing him. Yeah, Hunter Crowley was his boss, but that didn't give him the right to oversee every little action. In fact, truth be told, Irakli could run circles around said boss. He was already observing obvious missteps and potential threats to continuity. Irakli would cover for Crowley, of course. Everyone's reputation was at stake, not to mention the money, but he would not cover for him forever. At some point, someone would have to take the fall, and it wasn't going to be Irakli Guramishivili.

Chapter

30

Our conscience is but advice from the dead.
—Anthony Brivio

While Hunter Crowley and Irakli Guramishivili were drinking their breakfast beers, Nick Nucci was speaking to an elderly woman who had shown up first thing in the morning and insisted upon speaking with a detective. Of course, she didn't have an appointment, but it was obvious that he would not be able to have her make one; the woman had a look on her face that said, "Just try."

"Would you like some coffee or tea?" he asked.

"No, thank you. I don't want to take up more of your time than is absolutely necessary."

"Okay, thank you. What can I do for you?" Nucci asked, noting not for the first time how very old this woman was. She was smartly dressed in a suit that looked like it came from the 1960s.

"My name is Carmen Wesley. I have lived in and around Frederick all of my life. I am now alone. I had a young great-niece, and beautiful, I might add, but she died several nights ago in a car crash, going to her job at one of those horrendous superstores."

"I'm very sorry to hear that …"

The woman held up her gloved hand, paused for a second, and

then continued, "She was married to a man named Tommy Mitka. My great-niece, Lily, told me that he had a strange job. He would receive a phone call and then have to travel somewhere within the next few days. He would never tell her where he was going or when exactly he would return."

Nucci frowned, not understanding where this was going.

"He is nowhere to be found. Tommy seems to have disappeared. I have been to Lily and Tommy's house, but he has not been home since before her death. I could tell when I went in that he apparently had not been there in a while. There were only my great-niece's dishes in the sink. One coffee cup, one plate, and one set of silver. None of his clothes were dirty. I put padlocks on the doors so he would have to call me when he returned. Nothing. I buried Lily, alone. I don't even know if Tommy knows that she's no longer with us," Carmen said, putting an embroidered handkerchief to her watery eyes.

Detective Nucci didn't know where to begin. This was very unusual. Carmen had made some keen observations. She may be elderly, but she was sharp as a tack. "Well, Ms. Wesley, if you can give me the address and the key to the padlocks, I'll take a look to see if I can find any clues as to his absence."

"That is exactly what I would like," the woman said as she reached into her purse, which appeared to have come from the same era as the suit. "The address is in this envelope, along with the key and my telephone number. The house is right downtown." Nick accepted the envelope. "I have one other item that may be of help," Carmen added, reaching into her purse again. "However, it may be too far gone," she said as she handed the detective a smashed cellphone. "This was in Lily's purse. The accident was horrific, as you can see. Maybe you can still retrieve some numbers from it, see if the two spoke recently," she suggested, looking hopeful.

"I will certainly try," Nick said, accepting the damaged phone. "I will contact you after I've checked everything out."

The woman stood. "Thank you, Detective. You are a good young man."

And with that, she walked out of his office. Nick was going to escort her, but it was already too late. He looked out the window to see where she was going. She apparently had had a cab waiting. The driver was helping her into the back seat.

Nick poured himself a cup of coffee and sat back down at his desk. He opened the envelope and let the key drop out, thudding onto the wooden surface. Then the detective began his research on a Tommy Mitka.

Chapter

❖ 31 ❖

Think of it as a place where the dead are curated like a museum or library.
—Travis Nichols

Kayla met Henry and Parker at the National Museum of Civil War Medicine on Patrick Street. Cory Hansen, the executive director, met them on the ground floor. "I'm Parker Troxell, and these are my colleagues, Henry Marfoh and Kayla Dunn," Parker said.

"Nice to meet you; Cory Hansen here." They all shook hands and took the elevator to Cory's office on the third floor.

"Is it always so cold in this elevator?" Kayla asked.

Henry shot her a glance. He didn't feel any difference.

"Some visitors comment on strange feelings including cold in front of or in the elevator. Some leave the premises," Cory said matter-of-factly.

"That's interesting to know," Parker said. "They leave because they are frightened?"

"Some even bolt out of the building," Cory replied, motioning for the three to sit down in his office, as he seated himself.

Parker began, "First, we apologize for not getting over here sooner, but we have been totally consumed with another building, also under the foundation's auspices."

"I know," Cory said. "Polly told me a bit about Beacon's Way. That's fine. You're here now."

"So you must know that Polly did not want to come here, given the type of activity you described to her." Parker didn't add that she'd now taken a leave of absence. He felt that was her business.

"Yes. She said she was freaked out a bit. I'm only too happy to show you around. What's happening now is disturbing."

"I should have done my homework, but when was this building built?" Kayla asked.

"Sometime during the 1830s, though this floor wasn't constructed until 1892."

"But it's been renovated?" Parker asked, needing to confirm his understanding.

"Correct. We moved in here in 1996. It was renovated between 1998 and 2000."

"Do you believe the place is haunted?" Henry asked.

"Yes, most definitely. Employees have seen a woman in a long, gray dress. We've got security camera tapes that show a man with a hat who then disappears. Voices of children have been heard, as well. It's got a rather gruesome past, so it's understandable," Cory continued. "What I mean is that the man who owned the building, James Whitehall, was a furniture maker who also began an undertaking business during the Civil War, when he hired an embalmer to assist him, thereby turning it into a mortuary. In fact, it was a mortuary for almost a hundred years. People believe it became haunted during that period, for the obvious reasons."

Kayla felt goosebumps when she heard this. "How macabre."

"Yes, but someone had to do it. Given all of the makeshift hospitals that were set up in Frederick during the Civil War, around thirty in total, there were many, many deaths. Mostly from infections. You may or may not know that the Civil War transformed the practice of medicine in the United States, as well as elsewhere. Prior to that, there were no real hospitals; there was no such thing as triage, meaning the need to determine who is to be treated first. Sorry to be so blunt, but that's the concept, and that's how decisions were made about the wounded. Please take a tour of the museum when you get a chance. We hope we have explained what life was like back then for the soldiers, doctors, and nurses, the type of medicine, and what was invented to address all of the unmet needs that arose. I apologize for digressing, but you can tell I'm quite an advocate."

"Not at all," they said in unison, clearly fascinated by what he was describing. "I'm just sorry I haven't paid a visit yet," Henry commented.

Kayla and Parker nodded in agreement.

A few seconds of silence followed. "Well, would you like to show us what's happening here?" Parker asked.

"Yes, of course. Please follow me to the library," Cory said as he rose from his chair. He led them down the hall and into the library. "Normally, this is an uneventful place. I mean, it's a place where there are books, archives, and other research material; people come to read and sometimes conduct research. Nothing unusual about it ... until recently. Take a look."

The team entered the room and stopped. The bookshelf under the window was virtually empty; the books appeared to have fallen to the floor. The surrounding bookshelves were untouched, however. Similar to Beacon's Way, the ceiling paint was peeling.

Just then, a middle-aged woman walked in. "Oh, folks, I'd like to introduce Amanda Borst. She's been our librarian here since 2002. Amanda, please meet the Dulany Team: Parker, Henry, and Kayla."

"Nice to meet you," the comely woman said politely. "I'm glad you're here."

Kayla was taken aback. A fuzzy white aura surrounded the woman.

"What have you been experiencing?" Parker asked.

"I've been feeling things. Things I've never felt since I began working here."

"Please describe what it's like," Parker asked politely.

"I know this sounds ridiculous, but I feel as though something is hovering around me at times."

"What times?" Kayla wanted to know, looking around again at the fallen books.

Amanda thought for a second. "It's mainly when I'm putting the books back in place." Kayla looked over at Parker, who raised an eyebrow. "And I want you to know that I've fixed the books each morning since this began, which I'll do today, but by the time we return tomorrow, this is what it will look like."

Parker turned to Cory. "Have you seen anything on the security tapes?"

"I'll loan them to you, but no, just the books falling."

"Anything else, outside of the library?" Parker wondered.

"Nothing specific. But employees are saying that they feel the presence of something that they have not felt before. They can't describe it other than to say it's clammy."

"Clammy?"

"I myself have not experienced the sensation, but they say it's a heavy humid sensation that envelopes them. It's gone as quickly as it manifests itself."

"Is that different from your sensation?" Henry asked Amanda.

"Yes, I'm not feeling clamminess. I'm feeling as though something or someone is watching me. And as I said, it hovers for a period of time."

Parker turned back to Cory. "And the clammy incidents ... where do they occur?"

"Everything happens up here on the third floor."

"When did the ceiling start to peel?" Henry asked. "I mean, the moisture I see on it may be contributing to a clammy feeling. Did all the new paranormal activity start simultaneously?"

"Those are good questions," Cory responded. "I'd have to say the clammy feelings started about a week ago. The problem with these kinds of occurrences in this building is that you're used to the abnormal happening. I mean, we're all pretty aware of the paranormal repertoire that we have here. So while someone unaccustomed to the unusual would probably have been out the door immediately, it took a while to notice that we had something, someone new."

Amanda nodded in agreement. "But the falling library books started three days ago," she said. "And that's when I started to notice the peeling ceiling paint too."

"Anything else?" Parker asked.

"Oh, there is one other thing," Amanda said. "There's sometimes a clinking sound, in this room in particular."

"Clinking sound," Kayla repeated. "What do you think it is?"

"I don't know. I've wandered around trying to discover where it's emanating from, but it's too indistinct. Sometimes it's almost a grating sound along the floor. Other times, it's so muffled, it's barely audible."

"Did that happen the same time the book tossing began?" Henry asked.

"Yes. It occurs maybe two to three times a day. Again, it's subtle, but I do reflect on it eventually. It's analogous to what I was saying earlier. You get used to strange, abnormal occurrences, so it takes a while to recognize them. But it's definitely a new addition, along with the books and deterioration."

"Thanks, Amanda," Cory said as he turned to go. "Please follow me, and I'll get the tapes for you. I really am not allowed to turn them over to anyone but the police by law, so if you can review them quickly and get them back to me, I'd appreciate it. Just want to be on the safe side."

"Of course," Parker said.

As they filed out of the room, Kayla looked back at Amanda to say thanks, but she was already trying to straighten the books. *That's gotta be depressing,* she thought. *But that's not the real issue, is it?*

Chapter

32

"I'm starving," Henry commented as they left the museum. "You want to grab something at Nola's and then look at the security tapes?"

"Sounds good," Kayla agreed. Nola's was just down the street.

"Yeah, let's do that," Parker said. "Want to eat outside?"

Henry was definitely in agreement. Kayla thought it was getting a little too cold but didn't say anything. Winter would be here soon, and she didn't want to miss any chance to be outdoors. The street was busy as usual, especially because it was lunch time. And Frederick always had its share of tourists. The three sat down at the wrought iron table, adjacent to East Patrick Street. The waitress quickly took their orders.

"Well, first of all, I have to tell you that I observed a very impressive aura surrounding Amanda Borst," Kayla started.

Henry and Parker stared.

"What color?"

"Whitish." The two were quite stunned. White meant what one would think: purity, infinity. As an aura, it meant being sensitive to all aspects of life. "She's apparently a very understanding and open person, one who could attract the abnormal, the paranormal," she added.

"Well then, she's a good person to have there," Parker acknowledged. "We may continue to learn more from her."

Kayla hadn't known there was a name for the color she periodically saw around a person until she'd started working with the Dulany Team. One day, Parker and Henry had introduced her to a former client, Ted Becker. After he'd left, Kayla had asked if he'd always transmitted that brownish color. Both Parker and Henry had stopped in their tracks.

"You saw a color around him?" Parker had asked excitedly.

"Well … I think so," Kayla had responded, not knowing if this was a good thing or a bad thing and not really sure if she had seen it.

Sometimes, she perceived that some people exuded a particular color. This was something that she'd experienced all of her life, so Kayla didn't think to comment on it, until now. Later that day, Henry handed her some literature on auras. She'd read through it, recognizing the explanation that fields of energy surround all bodies, but that most people don't actually see them. Kayla recalled feeling goosebumps. Then she saw a list of colors with their respective moods described. Brown indicated stable but often boring.

"So would you say Ted is boring?" she'd asked.

Parker had nodded. "You have a very special gift," Henry had said, grinning.

But Kayla had seen no more until today.

Just then, their food arrived. "You felt that the elevator was cold?" Henry asked, as he dug into his Monte Cristo sandwich.

"Yeah, cold. But after the discussion, I started to wonder if maybe it wasn't only cold. Maybe there was a clamminess. It's hard to discern. But yeah, definitely something was up. Interesting that I'm not the first, either."

"Apparently not. It's amazing that some people just exit the building like that," Parker commented again.

The three were silent for a while, eating.

Then Kayla asked, "So what do you think? Is this a coincidental anomaly, or is the museum related to Beacon's Way?"

Parker swallowed. "I think they're related, but since we've never investigated a case similar to this, I want to analyze them in an independent fashion. Then when we have results from both, we can cross-reference any similarities. That will hopefully result in a confirmation, one way or the other."

Kayla nodded. "Makes sense."

"It does," Henry agreed, finishing his lunch.

"Now that we're done, let's go look at those tapes," Parker suggested. "I'm eager to see if we can find anything Cory might have missed."

They went to their office on East Street. This was an expanding part of Frederick. There were already new apartments being built in the vicinity, and a new business center was planned. One could reach the train station from it, as well, and there was a great Italian restaurant, Pistarro's, located down the street. The Tourist Center was also nearby.

The paranormal company's building was an old, two-story brick house. Parker and Henry had purchased it over ten years ago and transformed it into an office-cum-business building. There was a library, kitchen, research lab, and conference room, where they were sitting now. The white board already contained a list of the paranormal observations they had made or had been told about. Initials next to the observation indicated who it belonged to. In some cases, there were three initials, if each of them had seen, heard, or discovered it. Kayla liked to keep it in mind when she was looking at photos or even just thinking about a case. She took a photo of it to update her current list.

The conference room was where they went when they needed more than one perspective. Perhaps it was to hear an EVP or clarify a movement in a video, as they were getting ready to do now. Parker hit the On button. There was silence as they all stared, eyes wide open, hoping to see or even hear something.

The video camera was able to capture the entirety of the museum's library, which was a good thing. Suddenly, the bookshelf seemed to shudder. Then, slowly at first, the books began to tumble to the floor. The clock showed 4:16 a.m. After a couple of seconds, the remaining ones came flying down.

"Well, that didn't take long," Henry commented.

Then, nothing happened. It became clear that this was going to be a very boring session. Finally, after an elapse of time, Amanda walked into the library. You could see her shake her head as she saw the mess on the bookshelf and floor. She looked around.

"I'd look around too," Kayla whispered. Amanda slowly approached the bookshelf.

"What's the date?" Henry asked. "Oh, there it is in the corner. It's the first time this has happened, three days ago. She's pretty brave, but I guess just like she and Cory said, you get used to the unusual."

They watched breathlessly as Amanda started to pick up the books. Suddenly, she dropped one and looked around.

"I don't think she dropped it by accident," Kayla said, noting her apprehension.

"You're right," Henry agreed. "Look, she's picking up a set of three. There they go. Bam! Back to the floor." Amanda looked around again. Now she was hugging herself, rubbing her upper arms. "That may be in response to the feeling she has of something hovering."

"Maybe it's in response to being scared to death," Kayla commented.

Suddenly, Henry jumped. "Stop," he said. "What's that?"

Parker hit the Pause button.

"What?" he asked. "I don't see anything."

"There. There's something dark."

"Where?"

"It's a shadow on the table." The library had a table in the middle of the room. Kayla got up and went closer to the screen. Henry was right. There was a shadow on it. A shadow of a figure.

She backed away, somewhat apprehensively. "It could be someone standing in the hallway, looking in."

"Could be, but the light's not right for that. Anyway, let's just take a look at the security tape in the hallway," Parker suggested. He looked through a couple and pulled one out. Noting the time on the current tape, he fast-forwarded to the same time on the hallway tape. "See, there's no one."

"Let's go back and see what it does," Henry said eagerly. Parker complied. "Look, it just disappears," Henry noted.

Amanda looked up and then seemed more comfortable. This time, she was able to pick up the books and put them back on the shelf.

"It's also surprising that Cory didn't see it," Kayla thought aloud.

"Not really. He was probably watching Amanda the entire time," Henry speculated.

"Well then, I wonder why Amanda didn't tell us about it," Kayla continued.

"What?" Parker asked. "She doesn't know there's something there. She must have thought that she legitimately dropped the books. So in reality, she told us everything she knows. She feels a sensation of hovering. And by the looks of it, something, someone is hovering."

"Well, that specter won't be going anywhere soon," Kayla stated. "Amanda is too easy a target for it. Her openness is her failing in this case."

Chapter

33

The three flipped through the rest of the security tapes. On morning two and three, when Amanda began to clean up the bookshelves, the faintness of an entity appeared, always as a shadow on the table. It was strange. It always disappeared after a few minutes. The three were stumped. The reason for its presence was unknown. Nothing else appeared on the tapes, nothing that they could see. No sounds were made. The team decided to call it a day.

They were each heading to their respective cars when a Frederick police car with its lights spinning pulled up to the curb. Two officers, a male and female, jumped out and approached them, their ID badges held out in front. "Parker Troxell," the policewoman announced, rather than asked.

"Yes?" he responded, turning.

"You're under arrest for breaking and entering Beacon's Way. Put your hands behind your back," she said, pulling out her handcuffs.

"What?"

Uh-oh, Kayla thought.

"Henry," Parker called out as he was being handcuffed, "contact Otto Fritz and tell him to meet me ... where are we going?" he asked the police officer, interrupting himself.

"The police station on Council Street."

"Tell him to get over there ASAP," Parker snapped, clearly shaken. "I can explain everything," he said to the male officer, who was helping him into the back seat.

"Yeah, yeah, yeah, that's what they all say."

Kayla looked at Henry. He raised an eyebrow and clicked open his phone. She stood by, watching the police car drive off with Parker inside, while she overheard Henry talking to Otto, the team's lawyer. The team had felt that it was important to have a lawyer on retainer in case something turned up, and they needed one in a hurry. Never had anyone imagined it would be something like this. She was wondering how the police had found out about the break-in in the first place.

Henry clicked off the phone. "Otto's on his way. I'll meet him there."

"Will you call me when you hear something?"

"You bet."

Around eight o'clock that night, Henry rang Kayla.

"Parker's out, but the situation is not going to be resolved as quickly as we'd like."

"Why?"

"Apparently, the cops have a photo of Parker breaking into Beacon's Way."

"You're kidding. How can they tell it's him? It was in the middle of the night. Anyone could have been breaking in."

"The guy inside used a Polaroid. Parker's shiny, rubbery face takes up the entire shot. That coupled with one taken with a digital recording while he was pulling the plywood down cinched it."

"You mean the guy who was already inside, the criminal, or at least someone on par with Parker's criminality, caught him on camera and turned him in?"

"Bingo."

"But that's absurd. What about that guy?"

"Yeah, well, they have to go with the evidence they have. The photos were expressed mailed."

Kayla sighed, shaking her head. "So what's next?"

"Right now, it looks like the best approach is to have someone at Beacon's Way vouch for him."

"What does that mean? He was caught breaking in."

"Yeah, I know. Otto said it's a euphemism for saying that the foundation was aware of what he was going to do and agreed with him." Kayla remained quiet, wondering all the same how this was going to be achieved. Noting the silence, which Henry accurately construed to be skepticism, he continued, "It's the deal Otto cut, after much haggling."

"Cops don't haggle," Kayla stated.

"Maybe not, but lawyers do. Whatever. Parker just needs to meet Polly's replacement, Helga what's-her-name, and convince her of his good will on behalf of the foundation. Then everything will be okay. Meanwhile, Parker's going to be meeting with Otto tomorrow to try to strategize. He wants you to contact Cory to take photos of the museum and then we'll powder the third floor and set the equipment up tomorrow evening so we can review the findings at the museum on Sunday morning. But there's another problem."

"What?" Kayla didn't know if she could take anything else.

"Amanda Borst had a meltdown."

"Oh, my God," Kayla exclaimed. "What happened?"

"Apparently when she left this afternoon, she said she decided she didn't want to come to work anymore."

"But she seemed okay this morning."

"Dunno. Something happened, I guess."

"I told you her aura was white. She's attracting energy."

"But I'm not sure what we're supposed to do about it. It's not anything we have control over."

"Well, I don't know either, but I do know it's another sign," Kayla said flatly. "Another piece of the puzzle. Just some food for thought; it could be that it's not really the museum, per se, that's being haunted; it could be because Amanda is there. The spirits are attracted to her. It's not a coincidence."

"Maybe."

Chapter

**I have never yet heard of a murderer who was not
afraid of a ghost.**
—John Philpot Curran

While Parker was being arrested, Nick Nucci was not far away, inspecting the home belonging to Tommy and Lily Mitka. As he noted the same things Carmen had mentioned, he was glad she had not disturbed anything. The place looked like only one person was living in it, and that it had been a while at that, which of course he knew to be true. There was the dinner plate and glass in the sink with the silverware. Before he opened the refrigerator, Nick noted a calendar partly secured by a refrigerator magnet. He removed it and flipped through the months. Dates were highlighted in different colors, and there were appointments for dentists and doctors here and there. That was all. He opened the refrigerator and glanced inside. The food was starting to go bad. A half a bottle of white wine sat in the door.

There was only one toothbrush in the bathroom, though it was apparent that a man lived there, given the aftershave and razors in the drawer. It was also obvious that Tommy Mitka had not been here for the last days of Lily's life. In addition to the bedroom, a small room appeared to serve as a gym and office, with a Bowflex, rower, weights, and desk. Nick thumbed through some loose papers on the desk. They looked like old shopping lists. He stopped when he saw a sheet with "Port A, 12" scribbled on it. Nick pocketed it. Lily Mitka had died on the twelfth.

In the course of Nick's research on Tommy, he discovered that the man had graduated from Penn State with a degree in transportation engineering. The degree had not come cheaply. At one point, Nick discovered that Tommy owed well over $100,000 in student loans and accompanying interest. It seemed he was able to stay just ahead of the bills, with help from part-time jobs and his wife's earnings. Then, about four years ago, the loan had been paid off in full. At the same time, it became impossible to find out where the man was working. For the same past four years, the couple's IRS returns only listed Lily's salary. So where did Tommy get the money to pay off the loan? What did he do now? What kind of job did he have? Who did he work for? How was he able to hide his income? The couple could not live on Lily's salary alone. It was subsistence, at best.

Nick entered the living room and walked around it. He examined a photo of the happy couple on their wedding day. Carmen Wesley had not exaggerated; her great-niece was (or had been, he thought grimly) quite beautiful. Tommy was staring back at Nick, a slim man, a happy man. "Where are you?" Nick asked out loud, thinking that something bad must have happened. This man with his arm wrapped tightly around his wife would not have just left.

Nick jumped when his phone rang. He'd been concentrating so hard, it startled him.

"Nick, Sam here."

"Yeah? Did you get anything?"

"What do you think? I told you, you could count on me, bro." Sam was the department's best IT guy.

"What exactly?"

"The whole shebang."

"I'll be right there."

Chapter

35

"**N**o whining."

"We don't mean to whine," a young teenage girl whispered. "But sometimes it's hard."

"So what? There's nothing we can do about it, so it's not worth whining," a man explained.

"He's right." The group moved forward at a snail's pace. Then suddenly, less darkness.

"Oh, look, look how nice."

"Actual beds."

"Actual covers."

There was almost a sense of giddiness in the air.

"You were told it would be nicer, but don't forget who made it nicer for you," the man commanded. "Remember it was me. Especially when I come calling," he added, checking out one of the young women. She averted her eyes.

"Yes, sir," they all said in unison.

Chapter

36

"So look around you," Hunter said, leaning in conspiratorially.

"Yeah, so what? These are tourists."

"Of course they're tourists. And they're spending their hard-earned bucks at Volt, the most expensive restaurant in Frederick."

"Yeah, so what? They're not voting, and they're not spending their money at a superstore."

"I know that. But Frederick is expanding because of its tourism. People move here. People are moving here," Hunter added, sipping his wine and truly enjoying the full flavor, all the while studying his dinner guest for signs of capitulation.

Tayden Moore, an entrepreneur who was highly respected by residents for his visionary approach to expanding Frederick farther out from East Street, sighed heavily. "I just don't think the county executive is going to go for a fifth store."

"You know the planning commission has final say. Why would you even bring up the county executive?"

"He's got tentacles."

"So does anyone who's been in government for any length of time. I can assure you, my tentacles are longer than his. You can do this," Hunter added.

Just then the entrée arrived, so there was some silence as both men began to eat. Hunter took the opportunity to change the subject, since it had become redundant.

"Do you think Brian is here tonight?" he asked, looking around.

Brian was Brian Voltaggio, the renowned owner of the eponymous establishment. He was the fifth season's runner-up on Bravo's *Top Chef Masters* and the sixth season's runner-up on *Top Chef,* among other distinguished titles and awards.

"Don't know," Tayden responded, looking around. "I haven't seen him recently. He's got to make the rounds to his other restaurants as well. Or maybe he's looking for new ideas for recipes, like this veal I'm eating."

"Yeah, this pork belly does not disappoint," Hunter agreed, starting to feel sated but continuing to eat. He resumed the previous conversation over dessert and coffee: "Have you had a chance to check out the location of the superstores in Frederick County recently?"

"Of course. I know where all of them are located."

"Well then, you know that constructing one to the west is a necessity."

"It's not a necessity. No one lives out there."

"Jeez. You sound like you're Lewis or Clark. 'Out there' is where the next growth spurt will be. And those folks will relish not having to drive into Frederick to do their one-stop shopping, not to mention the employment opportunities available to those same folks."

Tayden slowly folded his napkin and placed it deliberately back on his lap. "Hunter, send me your proposal tomorrow morning, and I will read it, the whole thing, word for word."

Hunter slowly reached into his suit pocket and removed an envelope.

"It's all there," he said, handing it to Tayden. "I'll send an electronic version when I get home. You will see how economically sensible it is. The question you need to raise to the commission members is, 'If not now, when?' Somebody's going to build on that track of land. I should think you all would want it to be someone you know and trust," he added somberly.

Chapter

37

Cory readily agreed for Kayla to take photos. He looked much more concerned than he had the first time she'd met him. "I was sorry to hear about Amanda," Kayla began, once she had arrived at his office.

"It's a real shame," Cory agreed. "She has always been a very steadfast colleague and friend, to be quite honest, and now this. I just don't know how to help her."

"It's something she will have to come to grips with," Kayla said. "It's in her nature."

Cory looked surprised at hearing this. "You mean there's something internal that is affecting her, something that could harm her?"

"I presume so," Kayla said, realizing she really shouldn't be talking about someone's nature, so to speak. "I mean, it's real to her, right? I mean, well … you know what I mean. If you think it would help, Henry and I could go visit her. See if we notice anything you and your other colleagues might have missed." Kayla hoped he would say yes.

Cory nodded thoughtfully. "Yes, that might help. You're the experts. See what you think."

"Okay. We'll try. Of course, she might not want to see us, which would be her prerogative, but I think it would be helpful to talk with her directly." Cory nodded his agreement again. "Now, if you'll excuse me, I've got to get started," Kayla said, standing.

Cory smiled slightly and nodded.

Although the issues seemed to be occurring on the third floor, Kayla decided to take photos throughout the entire museum, just in case. Starting on the first floor, she snapped pictures of the various exhibits. The first exhibit described the types of medicine that were practiced when the Civil War started and the kind of medical education that existed at the time. *Not much on either account*, she noted. Continuing as though she were a tourist, Kayla learned about recruitment and camp life. The curators did a great job, literally setting the scenes with realistic mannequins. Then she went on to discover how the wounded were cared for in the dressing stations, what happened at the field hospitals, and the invention of the pavilion hospitals. There was also an entire display and presentation about the destruction imposed by the horrid Minie ball, named for the Frenchman Claude-Etienne Minie. This piece of ammunition decimated a person's anatomy beyond recognition; medical restoration was almost impossible. Bones became infected, and people died from their wounds even years later.

It was morbid in every sense, Kayla thought. Once she finished the cursory tour, she made a mental note to come back. *Too interesting not to*, she thought to herself. The museum was truly fascinating. She chided herself for not viewing it sooner.

Kayla returned to the third floor to tell Cory how impressed she was with the museum.

"I'm pleased that you were able to take the time to visit it," Cory replied. "I'm curious to see what your photos reveal."

"Yes, me too," Kayla said, turning to go.

"Oh," Cory said suddenly, a bit self-consciously. "I almost forgot. I need to ask a favor. Can you give me a ride to Skip's Auto Repair on Broadway Street? My car's ready to pick up. I could walk, but I've got a meeting shortly."

"Sure. I'd be happy to."

"So do you think you can get to the bottom of what's happening?" Cory asked after getting into her car.

"I'm sure of it." Kayla said with confidence, nodding. "This is a complex case, but we'll figure it out. We always do."

She pulled over when they got to the repair shop.

"Good," Cory said, sounding relieved. "Thanks so much," he said as he stepped out.

"My pleasure."

"Hey, what's that?" Cory asked, leaning into the back seat.

"What?"

"Is that a chain?"

"Oh, yeah. I found it in my yard after that hard rain a few nights ago. I forgot I threw it back there."

"Mind if I take a look?"

"Not at all." Kayla turned off the engine and came around just as Cory was pulling it out. In the sunlight, she could see for the first time that it was corroded.

"This is old," he said enthusiastically. "I mean very old."

"Really?"

"It was just lying there?"

"Uh-huh. I figured it surfaced due to the rain." She decided not to mention that she thought she'd seen a group of people passing through her yard that evening.

"Hmmm. It's pretty big to have been totally buried, but I guess so. Mind if I have one of our researchers check it out? Find out how old it is, what it might have been used for?"

"No, I mean no, of course not. I'm interested to know."

"Okay, thanks. I'll tell you as soon as I get the results," Cory said, carrying the chain as he headed to the garage.

Chapter

38

After dropping Cory, Kayla decided to drive to the closest superstore to search for a costume for Hunter's Halloween party. She had an idea, she just didn't know if the store would carry the items she needed, primarily a pipe of sorts and a funky hat. She could adjust them both accordingly, Kayla reasoned, as she pulled into the multi-acre-sized parking lot. As she parked, she thought about the museum and the current situation with Amanda. After the building the museum was housed in had become a mortuary for Civil War soldiers, it was known to have had reports of paranormal activity. Many said it was haunted. So far, the Dulany Team's investigation had discovered only two activities: the falling books and the shadow that hovered over Amanda. Was that presence affecting Amanda's well-being? If so, why? Were Beacon's Way and the museum related or a simple coincidence? Kayla sighed. She hoped they'd find, see, or hear something happening through the staging equipment.

Kayla recalled that this was the newest superstore in town; she hadn't had the need to come here until now. When she entered, she was a bit overwhelmed by the sheer size of it. This store had to be the biggest of them all. An employee approached her with a thin newspaper-like flier. "Here are our specials," he said politely. "Are you looking for anything in particular?" Tom asked, his name plate indicating his first name.

"Ummm, hats and smoking pipes."

"No pipes. No tobacco products … bad for kids. But yes, we have lots of hats. Men's or women's?"

"Men's."

"Okay, aisle 15 just on the other side of the firearms. You'll see hunting hats and lots more. Everything is over there," Tom stated, pointing and still pushing the advertisement flier.

"Thanks, no need to waste the paper," Kayla commented, dismissing the gesture as she walked toward the direction he'd indicated.

Once she reached the aisle, she started searching. *A lot of camouflage, but no thanks, just plain, please.* "Ah hah! Look at these dandy hats," she muttered.

She pulled her shoulder-length hair back and tried one on, seeing how it looked in the mirror. Then she turned sideways to view her profile. *Yes, this is starting to be something. You know what?* Kayla suddenly thought to herself. *The hat and pipe aren't going to cut it. I need a raincoat.* She kept the hat and walked out to the larger horizontal aisle at the back of the store, seeking some assistance. She was looking up and down each aisle as she walked. She saw a young man shelving towels. As she approached, he turned toward her and suddenly mouthed *"Help me."*

Kayla glanced around to see if indeed he was talking to her, but when she turned back to look at him, he was helping another customer, in a very normal, friendly way, wearing a polite smile. She continued staring, but he would not make eye contact again, even when the customer walked off. Kayla decided to approach him, but before she took the first step, the man picked up the ladder he'd been working from and headed through the double doors at the back of the store, all the while speaking on the store communicator, as if someone had contacted him for information.

Kayla looked around; was she slowly going crazy? *Maybe.* She started once again in search of raincoats and observed other store employees along the way. They all seemed happy enough. She decided that it had been her imagination and tried to shake it off. *Ah … finally, the raincoats.* Kayla found a trench coat in a color that perfectly matched the faux herringbone hat she held in her hand. She looked at the scarfs but decided that it wouldn't fit the outfit. *Too much. Yes, this would work.* She was pleased with herself.

When she checked out at the register, the clerk said perkily, "You have a nice rest of your day."

"Thanks so much."

"You're welcome."

Yeah, Kayla thought, *I imagined it.*

———•———

Kayla entered her house with her costume elements. She hadn't been able to find a pipe, but her neighbor, Burton, smoked one, so she was sure she could borrow one of his. In the meantime, she wanted to see if she could perfect the look with a bit of make-up. Fritchie was lying on the back of the couch. She watched as Kayla walked to the back room, not bothering to get up.

"Hi, Fritchie," she said. "You decided to stay put today?"

She had finally gotten used to the fact that Fritchie managed to move from the house to the darkroom through means only known to her. And every time the cat was in a different place from where she had left her, she swore she was going to go check out the basement, but there was always something more pressing to attend to. Kayla might have time today, but she doubted it.

Chapter

❊ 39 ❊

Helga Dorschner sat primly in her chair behind her large desk at the foundation's main office, looking none too pleased as she listened to Parker's detailed description of what happened at Beacon's Way, starting from the beginning of their connection with the house to the need for her to tell the police that his presence during the night of question was okay. "It was an effort to help out the foundation and nothing more. Simple as that. There's no other way we could figure out if something is happening down there."

"Well, it's obviously not as simple as you claim, or you wouldn't have been arrested. Tell me again who the person is who took the photos of you?"

Parker sighed. The woman did not listen, or she was just obtuse, he couldn't tell which. "I do not know who the person is. He or she, I suppose, was already in the house, which in and of itself is suspect since I had to remove the plywood over the broken window in order to let myself in."

"What broken window?"

"In the back door."

"And how was that broken?" she asked, tapping her pen on her blotter impatiently.

"We still don't know." Parker started thinking that a stay in jail might provide him with a much-needed respite. The woman did not belong on this side of the business. He wished Polly would come back.

"Well, let me take it up with the staff. I'll need their agreement, at the very least. If we do vouch for you, what are your plans to get inside the hatch door?"

"That's the crux of the problem. As I mentioned, the foundation won't provide a welder to remove the door for some time."

"Well, I'll see about that, too," she said, standing up.

Time to go. "Thank you again, Ms. Dorschner."

"You're welcome. I will be in touch."

Parker left with a smile on his face. *I might have gotten this resolved,* he thought to himself. She was a tough cookie but seemed to be reasonable enough … hopefully. And, hopefully, the team would soon find out what the hell was going on in the cellar at Beacon Way.

Chapter

40

While Parker was working with Otto to clarify the language for the foundation to legally vouch for his actions, based on his inference from Helga's response, Hunter Crowley was having coffee with Guy Hardy at a nearby Starbucks.

"What happened yesterday with Helga?" Hunter asked bluntly after they sat down.

Guy had set up an eavesdropping device in the woman's office, based on an urgent request from Hunter. How Hunter was able to know that Helga and Parker were meeting was beyond Guy's capabilities.

"Sounds like she's willing to consider helping him out of the charges," Guy replied, sliding the micro tape over to him.

"Well then, you're going to have raise hell," Hunter replied as he took a bite out of his cheese Danish.

"What do you mean? I can't control her decisions."

"You most certainly can, and it's by raising hell. Get a spine, man." Guy sat back. *Now what?* he wondered.

"You tell Fancy-Pants Helga that you will not have your maintenance responsibilities jeopardized by forgiving an intruder who wanted to do God knows what to one of the foundation's historical homes. If it is allowed this time, who knows how many more incidents may occur. It sets a dangerous precedent. End of story," Hunter concluded as he brushed the crumbs off his shirt while washing down the last bite with his coffee.

"But I'm not in the know. How would I broach the subject with her?"

"I've already solved 90 percent of your challenge. You should be able to figure the last 10 percent out yourself," Hunter replied, pocketing the tape. "Just make sure Troxell goes back to jail."

Chapter

41

That evening, after feeding Fritchie, Kayla walked to the masquerade party at Hunter's house, as it was located near the center of town. Tonight was the end of Daylight Savings Time, she mused. Ugh. She disliked the darkness of winter. As she rounded the corner, she was surprised by the slew of cars and people. Hunter's house was lit up like a jack-o'-lantern, she observed. *Should be referred to as a mansion*, she thought, as she walked up to the gate with her invitation. *Jeez, security? In Frederick? Seems a little over the top. No, actually, it was way over the top.* Kayla sighed. *Delusions of grandeur? Maybe.*

The security guard examined Kayla's invite, as though looking for counterfeit. "It's just an invitation to a party," she finally proclaimed.

He handed it back to her with no expression whatsoever. Kayla shook her head as she walked to the entrance. She remembered when this house sold. Everyone was surprised, since it appeared to be priced out of the market. Of course, they had not yet had the pleasure of meeting Hunter Crowley.

She recalled reading that the house was built in the early 1800s by a newcomer to Frederick. A man by the name of Jenkins had arrived with his family. The home's construction had been commissioned in advance, so the family was able to move in upon arrival. At least one Jenkins descendant always lived there until the last one, a spinster, died three or four years ago. She was close to a hundred years old. Annabelle Jenkins had willed it to the city, but because of its grandeur, the city decided to keep it residential; not to mention that it would have created zoning issues to make it available for private affairs. Because the Jenkins family line had died out, no one would comment on what the new buyer, Crowley, did to make his money. No one seemed to know. But rumor had it that he had refurbished the house to the hilt. Well, now was Kayla's chance to see what everyone talked about.

Whoa, she thought as soon as she had made it through the throng of costumed people still entering the home. Beautiful crown molding, huge windows, old and beautifully maintained wood floors with plush carpets, eclectic furniture, oil paintings that she figured were originals, and a winding staircase that looked like it belonged in *Gone with the Wind. Indeed. What a party; what a spread.*

Lights were flashing, and waiters and waitresses laden with drinks and food were roaming amongst the guests. Feeling a bit overwhelmed, Kayla immediately began looking around for people she might know, although with all of the unbelievable costumes, she figured it was going to be difficult. And she had not gone out of her way enough with her costume. This was obvious.

Suddenly, she saw John Dillinger approaching. Kayla felt her mouth open. The likeness was astounding. "Well done," she said to the man, enjoying the moment and wondering who had achieved such perfection.

"Why, thank you." She noticed that whoever it was had also been able to imitate a Midwestern accent. "Would you like to go to the movies with me?" he quipped.

Kayla laughed. "I don't think you'd make good company, especially afterwards," she commented, alluding to the fact that Dillinger had been shot and killed by police after exiting a theater.

"Have it your way," he said, smiling as he walked off.

"Come on, Kayla. Sherlock? Give me a break," Henry said, coming up behind her. Kayla turned, continuing to puff on her pipe.

"And you are?"

"Who do you think?"

"I don't know. It's not much of a costume."

"Show me the money," he quoted. "Show me the money."

"Cuba Gooding Jr.? Really?"

"Lots of people say I look like him."

"Again, really?"

"Yeah, really. Kayla, this is Patricia Ashburn," Henry said, changing the subject.

Kayla shook hands with a pretty, athletic black woman holding a tennis racket.

"Serena?" she guessed.

"Wait a second. How is it that you automatically know her and not me?" Henry asked, joking.

"Easy. You really do look like Serena," Kayla said.

"The tennis racket gave it away," Henry stated.

"What tennis racket?"

That got a laugh.

"We'll see you around," Henry said. "I want to go look for Parker and see how his costume turned out."

"Who is he?"

"You'll find out."

Kayla smiled to herself. She was actually beginning to enjoy the party, rather than think of it as an obligation. Just then, she heard a big, hearty laugh. It sounded a little familiar. Across the room she recognized a character very dear to her: Hagrid, a great character from the Harry Potter novels. Then she realized that it was Parker. He'd gone all out. She tried to locate Henry through the crowd. She saw him laughing and pointing. Patricia started to laugh too.

A waiter came by and offered champagne, wine, or beer. Kayla selected a white wine. *Ummm, it tastes good. A lot better than my brand.*

"Want to dance?"

Kayla turned to see Joe standing in front of her. Joe, as Andy Warhol, that is. It fit. Joe had naturally light blond hair, which helped to pull off the look. Kayla never would have thought of it, but it worked. Of course she wasn't an artist, so of course she wouldn't have thought of it.

"Last I saw you was Alive at Five. You look great," she said, giving him a hug.

"You do too, Sherlock."

"I'm starting to feel very inadequate. Everyone worked hard to pull this party off."

"Ah … don't sweat it. Some people went over the top," Joe whispered, nodding toward the top of the stairs.

"Who the hell is that?" Kayla asked, now whispering as well and watching in awe as a couple, arm in arm, came flowing down the stairs.

"Guess," Joe entreated.

"I really don't know. I don't even know who they're supposed to be," Kayla added, referring to the incredible costumes.

"Peter the Great and his wife, second wife, Catherine I."

"Oh." Kayla truly did not know what to think. "And who are they?"

"It's Eleanor and her new husband, Irakli," Joe explained.

"Oh … well, they look beautiful; I mean, handsome and beautiful."

"You think?" Joe asked.

"What's he like?"

"I don't know. Never met him."

"I didn't know they were married already," Kayla continued.

"Apparently, it was a very small wedding. Rumor has it that they are going skiing in the Alps for their honeymoon."

"Well, they enjoyed that little limelight," Kayla said when the couple finally moved into the crowd of partygoers. "I wonder where they got that uniform and that gorgeous dress."

"I heard that Irakli had them for some other event, so it was just a matter of having the gown altered to fit Eleanor."

"Well, she looks beautiful. I hope she's happy," Kayla replied. "Do you know if Buzz and Sally are here?"

"I saw them earlier."

"And?"

"Batman and Batwoman."

"Jeez. I better leave."

"Oh, stop. You're fine. Listen—I have to go find Greg."

"What did he come as?"

"Austin Powers."

Kayla laughed. "Okay, see you later." Just then she noticed Angie across the room. Amelia Earhart. That works. Kayla waved, and Angie waved back, showing a thumbs-up. *Nice of her*, Kayla thought as she walked over to look at an oil painting that had caught her eye.

"Do you think it's an original?"

"I don't know. Is it?" she asked, turning as she did so. "Oh, thank God," she said out loud. Finally, someone else who didn't get the memo that this was supposed to be an elaborate masquerade, noting that the man next to her was wearing a simple mask. "Not to offend, of course."

"No offense taken. I know. A lot of great costumes here. Yours is pretty good. It's more than a mask, at least."

"Do I know you?"

"You really don't recognize me? It's Nick. Nick Nucci. So I guess the mask does work," he replied, lifting his mask up for her to see.

"Oh. I'm sorry," Kayla said, flustered. "I apologize, Detective."

"No need to apologize," he replied, smiling as he reached out to shake her hand. "And yes, it's an original," he added, pointing to the painting.

"Well, it's obvious Hunter's rolling in dough, that's for sure," Kayla commented. "I didn't know you knew Hunter. I mean, I guess I didn't know how ..." Her voice trailed off.

"You mean, how did we come to run in the same circles? It's okay. Most people don't think detectives have much of a life outside of dark alleys and spying on others. At least that's how we're portrayed in the movies. I met Hunter when he joined the Rotary," Nick went on to explain. "I've been a member for over twelve years now, by the way."

Kayla had to smile. "You're right. About the impression of what it means to be a detective, I mean. And, yeah, I guess I don't think of detectives being members of the Rotary Club."

"Well, even though I'm not a business owner, having the police represented among businesses is good for the community, especially now, when there seems to be increasing hostilities between some police forces and the public they serve."

"It makes sense," Kayla agreed, nodding. "Speaking of which, have you seen our esteemed host yet?"

"You haven't? I thought I saw him talking with you earlier."

"Really?"

"Yeah. He's John Dillinger."

"Ohhhh." Kayla thought back to the little exchange with Hunter, somewhat resenting that she didn't know who she was talking with. "Why did he pick him, I wonder?"

"He fancies himself as a sort of Robin Hood. Bigger than life. Dillinger fills the bill."

"A Robin Hood? I kind of always considered him a blowhard," Kayla said.

Nick laughed out loud. "He's that too, believe me. But he thinks, at least he says he believes, that he has been contributing to the health and wealth of the community by being able to employ those who need work. That's why he says he wants to expand businesses around the area."

"Well, maybe," Kayla said, looking around to see if she could spot him again. She should have looked up, because Dillinger was on the landing, looking down at the two of them talking. "It is an excellent costume, I'll admit that," she added, "but maybe he should have dressed as Robin Hood, rather than a gangster. Maybe he also fancies himself a little dangerous."

"Touché."

"Anyway," Kayla said, sighing, "have you heard anything else?"

"No. I told you I would contact you, and I meant it. But ..."

"Yes?" She thought he was going to broach something unpleasant about the case.

"I was wondering if you'd like to have dinner with me, unless, of course, there's a significant other."

Kayla was blown away. *Me?* "Well, I would like that very much," she said. She noticed he looked extremely relieved. *He must have been nervous to ask me.*

"That's great," he said. "I was thinking tomorrow night? I can pick you up."

Kayla had no idea where or what she'd be doing tomorrow at dinnertime. "I'll just meet you," she suggested.

"That's fine, too. Let's say seven o'clock at Isabella's."

"Thank you, Nick."

"I look forward to it," he replied. "And I wanted to say …"

Just then, a man dressed in a space suit walked up. "Don't want to interrupt, but have you got a minute, Nick?" he asked.

"Of course …"

Kayla nodded. "I'll see you later."

"Okay."

Nick walked off with the rather clumsily clad man, who must have had very limited peripheral vision. Kayla had to smile. A waiter walked by with some fresh shrimp, and she couldn't resist. She took two and headed to the other side of the room. It soon became obvious that this was the place to be. Despite the roving staff, a bar had been set up next to an extensive spread of food. A huge fireplace was ablaze in the corner of the room, and several people, characters actually, were sitting around it. Nearby, two guests, Ulysses S. Grant and Robert E. Lee, were in a heated argument that had attracted a crowd. Lee kept arguing that Maryland had desired to secede, but Lincoln had outsmarted the members of her legislature.

"Not true. Not true at all," Grant stated, holding an unlit cigar.

"You obviously have not read the plaque in front of City Hall, much less studied your history," Lee drawled.

Kayla noticed that while the men appeared to be genuinely sincere about their discussion, they were also maintaining their accents.

"Lincoln suspended the writ of habeas corpus because of the impending Civil War. Then he used it against the State of Maryland by arresting certain politicians who wanted to vote for secession, thereby preventing the state's legislature from achieving a quorum when they were set to vote for secession."

A few people whistled and applauded.

"How dare you accuse Lincoln of manipulating the system in such a crude fashion?" Grant replied.

"You're both right and both wrong," another Civil War era costumed man interrupted.

Kayla realized it was Cory from the medical museum, but she didn't know who he was impersonating. Both men stopped to stare at the intruder.

"And you might be?" Grant asked, pretending to flick an ash off his cigar.

"I am Major Jonathon Letterman, father of battlefield medicine."

Wow, he doesn't miss an opportunity to publicize the museum, Kayla thought.

Dr. Letterman continued, "Lincoln did as you say, General Lee, but eventually, after much back and forth, the Union Congress made it legal. However, by that time, the damage had been done, and Maryland remained a Union state. Lincoln had no choice. He needed Maryland, or he would not have had a chance. Maryland was the buffer between Washington DC and the Confederacy. Of course, if your sympathies were with the Confederacy, then withdrawing the writ of habeas corpus in 1861, as Lincoln did, was viewed by many as treasonous. But since those states were no longer in the Union, their opinions did not matter."

Now another group of people began to clap.

Lee finally spoke: "Very well, then. Let's not fight the war all over again."

Grant laughed. "Yeah, that would be stupid," he agreed.

Kayla was standing next to the fireplace by now, not too far from Dr. Letterman (or, rather, Cory). As he turned away, he caught a glimpse of her.

"Hi, Kayla. I didn't see you there," he said.

She felt another guilty twinge of not having done enough with her costume. "Hey, Cory, that was a good interjection. I like your costume. Very fitting."

"Thanks. I do my best. Do you have a minute?"

"Sure."

"Here, let's sit over by the fire."

Kayla sat opposite Cory in one of the wing-backed chairs. "What's up?" she asked, leaning forward.

"Do you remember that heavy chain from your back seat?"

Now the man sounded worried, she noticed. "Yes. Of course I do."

"And you just found it lying on your lawn?"

"Yes. After a heavy rainstorm. You remember it was torrential. Why?"

"Well, that chain belongs to shackles."

"What? How do you know?"

"My researcher identified them. There's no doubt whatsoever."

"You mean maybe someone wearing shackles … someone who maybe escaped from some nearby prison," Kayla continued, as Cory shook his head no.

"No. None of that. But there is more. The chain is over 150 years old."

Kayla sat back in the chair, trying to digest what she was hearing. "Well, then, it must have surfaced during the storm, like I said at the beginning."

"Maybe … problem is, it would not have looked like that."

"Too corroded?"

"Not corroded enough. As you recall, the corrosion was obvious in the light, but you didn't even notice it before. After 150 years, the chain would have been almost unrecognizable."

"So what are you saying?"

Cory shook his head, as if trying to shake loose the confusion. "I don't know for sure. It's just that it looks like it's been around, meaning above ground, and perhaps in use more recently." By now, the crowd around the fireplace had grown twofold, and the music was almost deafening. Cory stood. "I'm going to call it a night, Kayla. But, well, even though Frederick is relatively safe, I'd make sure your doors and windows are locked before going to bed. You should do that anyway, but just a note of precaution."

"Jeez, Cory. Thanks, but it is only a chain."

"I know, but it's a suspicious chain. Just sayin'. Nice to see you again," he said with an outstretched hand. "I hope you and your team will be able to resolve all these unsettling occurrences."

"We will, Cory. I promise."

Kayla left shortly afterwards. When she got home, she unlocked the door and then locked it right behind her, with a whiff of panic. She had to laugh. Never had she behaved like this entering her house.

"Okay, Fritchie. We're going to stay here tonight. No darkroom."

The cat ran to the bedroom and leapt up on the bed. Kayla followed and soon fell dead asleep.

Chapter

42

**Some ghosts or felt presences may simply be the essence of
another living person projected outward while
sleeping.**
—Doug Dillon

It was Saturday morning, November 1. Kayla felt motivated to find something, anything that could get the team closer to resolving the big mystery: Why was old Frederick being inundated with new paranormal activity? Cory's read on the chain was the latest example. She made her way to Mount Olivet. Some other joggers were present, more than she had come across so far, due to it being a weekend, she reasoned. The air was crisp and the run invigorating. She even startled a ground hog that quickly ducked back into his tunnel, but not before voicing its displeasure at being disturbed.

Afterwards, she quickly showered. "Are you going to stay here in the house today?" Kayla asked Fritchie. "Please do," she entreated, giving the cat a big hug before heading off to pick up Henry.

Amanda Borst had reluctantly agreed to speak to the two of them that morning. They arrived at her house a little before the ten o'clock appointment.

"So what's the game plan?" Henry asked.

"Game plan? What game plan?" Kayla replied.

"You know, how will we approach this? Who takes the lead?" Henry asked.

Kayla decided she didn't want to play any games, and so she quashed that discussion immediately, saying, "I'll take the lead. I'll base it on her aura if I see it and, of course, on her demeanor."

"Right." Together they went up to the smallish row house and knocked. A dog barked. "I hope it's not some slobbery thing," Henry muttered.

Just then, Amanda opened the door. "Stay!" she called over her shoulder.

Uh-oh. While the woman still maintained a white hue, it seemed it was a bit darker, a bit gray. *A sign of transition or transformation,* Kayla noted.

"Please come in." Amanda had also lost weight. A golden retriever sat in the dining room, furiously wagging its tail, eagerly awaiting another command. "Okay, good dog, good Rusty."

That was it. It came wagging up to Kayla and Henry, and the two spent the next couple of minutes petting the sweet animal. Finally, Amanda called off the good dog, and the three sat down. The dog went to its bed, not far from where Amanda was sitting.

"Can I get you anything? Coffee, tea?"

"I'd like some tea, thank you," Kayla said.

"Nothing for me, thanks." Henry replied.

"Okay, I'll be back in a couple of minutes," Amanda said, getting up and heading through a previously closed door. Rusty trailed right behind her.

"When did you start drinking tea?" Henry asked quietly.

"I just wanted to look around a bit," Kayla said, as she started peering into framed photos.

There was one showing Amanda at the Frederick Street Festival, selling food items at the Five Pigs BBQ stand, and another showing her helping out at Oktoberfest. One photo was from a concert at Baker Park.

She looked really happy, Kayla observed. The photos were interspersed among a vast number of books. *Figures.* There was a coffee table book about Frederick on one of the end tables that Kayla recognized and lots of books about Maryland's role in the Civil War. Popular fiction novels occupied another shelf. Native American dreamcatchers hung from the two front windows.

"Boy, she's really engaged with the community," Kayla commented to Henry as she sat down.

Just then, Amanda and Rusty returned. Amanda handed the tea to Kayla.

"Thanks so much," Kayla said, standing to take it. "And thanks again for agreeing to meet with us. We know you haven't been feeling well. We thought maybe we could find out what seems to be affecting you and try to address it."

"Well, like I said to Cory and told you over the phone, it's a presence. After I talked with you all that morning at the museum, it got worse. Really bad," the woman explained, almost apologetically. "I had to get out of the building. And, well, I can't shake it. It's weighing me down. I feel like I'm being choked or smothered sometimes. I wake up in cold sweats. I feel someone is watching me during the day and that they're with me at night, literally. I'm having nightmares."

"Did you have those before … before the incident in the library started?" Kayla asked.

Amanda thought for a while. "I'm prone to having nightmares, but the difference is that these are much more real, as if I'm really there."

Kayla asked, "What's their nature?"

"Honestly, it's not clear to me. I seem to be with people who are running away from something. I never find out what it is. In fact, part of the reason that it's a nightmare is because I'm blind during it. Not literally. What I mean is that I can't open my eyes to see what's happening. I keep trying to open them, but I just can't. It's awful," she said, dabbing her eyes with a tissue.

"That does sound awful," Henry agreed. Kayla practically kicked him. He caught the gesture and added, "I've had bad nightmares since I was a kid."

"Do the people talk?" Kayla asked, trying to keep Amanda engaged.

"They do, but I can't understand them. It's another language, though at times I catch an English-sounding word here and there; it's not enough to grasp the meaning."

"If you don't mind, is there anything else associated with them that you can think of?"

"Noooo. But I'm afraid. Of what, I don't even know."

"Maybe it would help if you would go back to work," Henry suggested.

"You know, I thought that too. But I'm so tired because of the lack of sleep that I can't get up in time to go to work."

"Why don't you ask Cory if you can work part-time?" Kayla offered. "I know he misses you, as do your other colleagues. Maybe you could go in at ten o'clock or something like that. Then someone else can rearrange the books if need be, I mean if they are still falling down, or whatever is happening to them."

For the first time since they arrived, Amanda actually looked happy. Her face literally brightened as she thought of this possibility. "I don't know why I didn't think to ask him," she said. "That's a great idea. Thank you so much."

"It's our pleasure," Kayla replied, smiling. "Is there anything else you can think of, anything at all?"

Amanda shook her head no. She looked as though she was pretty much done meeting with them.

"You know, it's been great talking with you," Kayla said, standing. "Is it okay if we stay in touch, in case we have questions or you need to talk with us?"

Amanda slowly nodded. "That would be okay. Thanks."

The two petted Rusty again and left. They could hear Amanda lock her door after them.

"What do you think?" Henry asked as they got into Kayla's car.

"I think she's being used as a conduit from the past, given the museum and all."

"Yeah. Spooky."

They headed to the office. Parker had said he'd meet them there.

———————•———————

They found the man sitting at his desk, appearing quite defeated.

"What's up?" Kayla asked. "I loved your costume last night, by the way."

"Thanks. Listen—I thought I had the foundation on my side, but they've just informed me that they will not support me."

"What?" Henry and Kayla said in unison.

"Yeah. Helga said that they don't want to set a precedent. It will jeopardize their ability to ensure security in the future."

"But they know it was you. How many other times have their buildings been broken into?" Kayla asked, sounding exasperated.

"She mentioned the fact that someone was already in Beacon's Way, by way of an explanation."

"That's absurd. Someone just got in there to set you up," Henry commented.

Parker looked up after hearing this comment. "You know, I think you're right. This means someone had been watching the place. Someone got in, or was in, while I was trying to get in."

"Well, I don't know about that, but somehow we've been observed," Henry continued. "We've not only been seen, I think we've been heard. We've talked about all this before."

"Well, it's too late now," Parker said, slumping again.

"What's going to happen?" Henry asked.

"The arraignment is Monday."

"Oh, Parker, I'm sorry. What's Otto say?" Kayla asked.

"He told me to plead not guilty."

"So … that's good, right?" Kayla continued.

"It will just delay the inevitable."

"Which is?" Henry asked.

"Six months to a year."

"I don't know," Henry mused. "We should be able to figure something out by then. Maybe we'll be heroes, and the foundation will have to find a way to get you pardoned. I wouldn't let it get you down."

Kayla marveled at how upbeat Henry could be, even when he was looking obvious obstacles right in the face.

"Maybe you're right," Parker agreed. "I do have some time, maybe. So let's see. Let's try to get this case solved. Now it's personal," he added, trying to shake his own gloom off.

"Agreed," Kayla responded, with enthusiasm this time. "I wanted to talk with you last night to find out the status of your arrest, but your obvious enjoyment of being Hagrid told me no shop talk."

"I really appreciate that," Parker said, grinning. "It was a good party, don't you think?" he asked, looking at the two of them.

Henry nodded with a huge smile.

"It was, until I talked with Cory," Kayla commented.

"Why?"

Kayla proceeded to tell both of them about the chain. Again, she refrained from describing the people she thought she saw in her yard that stormy night, which now seemed so long ago. The further she got from the incident time-wise, the more incongruous it appeared.

"You know, I don't know Cory, but to me that's a bit extreme," Parker concluded.

"Yeah, agreed," Henry said. "Unless there's something he's not telling you."

"Thanks, Henry. Just enough doubt so I can't put it to rest," Kayla joked.

"Didn't mean to imply anything. Just strange. Maybe we can get a look at it next time we're there."

"I'm sure we can. It's mine. And by the way, Parker, we had a good discussion with Amanda."

Parker looked pleased. "Yeah? How's she doing? I should have asked sooner."

Kayla relayed their meeting, with Henry interjecting observations here and there. She added her remark about Amanda's aura and its possible transition, which she had not yet relayed to Henry.

"I think we'll have to just wait and see which color it turns into," she concluded.

Parker agreed that if Amanda went back to work, she might start to feel better. "I think Amanda Borst is someone we definitely need to stay in touch with," he said. Kayla and Henry nodded. "And you know what else I think?" Parker asked, looking at his watch. "I think we should call it a day."

"That's an excellent idea," Henry said.

"Yeah," Kayla added.

Chapter

43

The walk to Isabella's Restaurant was short. Kayla hadn't been able to decide what to wear and finally just put on jeans, a sweater, boots, and a leather jacket. The weather was turning wintry, and it was truly cold this evening. She grew nervous as she saw Nick sitting at the window as she approached.

Nick stood as she entered. "Hey. How are you Kayla? Recovered from the party?"

"Yeah. How about Mr. Astronaut? Did he make it through the evening?"

"Nah. He ditched it after we started talking. Well, at least the helmet."

"Yeah. He looked pretty encumbered. I once wore a bird cage on my head for Halloween. I was supposed to be headless, so the cage became my shoulders, and I carried a pumpkin with a mask on it as my head. It was my father's suggestion, but I loved the idea, so I only have myself to blame."

"Blame yourself? For what?"

"For the pain. It was very painful, no matter how I tried to cushion it. Then there was the occasional 'Hey, that person is wearing a birdcage,' which actually sounds as dumb as it was."

Nick thought it was pretty funny. "I can see why you picked Sherlock."

"No kidding."

Just then, the waitress approached and asked, "Anything to drink?"

"I'll have a house chardonnay," Kayla said. Nick asked for a Flying Dog beer.

"So how has your weekend been so far?" he started.

"Good. We knocked off early today."

"Are you … busy then?"

"Oh, you wouldn't believe it."

"Well, tell me."

Kayla proceeded to describe all the goings-on at Beacon's Way but caught herself when she got to the cellar. Abruptly, she stopped.

"And … don't keep me hanging."

"I just realized. Maybe I shouldn't be discussing all of this. I mean, everything is inconclusive, and I …"

"Kayla, believe me—I'm not going to mention your activities to anyone. I mean … there's no one that I'd be talking to about them, no matter what. I do find this all very interesting. I'm truly fascinated."

Kayla took another sip of her wine. She felt torn. She was enjoying this evening, but should she divulge more to a man she barely knew? But he was a detective, after all. *Yeah. It's okay. Who would want to listen to any of this anyway? Most people were nonbelievers. And like he said, who was he going to tell?*

So she continued her description, including the teams' suspicions regarding the hatch door, the broken window glass on the outside, the boy crouching in the photo, and finally, the part about her break-in, where the trompe l'oeil had made a swing for her, and then most recently, Parker's unfortunate break-in, for which he was being charged by the police.

"My God. I had no idea this type of activity could be observed, tracked, or investigated, or that it occurred at all."

"Well, you asked," Kayla replied, laughing. "That's just one of the places we're checking out. Yeah, something's up in Frederick."

A shadow passed Nick's face. "Maybe it's ghosts, but maybe it's more."

"Yeah, we've been debating that." Kayla went on to explain her theory about the meaning of trompe l'oeil. "It seems deception, in general and specifically, might be the impetus for the activity. We just don't know what it relates to and why."

Nick sat thoughtfully. The waiter arrived to take their orders. They decided to share some tapas and ordered two each.

"I know I said I won't discuss your cases with anyone," Nick started, "but I do feel obligated to inform you that you are treading on what may be dangerous ground. I'm sure you know this."

Kayla nodded.

"I don't think it's good that there was someone, alive, well, a live person, who was hiding in the cellar. And whether it's that person or another person who broke into the house is still unknown. I'd like to help you, in other words; you and the team, that is."

Kayla was cautious. "How, exactly?"

"Well, without knowing what's going on with the other buildings, the first thing that needs to be done is to dust the basement at Beacon's Way for prints. We need to see if we can ID the fella who was in there, not to mention any other folks who have been there, if any."

Kayla immediately noticed the use of the word "we." Just then, their tapas arrived. There were potatoes, salmon, sautéed spinach, and meatballs, all of them ample in size to split and all delicious.

"And, based on those results," Nick continued as he served up the salmon, "there may be more investigations."

With a mouth full of food, Kayla shook her head no. Once she could talk, she explained that Parker would never agree to something like that. His investigative approach was a purposeful one, and he would see an outsider only as interference.

Upon hearing this, Nick chewed thoughtfully and then frowned. "Kayla, what if I could help Parker?" he asked.

"How?"

"I mean help him with the breaking and entering charges."

"Ohhhhh."

"I mean, I could explain them away, since there was no malice involved in the event."

"He'd be so relieved, but he might turn you down on principle."

"Well, obviously, I don't know him, and he doesn't know me, but I would think working with me would be preferable to jail time."

"You're right, of course," Kayla agreed. "We're meeting at the museum tomorrow, so I'll ask him. He'll want to know in detail how you would want to participate."

"I would not interfere in any way with your investigation; that I can assure you and him."

Just then, the waitress came to clear away some dishes and ask about dessert.

"Of course we want dessert, don't we?" Nick asked.

"Yep," Kayla said, smiling. "Good thing I left room for it."

After perusing the menu, the couple selected a lemon crème brûlée with fresh strawberries to split. It was mouthwatering.

Chapter

44

Ghosts were created when the first man woke in the night.
—J. M. Barrie

Kayla awoke refreshed. She and Nick had walked up and down Market Street after dinner, window shopping and chatting all the while. He was an interesting person. She had found out that he liked to swim and did so religiously. He also liked hiking, as did Kayla. They decided they would go to Gambrill State Park next weekend, if neither had to work.

After that, he had walked her home. She said good-bye at the door. Kayla would have invited him in, but her house was a mess, and she was embarrassed.

The first thing she did after her jog the next morning was to call Parker and tell him about Nick's offer.

"I will be happy to meet with him," Parker had said immediately. Kayla was surprised but figured the idea of spending time in the clinker must be overwhelming. "Find out when it's convenient. You and Henry should be present to so we all know what he wants to do."

"That's great, Parker. Will do," Kayla said, hanging up.

As she drove to the museum, she called Nick.

"You're not driving and talking are you, Kayla?"

"Nope," she said, smiling as she pulled into a parking space along a side street next to the museum. "Parker wants to meet," she explained. "What's a good time for you?"

"This afternoon, say, five o'clock? I'm at the Maryland State Police Barrack B. It's on East Airport Drive."

"I'll let them know. We're all coming, if that's okay."

"The more, the merrier."

"Okay."

Kayla arrived at the museum at the same time Cory did. "Hi, Cory. How are you?"

"Well, we'll see once we get in," he said, smiling as he unlocked the door for her. "How are you doing?"

"Great. We need to wait for Henry and Parker, in case there are abnormalities," she explained. "They'll be here in no time. Oh, they're just pulling up," she noted. It was early. Far earlier than the opening hours for the museum.

"What can we expect?" Cory asked.

"First, we'll see how much activity occurred last night, if any, from the powder on the floor. It will be in the form of footprints," Kayla explained. Cory nodded. "By the way, did Amanda contact you?"

"She did," he said, smiling again. "I think it's a great idea to have her work part-time. Thanks for thinking of it. She said she'd like to start next Wednesday. How did she seem?"

"Okay. She was a little hesitant at first, but she opened up."

"Good."

Just then, Parker and Henry walked up. "How are you doing, Cory?" Parker asked.

"Good. Well, at least I think so. Are we ready to go?"

"Yes, of course." The four stood and waited for the elevator. Kayla felt the cold again and shivered slightly. They gingerly exited the elevator when they reached the third floor but stopped dead in their tracks. There were footprints everywhere.

"Incredible," a visibly shaken Cory whispered. "I knew the place was haunted, but it looks like there was so much activity here last night that they must have run into each other."

"Kayla, are you getting this?" Parker commented, not realizing that she was already snapping away.

"You know it," she responded, still conscious of the goosebumps on her upper arms. She looked over at Henry. Even the unflappable comedian looked quite startled. He was standing still and just shaking his head, hands on hips.

"Okay, try to avoid stepping directly on any footprints," Parker recommended. "I know that sounds impossible, but at least try. Let's go look at the library." Surprisingly, the books had remained on the shelves. There was only one set of footprints. It appeared that the spirit had paced around the conference table at least three times, and three times it had stopped in front of the book shelf but had not disturbed them.

"Maybe it was interested in some reading," Henry quipped.

"Maybe it's waiting for Amanda," Kayla suggested.

"Ha! That would be interesting," Henry replied.

"Let's move on to the next room," Parker suggested. "Tiptoe if you have to," he added.

Kayla almost laughed out loud. The comment conjured up a funny image, especially of the beefy Parker. The offices, including Cory's, displayed no footprints. But when they got to the rear of the floor, with its long, sloping hallway, they discovered something entirely different, something that once again astounded them.

"What is it?" Henry asked.

Kayla zoomed in and snapped several shots. Parker knelt to observe the indentations more closely. "I'm stumped," he said, looking up at Cory. "Hey, are you okay?" Parker asked, suddenly alarmed.

The man had turned white.

"They're wagon tracks," he replied hoarsely. "Wagon tracks. Wagons were used on this hallway to carry the dead during the Civil War."

Kayla suddenly felt cold, very cold. But it wasn't just her. She saw Henry wrap his arms around himself, as well.

Parker stood up and just stared. "What in the name of heaven is going on?" he asked, more to himself than to anyone else.

"Maybe it's always this way," Henry suggested. "I mean, we see it because of the powder, but maybe it happens frequently, or all the time."

Parker zipped up his jacket. *He's cold too*, Kayla thought.

Cory was now a shade of gray, looking like he was coming out of his shock. "No wonder stuff is happening all of the time. This place is … infested," he said, finding a word that suited his need. Just then, he pointed to an open window far above them. "Things like that," he said.

They all stared.

"What about it?" Kayla asked.

"We've tried to close that window on numerous occasions. Let me restate that. We have closed that window on numerous occasions. We have even nailed it shut. But nevertheless, it always returns to its current open position."

Kayla felt the hairs on the back of her neck raise up. *What was the rationale behind that, at least from a spirit's perspective?*

Then and only then did Kayla see the figure at the end of the hall, or rather the manifestation of a figure. She tapped Henry's shoulder. He turned and saw her hand trembling as she pointed a finger at the wall.

It was a trompe l'oeil. A dark figure this time. A small black person? Parker and Cory had seen it, too. Kayla snapped numerous photos, trying to walk around it without disturbing too much. Save for the clicking of her cameras, silence ensued. Cory sighed when she finished, shaking his head. Finally, he suggested they return to his office.

"I'll be frank," Parker started, once they were all seated. "We've never come across anything other than footprints on the powder. This is new for us. I can say it shows extraordinary energy being generated in this building. The number of prints, the wagon tracks, the falling books, the painted figure, and even the window, though it may not be related to the most recent … disturbances, are phenomenal. Yes, I know the history of the place lends itself to the paranormal, but again … well, as you said earlier, Cory, it's very busy. Why just now? We don't know.

It's not to say we won't find out; don't get me wrong. We have yet to be stymied," he said proudly.

"I appreciate it," Cory said. "I sincerely do. But now I almost wish I didn't know this stuff was happening. It makes you ... paranoid, I guess. I mean, it's hard not to think that they're all around here, all of the time."

"They are," Parker and Henry said in unison, nodding. It was evident that Cory was disconcerted to hear this.

"Well, but ... why are they here? Why are some of them here and the vast majority not here? I mean, if all of the people who died here remained, it would be much more crowded, though the number is already overwhelming."

"Ghosts, spirits, energy, whatever you want to think of them, or it, manifest themselves for a variety of reasons. Maybe there's unfinished business, or they're too familiar with the place and its former mission and don't want to leave; in some cases, they don't know they're dead," Parker explained.

"Or they're trying to send a message," Kayla added. Parker nodded. "Sometimes, they have a goal in mind. We just haven't detected enough clues to know what that might be. That's why I'm saying, we will figure this out. Don't worry."

The director sat silently, staring at his hands on his desk for what seemed to be several minutes. Kayla glanced over at Henry, but he just raised his shoulders as if to say, "Let's just wait." Parker remained silent as well.

"So what now?" Cory finally asked, shaking his head as if to erase what he had been thinking.

"We'll be going to review our results, look at the camera shots, listen to the recordings, and then brainstorm, if you will," Parker responded. "We have to do this over and over again until we see a pattern. What we've observed here today and what we may see and hear could provide the catalyst to understanding more about what is happening, which gets us closer to the answer or answers."

Cory nodded thoughtfully. "Okay ... Okay. Something is happening here that has not occurred in the past, and I for one want to understand it … and stop it, whatever it takes. So I'd really appreciate it if we can find out sooner than later. I know it can't be easy," he finished, smiling wryly.

"We will most certainly try. It's our job," Parker answered simply, standing up.

"I presume it's okay to walk on the powder now?"

"Yes," Parker replied. "We have the photos. I'll have a couple of guys come to clean up and remove the plastic."

"Thank you all again," Cory said, standing as well.

The team filed out with the most explosive collection of material they had ever assembled.

Chapter

Kayla followed Parker and Henry to their office. Once seated, Parker could not restrain himself, even though they had just come from one of the most amazing investigative sites of their careers; the idea that he might not have to face jail time was just too good. "Have you talked to your … investigator?" Parker asked eagerly. "I told Henry about it on the way to the museum."

"Good job, Kayla," Henry said, smiling.

"I didn't do anything."

"You know what I mean," Henry quipped, winking.

"Cut it out," Kayla replied, smiling. She relayed her most recent conversation with Nick. "So we'll meet him there at five this afternoon," she concluded.

Both men nodded.

"Now," Parker began, "let's get back to the museum. What do you think, now that we have some overlap between the two sites, given the painted figure? The …" he looked over at Kayla; "the trompe l'oeil."

Henry started, "I think what we can say is that there is an abundance of paranormal activity in both places."

"In addition," Kayla continued, "Beacon's Way has human activity of a malicious nature. Something bad exists. We're also beset by barriers to our investigation. We've pretty much decided someone is somehow spying on us."

"How?" Parker asked. "How is that happening, do you think?"

"Hidden cameras … bugs," Henry suggested, looking like he was actually enjoying the idea of a more sinister, spy-like image of the paranormal.

Parker shook his head. "That's hard to believe and harder to pull off. You said Polly told you that the keys have only been in her possession, right? So they close up the house for the season, and then one day, out of the blue, paranormal activity starts to occur. If someone had gotten in there to plant cameras or bugs, what would be the rationale? We weren't even on the scene yet."

"Yeah, you're right," Henry agreed.

"Well, never mind; it's happening somehow. So what else do we have?" Kayla asked, exasperated. "Are the two situations related or not? I say yes."

"I do, too," Parker commented, thoughtfully. Henry nodded yes.

"It's too weird to have two trompe l'oeils appear over the course of our investigations. It seems to be a message about deception, but deception about what?" Kayla asked.

"Well, we've got the Civil War and slavery as a start, where a lot of deception must have occurred. Then there's the fact that we know the ghosts or spirits or whatever seem to want to deceive us," Henry suggested.

"I wonder if all of the activity at the museum is related to trying to send a message, or that a lot of that stuff goes on regardless. I mean, there seem to be two distinct activities that are related to our investigation," Kayla offered. "It's the books, or rather as I believe Amanda herself, and now the trompe l'oeil. At Beacon's Way, it's the downstairs basement and the trompe l'oeil.

"And the hatch door," Parker added. "There's something about that room down there."

"And the hatch door," Kayla added.

"Oh," Parker said jumping up, "it's getting close to five. We've got to go."

Chapter
46

Kayla introduced the Dulany Team to Nick in the reception room of the Maryland State Police, Barrack B, which was empty. Nick saw the three of them looking around because it was empty.

"Fortunately, it's Frederick," he said. "We just have a skeleton crew on Sundays. Please follow me to my office," he added, turning. "Can I get anyone some coffee, water?" Nick asked after they were seated at a small round table across from his desk.

No one wanted anything. Kayla noticed that Nick's desk was not overly cluttered, but there was a pile of files in one corner of it. There appeared to be what looked like a mangled cellphone on top of it. The computer screen was huge. A desk lamp sat next to it. She looked around. Nick was obviously not that big on décor. Two or three pictures hung here and there on paneled walls, mostly outdoor scenes. A group of photos which she could not discern from her seat filled a small portion of the wall behind his desk. There were no plants. The wood floor cried out for a rug or two.

Nick began: "Kayla's told me about your current investigations. Not only do they sound interesting, as I mentioned to her," he said, looking over and smiling, "there appears to be some actual real-life inconsistencies and abnormalities that may hinge on the criminal."

Parker frowned.

"Four incidents in particular are worrisome; one, the photo of the person in the basement of Beacon's Way, along with the sealed hatch door, the broken window, and the fact that you were almost accosted, Parker."

"Well, I don't know if all of those are criminal, per se," Parker said, a bit defensively.

"I don't either," Nick responded. "But that's just it. They need to be investigated by a professional in order to determine whether there was foul play. Hopefully, none has been committed. But if it is discovered that something nefarious has occurred, we need to find out why and who."

There's that "we" again, Kayla thought.

Parker sighed slightly.

"Listen, Parker, I know you're between a rock and a hard place here," Nick continued. "I checked your file. The arrest is legitimate, but there are holes in it that I think I can leverage to get your case dropped. And I will work to do that regardless of whether you allow me to check out Beacon's Way."

Well, that's decent, Kayla thought, appreciating Nick Nucci even more.

"Believe me—I would not want someone to barge in on my investigations," Nick added, looking around at each of them. "And that's not what I'm suggesting I want to do. But it couldn't hurt to have me dust for prints, at the very least."

"What else would you like to do?" Henry asked.

"I'd like to just walk around the place, see if there is anything that catches my eye that you may have missed because you have a different focus, a different objective in mind."

All eyes were on Parker. "What do you think, Kayla? Henry?" he asked.

"I'm all for it," Henry said, grinning. "We might learn a thing or two."

"Same here," Kayla replied, smiling as well.

"Thank you, Detective," Parker began.

"It's just Nick."

"Well, thank you, Nick. I'm with my team. It would be nice to learn more and to find out if anything is going on that we cannot determine on our own. I'd really like to get off the hook for that arrest, no doubt about that, and I'd love to get under that hatch door. We would appreciate your help, in other words."

"It's a deal, then," Nick said, standing up to shake hands. "I think we can all respect our work and independence. I'll do everything I can to waive the arrest and to get into the hatch door, with approval from the foundation, of course. When can I start at Beacon's Way?"

"Why not tomorrow? We can meet you there on your schedule."

"How about nine?"

The Dulany Team nodded yes. The deal had indeed been struck. *This was going to be a win-win,* Kayla thought.

Nick sat thoughtfully at his desk after the Dulany Team left. He perused the printout that Sam had given him of the phone calls Lily Mitka had made and received for the ten days prior to her death. There were lots of calls. Nick cross-referenced one of them with Lily's Great-Aunt Carmen, whose number had been in the phone book. They had obviously been close. Three other numbers were called or received frequently. One had to be her husband's, Tommy Mitka. And, one of those three, in particular, had caught his attention. It was from Toronto. It was extremely short; lasting only twenty-one seconds. Now he needed to confirm who the number belonged to and to acquire that person's phone record to find out who that person had called other than Lily, and who had called that person?

Back to Sam.

Chapter

47

Kayla drove home, feeling satisfied that Nick would be able to conduct his investigation like he'd wanted to. Did she think they'd find anything because of it? She doubted it. While there would be fingerprints all over the house, so what? None of them would likely belong to a criminal. The kid in the basement would have left prints, but how could Nick match them to anyone if that person didn't have a record, which was probably the case. Most likely, the person waiting for Parker wore gloves.

Fritchie was in the house this evening, where Kayla had left her. "Are you ready to get to work?" she asked as she fed the cat, her new best friend.

She still hadn't had time to develop the photos she'd taken from the museum. *When was it?* Kayla thought. *Eons ago, it seemed.* After a quick dinner herself, Kayla picked Fritchie up and carried her into the darkroom. She was eager to see if anything else from the museum showed up in her photos. Given that winter was coming on, Kayla thought maybe she should get some wood for the fireplace. She had rarely used it in the past, but it seemed that the team had their work cut out for them this winter, meaning she most likely would be spending more time in the room.

"Would you like that, Fritchie?" she asked. "Want a warm fire in here?" The cat blinked and continued to stare at Kayla from her perch on the desktop, purring loudly. "Well, I suppose it would do us both good," she concluded out loud.

Kayla developed her photos with her mind elsewhere. She was recounting what she knew of Dorothea Lange, her hero. As a child, the woman had suffered from polio, which deformed her slightly. Lange claimed this malady had strengthened her character. Kayla liked to think that by strengthened character, Lange meant empathy. It had to be, Kayla figured, because the photographer had the ability to capture utter despair, or pain, or sadness, so beautifully. People changed because of her work. Policies were adopted because of her work.

Kayla still wanted to make a difference too. She wanted to make an impact, she thought as she swished her last photo in the chemical solution. So far, nothing from these photographs had caught her eye. She hung this last one up and started to look at them with her magnifying glass as they dried. Outside, she suddenly heard the rustle of leaves and limbs. Within a short time, gusts could be heard. She stopped working and went to a window. A storm was brewing. Leaves were falling like rain. She hoped, really hoped that they would not all be gone tomorrow because of this. That would be depressing; bare trees made her feel lonely.

When she returned to the hanging photos, she was startled to see that Fritchie was walking under the pictures, looking up at them with her tail twitching. When she reached the end of the line of photos, she turned and walked back beneath them, looking up all the time. Kayla approached the photos with a new inquisitiveness. Upon doing so, she noticed something that she would not have seen up close with the magnifying glass. Each of the photos displayed a large shadow, albeit faint. She studied each one, trying to discern what made the shadow, but couldn't find anything. They loomed enigmatically.

Chapter

48

Hunter hung up from his counterpart in Russia. Another shipment was being prepared, and an installment was necessary. The amount did not concern him, though it was seven figures. Hunter went online and transferred it in full from his Bermuda account. This time, the package was coming through Mexico. Hunter tried to visualize the hulking Irakli going to the Port of Rosarito to facilitate its pickup. The plan was that Irakli would stealthily transfer it to Leonardo Valdez in southern California, where it would then be distributed. Would Irakli succeed? Hunter chuckled cynically to himself. Maybe Irakli wasn't as good as he said he was. Hunter almost wanted the man to fail, though it would cost him a small fortune. He reflected at his turn of heart for Irakli. They'd only spoken twice since their last face-to-face meeting. Irakli had been rude and dismissive, *the ingrate*. And there was the fact that Hunter still felt … intimidated? Or was he afraid? Being afraid was not an emotion Hunter felt very often, and he did not like it. Yeah, so if Irakli were to fail, he might not care that much. He'd be rid of a growing thorn in his side.

Chapter
49

The boundaries which divide Life from Death are at best shadowy and vague. Who shall say where the one ends, and where the other begins?
—Edgar Allan Poe

"Thanks for coming early," Kayla said to Parker and Henry as she inserted the key into Beacon's Way. "You need to see these photos from the museum before Nick comes," she added as she led them to the kitchen. There were six photos lying on the table. "I decided to check out all three floors just in case. Guess what? There are tons of spirits around, if that's the right word for describing them, but they're all confined to the third floor."

Parker and Henry stared at the photos but didn't say anything. Finally, Parker cleared his throat and said, "I don't see anything."

"Me either," Henry agreed.

"I know," Kayla said. "It's difficult. Let me help." She picked up one of the photos and, holding it in front of her, backed up. "Do you see it now?" she asked.

"Jeez," Henry said. "What the hell is that?"

Parker squinted and then saw it, too.

"I don't know, but I bet it's what's making the staff feel clammy. It's similar to the shadow we see watching Amanda, but that one is much more distinct. These," and with that Kayla waved her hand across all of the photos, "are much more amorphous. That's why it's so hard to see them. And I did wonder if something is causing the shadow, an object in other words, but there's nothing that big up there. You've been there. This thing covers the ceiling, wall, and floor."

"You still don't think it's the museum that is attracting this activity?" Henry asked.

"Right. I think they're interested in Amanda. She's the attraction, and I mean that literally."

"But she hasn't even been there lately," Parker argued, arms across his chest.

"No, but her energy is still there. They're waiting for her return. And who's to say that she doesn't have some of these lurking in her house? Maybe that's why she's so … disturbed."

Henry started to nod.

"It's just a theory. But the photos don't lie. We've got more than we bargained for in the museum. It's busier than Grand Central Station," Kayla concluded, as she shuffled her photos back into her satchel.

<hr>

Nick pulled up to Beacon's Way, noting that the team was already there. He knocked at the door. Henry opened it.

"Come on in, we're having coffee," he said, shaking hands. "I got some for you, too."

"Thanks. I appreciate it."

"Let us show you around the house first, and then you can decide where and what you'd like to do," Parker started after they'd finished their coffee.

They marched up to the cupola. "Wow! This room does not disappoint," Nick exclaimed, noting the icicles and the figure in the corner with the teardrop.

"Yeah, we've never seen anything like this," Parker explained. "Then there's this master bedroom. The armoire has moved back and forth at least once that we know of."

"I also photographed an outline, or indentation, of a figure lying on this bed," Kayla said.

Nick nodded, thoughtfully.

They went back downstairs and headed outside; the house continued to show signs of degradation: more broken tiles, more sagging in the frame. After coming back in, they could see more paint chips had fallen in the grand living room.

"You ready to see the basement?" Parker asked, looking at Nick.

"You bet. This has all been illuminating to say the least, but yes, let's go to the cellar."

"You have to use a lantern. I can't for the life of me get the electricity to work down there," Parker explained.

"No problem."

"Well, it might be, but we'll see," Parker commented. "I mean for what you want to accomplish."

Nick nodded.

The four gingerly made their way down the steep, narrow steps. Again, Kayla could not help but feel like the lanterns and stairway created a scene reminiscent of centuries past. It was spooky in and of itself. The whole cellar seemed worse than ever, she felt. It portrayed a sense of gloom, of doom. It made her sad.

Kayla had shown the photo of the boy behind the washing machine to Nick at the beginning of the tour.

"So he crouched here," Nick said as he pulled out his yellow police tape and placed it around the area. "This is for my team so they can see where to dust," he explained. "And thanks for loaning the photo, Kayla," he added as he carefully stapled it to the suspended tape. "Where's the hatch door?" he asked.

"Next room," Parker responded.

As Nick examined it, Parker reiterated that he just had wanted to examine the inside of the area under the door, just to confirm exactly what Nick wanted to confirm: that there was no foul play.

"I get you," Nick concurred, feeling the seal as they had all done before. "We'll try working with the foundation to help them understand that we need to get into this now," he added, looking at all of them. "My team will arrive in fifteen minutes. I also want to tape around the back door." The four moved out and back upstairs.

"Is there anything else that caught your attention?" Kayla asked.

"No. I didn't see anything that seemed humanly out of the ordinary," Nick replied. "I know it's a long shot with these prints and investigation, but we have to start somewhere." Just then, the doorbell rang. Nick looked at his watch. "They're early. Good."

For the next few hours, the Dulany Team watched Nick's colleagues dust for prints and look for blood. The latter would have shown up immediately. There was none.

"Looks like on TV," Henry commented to Nick.

Nick nodded. "Just like. It's the analyses that differ. On TV, the research turns up unbelievable findings in a short period of time. It's necessary to carry the story forward. In real life, however, it's hardly ever like that."

"Understood," Henry replied, nodding. "Understood."

As Nick's team was wrapping up, Parker's phone rang. He winced when he saw the caller. "Hello, Ms. Dorschner. Uh … the William Tyler Page house? On Record Street? Yes, of course. Um, okay, we'll meet you there in ten minutes or so."

"Now what?" Henry asked.

"She didn't say," Parker replied. "But she sounded as distraught as Polly used to. Something's up. Listen—I'd rather not go right now … given the case and all. Plus, I need to wrap up here with Nick. You two can handle it."

Kayla glanced at Henry, but he showed no expression.

"Okay, sure," she said. "I'll just say good-bye to Nick."

Nick was still examining the back door, with gloved hands and bright light.

"Listen—we've been called to go to the William Tyler Page home. So I'll say good-bye now."

Nick stood. "Well, okay. I wanted to say that unfortunately, I won't be able to go hiking this weekend."

"That's okay," Kayla replied quickly but deep down feeling rejection.

"Yeah, I've got a ton of work to do on another case … another possible murder, but not here in Frederick."

"Oh."

"Yeah, someone from Frederick, though."

"Oh."

"I know it must sound boring, but would you like to go to dinner again? Saturday night?"

"Sure," Kayla said, feeling relief. She liked him.

"Okay, I'll call later in the week. Think of where you want to go."

"Okay, great. And Nick, thanks."

"What for?"

"Parker."

"Sure."

Hunter Crowley watched with alarm as Nick Nucci and the other three walked toward the third room in the basement. What they were saying did not make him a happy man. Within the hour, he observed with fury as the detective's team dusted for prints. *Son of a …* he thought as he paced. *Son of a …*

Chapter

50

Kayla and Henry pulled up to a parking space in front of the William Page house on Record Street. Kayla loaded the meter for a full two hours. "Who knows how long this is going to take?" she said, looking at Henry.

He nodded. They walked up the stairs and knocked on the door. A tall brunette woman in a smart suit answered. She looked to be in her early forties. "Are you the Dulany Team?" she asked, looking over Kayla's shoulder. "Where's Parker?"

"He's still with another client," Kayla replied. "He'll try to make it when he's finished. I'm Kayla Dunn, and this is Henry Marfoh. Are you Helga?"

"Yes, please come in. Please join us in the living room."

Kayla and Henry walked into a large room with twelve-foot-high ceilings, a huge fireplace, and entrance to a dining room that was just as big. Kayla didn't think she'd ever been in a mansion like this where people actually lived. Helga introduced Kayla to the owners, Danielle and Mathew. They both stood up and shook hands with Kayla and Henry.

"Thank you for coming," Danielle said.

"You're welcome," Henry replied. "It's our pleasure."

"Please have a seat," Mathew said, motioning to chairs.

Helga started, "I've come here at the request of Mathew and

Danielle. Given this is one of Frederick's heritage houses, we always want to ensure that they are well-kept and maintain the necessary historical appearance, reflecting the era in which they were built. This one, by the way, was erected in 1812. And of course, it was where William Tyler Page, author of the American's Creed, was born," she said, smiling at Danielle and Mathew.

"The house has quite a history," Danielle added. "Quite an esteemed one, with Dr. William Tyler, William Tyler Page's grandfather, living nearby as well as owning most of the houses on Record Street. And William's great-grandfather, of course, was the tenth president," she added.

Kayla wondered what all this had to do with what they were here for. Wanting to get back to the point, she coughed slightly and looked at Helga. "Is there a maintenance issue?" she asked, trying to gently change the subject.

"To a certain degree. There's a window that keeps opening on its own. No matter how much we try to keep it closed," Mathew explained.

Henry and Kayla exchanged subtle eye contact. This was similar to the window situation at the museum, though that had been going on for quite a while. "When did this start?" Kayla asked.

"About a week ago. We're not sure because at first we each just closed it, not thinking twice about it, but then Danielle asked me to fix it, and we realized we'd both been closing and reclosing it for a while, usually in the morning."

"So it happens at night?"

The two nodded.

"When you go to bed, you check it?" Kayla continued.

"We do now," Mathew replied, nodding.

"Where is the window?"

"It's in the office on the second floor facing Record Street."

"Is there anything else?" Kayla was beginning to think that this was going to be pretty easy.

The couple exchanged a glance.

Henry quickly jumped in and said "Don't worry. We've heard and seen everything, believe me."

"It's voices," Danielle said.

"Well, not really voices, the noise is too muffled, but it sounds human," Mathew said, correcting his wife.

She nodded in agreement. "It sounds like sobbing with some garbled words."

"A muffled sobbing, coupled with a creaking sound. Rhythmic creaking," Mathew added.

"Where is all of this happening?" Henry asked.

"In the back room, the apartment," Danielle said, motioning behind her.

"When did it start?" Kayla asked.

"About a week ago, same as the window, we think," Danielle responded. "I heard it first. Of course, I thought it was my imagination, but the second night, I got up to investigate."

"And?" Henry asked.

"Well, it was more than strange. As I approached the room, the activity began to subside, as though in reaction to my presence."

"So the next night, I told Danielle to wake me if she heard it, and she did," Mathew interjected.

"So you both went to check it out the next time you heard it?" Henry asked.

"Yeah. And I can tell you, it's real," Mathew replied. "I mean really there. Don't know what it is," he added, shrugging his shoulders.

"Well, let's go look," Henry said. "We'll check that window first."

They walked up the wide staircase, Danielle and Mathew leading the way. Helga hung back with Kayla and Henry and whispered, "I want to nip this in the bud. We've got enough problems."

Kayla and Henry didn't respond because it was hard to consider "nipping" paranormal activity in the bud.

They entered the tidy office, which faced Court Street. A large window, opened slightly, took up most of the wall. Henry and Kayla walked over to it. Henry raised it more, noting how easily it slid up the frame. Then he examined the lock.

"Have you used anything else to restrain it?" he asked, turning to the couple.

"That piece of wood," Mathew explained, pointing. "We wedged it in. But it seems to fall out during the night, since it's on the floor when we come in here in the morning. And the window is open."

"You don't hear the wood fall?"

"No. Strange, huh?"

"How far is the window opened?"

"Wide. All the way to the top."

"Well, we'll certainly want to examine it with our equipment," Henry responded, looking at Kayla. "Let's go see the apartment now."

"It connects up here, too," Mathew explained as he opened a door to a dark hallway. He flipped on a switch. The five of them moved through it single file and then entered a bedroom.

"The place where it occurs is past the stairs," Danielle said, now leading the way. They followed her through another hallway, a small room, and then into another bedroom. Kayla stopped when she entered it. To her, the room felt like it was lived in.

"Does someone occupy it?" she asked.

"Oh, no. It's a guest room," Danielle explained.

The room had a king-size bed, two nightstands, a dresser, and a long table. There was a lamp on each nightstand, one on the table, and an overhead light. The ceilings were at least ten feet high. Thin curtains covered the two large windows with shutters. A single closet door was located on the wall adjacent to the hall. The floor was wood, similar to all of the other floors, though it looked older or perhaps had just not been polished recently.

Henry walked around the bed. "Can you tell where the noise is emanating from?"

"No, as I mentioned, it's muffled to begin with and always starts to subside when we get close," Danielle answered.

Henry stopped next to the side of the bed opposite the entrance and knelt.

"Do you know what made these marks?" he asked, rubbing his hand over something on the floor.

Everyone rushed to see what he was referring to, which made it too crowded for anyone to see anything. Kayla backed off and turned on the overhead light. She noticed that Helga was working her phone.

"I've never noticed that before," Mathew said, now squatting as well. "Have you, Danielle?"

She leaned over his shoulder and could just make out what all the fuss was about: a thin groove in the floor, actually two grooves. "It's just scarred," she said. "The floors are over a hundred and eighty years old."

"I'm sorry to say, but it doesn't appear to be scarred," Henry said. "I'm an architectural engineer. I've worked in and around wood for years, and this is relatively fresh."

"Well, if that's the case, what made the marks?" Mathew wondered.

"It could be one of a dozen things. But it's not old," Henry replied. Kayla saw Helga look at her cellphone and punch in some message. Polly, she was not. "We'll get our equipment in here, too," Henry added, looking around.

"Okay, sure," Mathew agreed. "Whatever needs to be done. We just want everything back to normal."

Henry looked at Kayla and raised an eyebrow. "What we will do is try to find the cause of the activity, what is forcing the window open, and what is making the noise," he said.

"As far as making the occurrences go away, that depends on the cause," Kayla explained.

"Well, whatever," Mathew replied. "Once we know what it is, I'll take care of it if need be. Not to worry."

Kayla surveyed the room as he spoke. "Have you checked the closet?"

"No," Danielle replied. "I never thought to do that. Why do you ask?"

"Well, you said the noise sounded muffled. I just thought maybe the activity occurred somewhere more enclosed. So let's take a look."

Danielle opened the small closet in the corner and pulled an overhead string to turn the light bulb on. There were two winter coats hanging in the corner, two carry-on suitcases on the floor, a blanket on the shelf above, and, surprisingly (or maybe not so much), a trompe l'oeil. Danielle gasped slightly.

"What is it?" Mathew asked, leaning over her shoulder.

"It's a painting," Danielle responded.

"Actually, it's more than a painting. It's a trompe l'oeil," Kayla explained. "So you didn't know it was there?"

"Of course not," Danielle replied, almost defensively. "I've never seen it before."

This tromp l'oeil was the most well-done of the three that Kayla had observed. It was a girl for sure, which was different from the other shapes, which were not so specific, at least in terms of gender. Large eyes, similar to the others. Definitely a tear. Kayla looked at Henry. He looked at her with trepidation. If it could have been possible, he would have been white as a ghost. This was another first.

"We'll definitely be checking this room out with our instruments," Kayla said again, trying to mitigate the fear that had obviously permeated throughout the room. Even Helga looked concerned. "We'll be able to tell a lot more once our investigation is completed," she added, already wondering when they were going to find the time.

"But who could have done something like this?" Danielle asked. "I mean, it had to have taken time. It required, well, for God's sake, it required a lot of work."

"And a light," Mathew added.

Kayla frowned. "Maybe not. Let's go back to the living room," she suggested, as she glanced around.

Danielle and Mathew were obviously shocked. Helga looked very nervous, even scared. Henry, however, was regaining his composure. They filed out of the room. Helga practically ran down the stairs.

"Please have a seat," Danielle said, gesturing and then sitting down as well. Silence followed.

Finally, Henry broke it. "Is there something else?" he asked.

Kayla hoped there wasn't. But Danielle nodded yes. Then reaching into her pocket, she approached the pair and handed them a photo.

"It's this."

Henry and Kayla observed a white woman and a black woman staring back at them. The white woman held an infant, swaddled in multiple layers of cloth, its white face staring up at her.

"Who are they?" Henry asked.

"I have no idea. This photo just showed up in the pocket of my robe."

"I think you just forgot you put it there," Mathew muttered.

"I told you that would be ridiculous," Danielle replied, glaring. "I've never seen it before."

"It's likely to be an apport, given what else is going on." Henry said excitedly, standing up. "I mistakenly said we'd seen and heard everything, but this is new. This truly is a first."

Kayla had never seen Henry so animated, almost giddy.

"What's an apport?" Danielle asked. Kayla silently admitted that she did not know, either.

"It's when an object appears through spiritual means." Danielle sat down upon hearing this. "It is known to occur on very rare occasions, often at séances. Most of those cases have been determined to be fraudulent."

Kayla saw Mathew sigh. He obviously did not believe this explanation.

"But … what does it mean? Why me?"

"Don't know," Henry replied. "The opposite also happens. Spirits take something, and it shows up somewhere else. That's called asport. An apport is very, very rare. As I said, during our ten years in the business, we've never come across one."

"You've never seen this photo before or these people?" Kayla asked.

"No, never, ever."

"Well, they're obviously from another era," Kayla replied. "Do you mind if I use the photo for research? I may be able to find out who they are."

"Yes, of course."

Kayla stared at the photo again and turned it over. Nothing. She put it in her bag. *Who were they? What was their significance?*

"Are you frightened by these developments?" Kayla asked.

"Yes, I am now. I'd like to know who was in my guest room painting a picture," Danielle replied, glancing over at Mathew. He nodded.

"So is that it?" Helga asked, having regained her composure, along with her impatience.

"Isn't that enough?" Danielle asked.

"Yes, it is," Helga agreed, still glancing at her phone.

"We'll contact you again after we've talked with Parker about when we can set up our investigative equipment," Henry said.

"We'll be here."

"Okay, that sounds good, then," Kayla said as the couple showed them the way out.

———◆———

After the three were outside, Helga said, "Well, keep me posted. Let's hope you can button this up sooner than later."

Does this look like it can just be buttoned up? That would be magic, not a paranormal investigation, Kayla thought, but she held her tongue. "We'll certainly do everything we can," she replied.

"Thank you," Helga said as she rolled up her window and sped off.

"What a piece of work she is," Henry noted as he shook his head. "And what a mess this house is. I have to admit, that picture in the closet really took me aback."

"I know," Kayla said, shaking her head. "And you know what's even spookier?"

"I don't know if I want to know."

"Well, I'll confide in you anyway. In the slightest way, the girl looks like the body I discovered in Carroll Creek."

"Oh, my God. Seriously?"

"Yeah."

"Let's go grab a cool one. I'm sure you could use one, and I know I can. How about Magoo's? It's just around the corner."

"I'm with you," Kayla agreed as she refed the meter.

Chapter

G uy Hardy was reacting to Hunter's newest and most asinine demand yet: "Let me get this straight. You want me to break into Beacon's Way, bust into the hatch door in the cellar, clean it out with bleach, and then take out the stairs?"

"You know you don't have to break into Beacon's Way."

"What do you mean?"

"You have a key."

"Jeez. Hunter, this is too much. I work forty hours a week."

"Yes, and you're in charge because of me. You can give yourself whatever assignment you please."

Guy sighed. "When am I supposed to do this?"

"Yesterday. I mean it. Get over there and get it done. You're going to need a blowtorch for the hatch door."

"How am I supposed to get out of there once the stairs are gone?"

"You figure it out."

"What if someone comes in the house and tries to go down there after the stairs are gone? He could break his neck."

"Exactly."

Two hours later, Hunter watched as Guy entered the cellar, carrying bleach and a blowtorch. Hunter couldn't hear the man, since he was talking under his breath, but he could imagine what he was saying, and it was not complimentary in the least, especially about him. Hunter frowned. *Not good, my friend. Not good.*

Chapter

52

The next morning, the Dulany Team met at their office. Both Henry and Kayla told Parker what they had observed at the William Tyler Page home, including Helga's impatience and the concerned looks Mathew and Danielle had shared.

"It's definitely troubling," Henry commented.

"I'd say a little more than troubling," Kayla replied. "There are a lot of paranormal occurrences happening there."

"Have you had a chance to examine the photo Danielle found in her pocket?" Parker asked. "The one of the ladies and the baby? It might be some sort of clue."

"No," Kayla said. "I've got it on my desk at home. It's next." Parker nodded. "But," she continued, "I would like to throw something out for consideration, something that might shed some light on things."

Parker and Henry looked keenly interested.

"Please do," Parker responded. "Anything would be better than nothing, which is where we are just about now."

"Well, you didn't see it, Parker, but the trompe l'oeil in the William Tyler Page home was the most detailed yet. I mentioned to Henry that the figure was uncannily similar to the body I found in Carroll Creek." A shadow passed across Parker's face upon hearing this piece of news. "But the point I want to make is that now, we have a connection. It's very strange. A trompe l'oeil has been discovered in all three buildings. Furthermore, all appear to be crying, a tear running down their face. One of these figures actually reached out to me, or at least through me, but not in a harmful way. However, last night, as I was reviewing these three figures, it dawned on me that we might be missing something, that the figures themselves are not what we're supposed to concentrate on."

Parker and Henry both looked very curious.

"When you consider the literal translation of trompe l'oeil, *deceive the eye*, we keep thinking deception," she continued. "I don't think we're off on that interpretation, but maybe we should consider the word 'literal.' Maybe it's our eyes that have been deceived. Maybe whatever is happening, the paranormal activity or whatever is causing the paranormal activity, we are already part of it but don't know it. Maybe it's that personal. We're the only ones that the spirits are talking to at this point. They're talking to *us*."

Silence. Parker and Henry had nothing to say.

"The spirits are telling us that we're needed to do something."

"Kayla, you may be right. If so, then it's something extremely urgent," Parker remarked.

"If you're right," Henry commented, "then the spirits must think we're stupid."

"Why do you say that?" Kayla asked.

"Because we're not getting it, and they have to keep adding to the repertoire," Henry explained.

That made both Kayla and Parker laugh.

"So we need to get a move on," Parker agreed. "How soon can we set the Page house up for our investigation?"

"Tomorrow night," Henry replied. "I called them yesterday evening after I returned home, and they said that would be best. They're planning on leaving town for the coast soon."

"So wouldn't that be a better time?" Kayla asked.

"Yes, but they want it done as soon as possible. And now, so do we. And they are keenly interested in actually observing the findings. You can't blame them. They'll stay with relatives tomorrow evening. We'll meet them the following morning."

"I'll try to find out who the women and baby in the photo are," Kayla added. "Let's hope that can shed some light on … on something. Even if I can determine the era when it was taken, that could be of some help. Maybe a big help."

"I agree," Parker commented. "Let's get set up tomorrow and then meet Mathew and Danielle at the house the following morning at ten o'clock."

Chapter

53

Beware the man who walks lockstep with the Devil.
—Candice Tolbert

Nick was on speakerphone with Sam as he drove to one of the superstores in Frederick.

"Nick, I was able to turn the phone on, but it's encrypted."

"The phone is encrypted?"

"Yes, that's what I'm saying. Once we figure the code out, then we can see what calls were made. But I'm guessing that some of them will be encrypted, too. You're on to something, which is beginning to feel pretty nefarious, Nick. Sure you want to pursue it?"

"Absolutely. How long will it take to figure the code out, do you think?"

"I'm not sure. I have a buddy who specializes in this sort of thing. I'm going to contact her. She's good. Very good. So here's hoping."

"Okay, thanks," Nick replied just as he pulled in and parked. This was the store Lily Mitka had worked in. Nick had checked into the accident. It was definitely a hit-and-run, but the cop investigating it had been unable to find any witnesses, and the paint type from the other vehicle was a dime a dozen. No clues.

Nick walked in, showed his badge, and asked for the manager.

Monroe Cobb arrived within minutes, a balding man with a sizable girth, maybe thirty-five years of age, Nick figured. They shook hands.

"What can I do for you, Detective?" Cobb asked.

"May we speak privately?"

"Sure. My office is this way." The two walked together past the fast food restaurant and around the corner, where a sign indicated STAFF ONLY. Cobb opened the door for Nick. "It's this way," Cobb motioned, opening yet another door that said MANAGER. No names or photos were placed on it. Nick figured there had to be two or three managers in order to run the huge store, which was open 24/7.

There was only one desk with an office chair, two plastic chairs, and a small coffee table. Cheap. All of the furniture looked like it came from the store, the kind of furniture that comes in a box to be assembled. No pictures hung on the wall, but a large clock was opposite the desk. Given only one desk, the office was a mess, with papers piled up everywhere among half-empty coffee cups, confirming Nick's guess on the staffing. *It must be hard to share a desk*, he thought.

"Please, have a seat," Cobb offered, sitting in one of the chairs. "Anything I can get for you? Coffee? Soft drink?"

"No, thanks. I just have a few questions."

"Please, go ahead."

"What can you tell me about Lily Mitka?"

"Who?"

"Lily Mitka. She was an employee here," Nick explained. "She recently died in an automobile accident."

"I didn't know her, sir. We have a very … mobile workforce."

"What does that mean?"

"Um," Cobb began, clearing his throat, "it means that the workers, the … employees, have different hours, different days of the week. I'm one of four managers, so I may never have been on the floor when she was working here. I'm sorry about her accident."

"Yes, well, if you can find her schedule for me, I'd like to talk to some people who worked with her. In fact, I would like a comprehensive list of all employees so I can cross-reference information."

"Certainly," the man said as he stood.

"I have another person of interest I'd like to inquire about," Nick said as he pulled a photo from his front pocket.

"Oh?" Cobb said, sitting back down.

He handed the manager the photo of Jane Doe and asked, "Do you happen to know if this person worked here?"

Cobb took the photo and gasped, saying, "Good Lord! Is she dead too?"

"Unfortunately, yes," Nick said.

"I don't know her," Cobb said, handing the photo back to Nick, his hand trembling.

"You didn't look very closely."

"I saw enough."

"Well, I need to see your entire roster of employees, if I may, with photos if they are part of the file. It's possible I might recognize a name or a face."

"Sure. Do you want the schedule and list now?" Cobb asked, still visibly shaken.

"If possible."

"I'll have my assistant get copies for you. It will only take a few minutes."

"That's fine. I wanted to look around the store anyway."

"Okay, sure. Um, they'll be here on my desk in case I'm not back when you're ready."

"Thanks much," Nick said, standing up and extending his hand. The two shook, and Nick left. He imagined Cobb wouldn't be there when he came back.

Sometimes, even though there's no external indication that one is a cop, people can sense it, perhaps especially if they have something to hide. This definitely seemed to be the case as Nick wandered around. He saw one young man stocking paper towels glance at him and then turn quickly and slip into a back room. An older woman practically ran down the aisle to disappear around the corner, after seeing him coming.

Nick walked up to a cashier who was waiting for his next customer.

"Excuse me, sir," Nick said to the affable-looking man, who showed no sign of evasion. His name tag indicated his name was Roger. "I have a couple of questions, if you don't mind." He showed his badge.

"Shoot," the man said with a smile.

"Did you ever work with this woman?" Nick asked, showing the photo of Lily.

"Ah, Lily Mitka. Everyone was so sorry to hear about her death," Roger said. "She was very kind and so beautiful."

"Did you go to her funeral?"

"No. We were all pretty upset that we didn't know about it until it was all over, burial and all. She didn't show up to work, but no one thought anything about it. The schedules are so screwed up, you really don't know who is going to be on your shift."

"Did she talk about her husband, Tommy?"

"All the time. Anyone who knew Lily used to joke that he must have secretly planted a love potion on her. She was head over heels in love. That poor man. He must be devastated."

Nick let that one go. "What did, I mean, what does he do?"

"I don't know. To be quite honest, I'm not sure Lily knew. She just said he traveled a lot and made lots of money when he did. It wasn't a steady job, whatever it was."

Nick nodded thoughtfully. Just then, a customer came up to the register. "Well, Roger, thanks for the chat."

"You bet."

Nick continued his stroll around the store. Employees continued to avoid him. He finally was able to corner a young sales clerk by waiting to talk to her after she helped someone else. "Excuse me, miss," he asked the petite Latino woman. Her name tag indicated Rosa.

"*Si?*" She didn't look at him. Nick was beginning to think he had something on his face or his fly was open.

"I'm Detective Nucci. I'd like to ask you a couple of questions. Do you speak English?"

"Si, I mean, yes."

"Did you know Lily Mitka?" Rosa shook her head no. "Do you know anyone who's working today who knew her?"

She shook her head again.

"I have one more question. I don't want to frighten you, Rosa, but I would like you to look at a photo of a body. Will that be okay?"

"Okay."

"Do you know this person?" Nick asked, showing her the photo.

Rosa gasped when she saw Jane Doe's picture.

"What happened to her?" she asked.

"She was murdered."

Tears filled Rosa's eyes, and her lower lip quivered.

"Maybe we can go somewhere and talk," Nick suggested.

Rosa shook her head no while looking around furtively.

"I can't. I need to keep working."

"What is her name?" Nick asked.

"Kamala."

"Last name?"

The woman shook her head no again.

"Did she have family around here?"

Rosa shrugged.

"How do you know her? Did she work here?"

"I have to go." Rosa turned on her heel and rushed off.

Nick sighed. He might have to invite her to the station. She seemed afraid, first of him but then, later, afraid of something else. He would try to find another way.

———— •◦• ————

Nick left the superstore with the employees' schedules and a roster of all the workers' names. He sat in his car to peruse them. The first thing he noticed was that no one had bothered to remove Lily's name from the employee roster. She was still on the list, but when he checked the schedule, she was not there. Then Nick reviewed the schedule again, this time for a different reason. *Ah ha*, he thought as he looked at his watch. Another thirty minutes and Rosa would be off the clock. Time for another chat.

Nick waited in view of the store's exit. After a while, Rosa exited and walked into the parking lot. *Oh, going to the bus stop*, Nick assumed. He walked quickly and was alongside her within seconds. She physically jumped when she saw him.

"Hello, Rosa. What can you tell me …?"

"She worked in warehouse," Rosa said quickly. "Go," she yelled, swinging her purse at him. "Leave me alone."

Nick stopped, stunned. Technically, she could be booked for assaulting an officer, but she didn't seem to care. He was baffled.

Chapter

Kayla was just pulling into her drive when her cell rang. She turned off the ignition and checked it. "Oh, hi, Danielle," she answered. "How are you?"

"Fine, I suppose."

"What can I do for you? Henry is organizing the team to set up your house for tomorrow evening's investigation. I guess he contacted you?"

"Yes."

"Oh, good ..."

"Listen—you have that photo, the one of the baby?"

"Yes, of course. I was just getting ready to see what I could find out about it."

"Well, I may be able to save you some time."

"*Always* appreciated," Kayla replied, still sitting in her car and listening carefully.

"The baby is William Tyler Page. He was actually born here. Here in the house. I know now I should have mentioned this, but there was so much going on during our meeting that it slipped my mind.

"The woman holding him," she continued, "is his mother, Nannie Christian Page. Her father was Dr. William B. Tyler Sr. He owned most of Record Street and made sure his children each had a home here. He lived next to the Spite house on Church Street."

Kayla's mind was racing as she tried to put these facts into some kind of context. "And the black woman?"

"I can't find anything on her. My guess is she was the nanny or maybe the maid."

"Yes, that makes sense. Everything seems quite normal, actually, so we're back to square one. How, and more importantly, why did it end up in your pocket?"

"That I still do not know. But I have some questions."

We all do, Kayla thought. "Go ahead."

"Do you think there's any way we can find out where William Tyler Page was born in the house? I mean, maybe the rocking is coming from his crib or something."

"That could be, but you've lived in the house for some twenty-odd years. Why would he show up now?"

"I know. I'm just grasping. I was excited to find out who was in the photo, so I started to speculate from there."

"It's good," Kayla said, making a mental note to try to find out. "It's a good start. Let's see what information we get from the videos and other investigative approaches. And then maybe we can factor that in."

"Okay. Sounds good. I just wanted to touch base … in case it helped."

"It does help," Kayla assured Danielle. "We'll meet you there in a couple of days. Does ten o'clock work for you?"

"Yes, that's fine."

"Okay, great. Thank you so much. Have a nice evening."

"Thanks. You too."

Kayla wanted to investigate the photo herself. Danielle had provided a good lead and therefore had definitely saved her time, but it wasn't enough. There must be something in that photo that could provide a clue. *There had to be.*

The first thing Kayla did once she and Fritchie were in the darkroom was to make an enlarged copy of the photo so she could look at it on the easel. Sometimes examining a photo with a magnifying glass just wasn't enough. In this case, she wanted to look at the two women. Okay, so the white woman was William Tyler Page's mother, but who was the black woman? She must have a name. She didn't look all that happy. Neither did the mother. But back then, no one smiled for the camera. The black woman was well-dressed. And she was physically quite close to the mother and baby in a comfortable sort of way.

Kayla decided she needed to do some research, so she sat down at her laptop to investigate the Tyler family. Ah ha! Nannie C. Tyler was born in 1830; her father was Dr. William B. Tyler, Sr., just as Danielle had reported. Nannie had eight siblings, and her husband's name was Walker Yates Page. *It was coincidental that the woman's name was Nannie, in an earie kind of way*, Kayla thought. She noted, again, that William Tyler Page was indeed born at 111 Record Street.

Kayla read more about Dr. Tyler Sr., since there was scant material about Nannie. Dr. Tyler owned most or all of Record Street and the land that was currently Baker Park. *Ohhhh*. Kayla had never known that piece of history. There was information about Dr. Tyler Sr.'s political aspirations, which had been notable. He had run for governor of Maryland and lost by a mere thirty-one votes. *Hmmm*, Kayla thought. So, as Henry had commented, the Tylers were a notable family. One of the cornerstones of Frederick.

It was then that Kayla decided to query "All Saints Episcopal Church," because she knew the church was as old as Frederick and many well-known affluent families had been members. There must be history. Bingo! The church was founded in 1742 and was the oldest Episcopal Church in western Maryland. Then quite by chance, she came across an article titled "Trail of Souls." It described some of the congregants, stating that many were heroes of the time: Francis Scott Key; his sister, who married the first Maryland governor; Mrs. Roger Taney, whose husband was the chief justice responsible for the Dred Scott decision; and here again, the Tylers. Dr. William B. Tyler. Kayla was excited. She could feel her heart beating. *Uh-oh*. She next read something that simply had not occurred to her: All of these "heroes" were slave owners. Dr. Tyler owned four. Kayla raced through one document after another, looking for more information on the slaves.

She had almost given up when the photo that had ended up in Danielle's pocket, the apport, popped up on the computer screen. For a second, she didn't recognize what she was looking at. It was like seeing double. She had the same photo up on the easel, and now this. It deserved the second glance that she gave it. Once reality sunk in, Kayla's hands began to tremble. She discovered that the black woman's name was Laura Frazier. She was the fifth child of Charles and Milly Frazier, and she lived with the Page family.

"Lived with?" Kayla wondered aloud. She stood up and began to pace.

Fritchie watched her with interest. The impact of this discovery was overwhelming. It was almost too troubling for Kayla to grasp. She knew Washington, Jefferson, and others owned slaves, but that was different somehow. This was … well, this was personal. Kayla returned to the computer and began a new search: "Charles and Milly Frazier."

———————◦———————

Kayla discovered from her research that Laura Frazier was buried in the Fairview Cemetery, the largest African American cemetery in Frederick. So bright and early the next morning, having decided to skip her run, she drove to the cemetery to find Laura's grave.

It was barely sunrise. *Kind of spooky*, she thought as she stepped from her car. The well-kept cemetery was located on Gas House Pike, which was on the east side of town, out where a lot of expansion was occurring. She had looked for Laura's plot online, but for some reason, it did not show up. Kayla had read that the cemetery had been refurbished in 2014 as a community service project.

Kayla walked up the narrow paved road to the back of the cemetery and started to methodically crisscross the rows in search of Laura. She'd read that there were around fourteen hundred people buried here, so this was going to take some time. A lot of the tombstones were illegible. She often had to squat to trace the faded carving to determine what the name was. Birds in nearby trees were already chirping wildly. A few people came by walking their dogs, mostly; no one was visiting.

After two hours or so, Kayla saw it. The headstone was not what she'd expected, for several reasons. First, it was new, certainly relatively so. She wondered who must have had it made. Furthermore, there were several names on it. The stone explained that Alice Frazier Bouldin and Laura Frazier Downs were the daughters of Milly and Charles Frazier. Yes, Kayla knew that to be true. At least that Milly and Charles were Laura's parents. She had not come across Alice's name before.

Furthermore, there was another name, William Downs, Laura's husband. Kayla took a couple of photos. She circled around it, and lo and behold, more names: Peter Frazier, brother of Charles, was noted, and Hannah Frazier, Peter's wife. No wonder Laura Frazier had not shown up online; she was among many family members as well as her husband all seemingly buried in the same plot.

But then, Kayla read the short poem that had been carved below the names on the tombstone, the side with Peter and Hannah's names:

NO LIE IS STRONG ENOUGH TO KILL
THE ROOTS THAT WORK BELOW,
FROM YOUR RICH DUST AND SLAUGHTERED WILL
A TREE WITH TONGUES WILL GROW

Oh my God. Kayla felt like she'd been kicked in the gut. This was not just a rebuke. It was a shout out to the complacency that occurs when one group dominates another, spreading its history while denying the history of others, she thought. Kayla considered the history of the Page house and the messages and activity there. The poem fit it so well. Kayla took a photo of this side of the stone to capture that poem.

Chapter
55

Memories come back, pressing in on you, like ghost faces in the darkness pushing up the glass, trying to get into the lit room.
—Julia Green

Henry was waiting for Kayla at 111 Record Street. He wanted to brief her on what he'd set up for the investigation. It was just half past nine. "Hiya," he said as she got out of her car. "Just to let you know, we're on our own. Parker called and told us to handle this. He said he needed to meet with Otto."

"Why? I thought Nick, I mean Detective Nucci, was going to take care of things."

Henry smiled but didn't tease Kayla about her growing relationship with the detective. "Dunno. Maybe lining up all of his ducks. Just in case the detective can't pull it off, or maybe to help him do just that."

"Yeah, okay," Kayla said as she handed Henry a coffee.

"Thanks. Did you jog?" he asked, changing the subject to small talk.

"Not this morning."

"But you're still jogging in the cemetery?"

"Yep," she said, sitting on the porch as she took the lid off her coffee. It smelled delicious. The morning looked innocent, she thought, as she sipped it. Crisp, some autumn leaves still hanging in there. The street was filled with their colors.

"Anyone else there?" he asked.

"You mean besides …"

"Yeah, besides those buried there."

"Usually. All in all, there's a total of eight miles of paths throughout the cemetery. Did you know the population buried there is larger than that of Annapolis?"

"No, but I also didn't know you referred to a cemetery's inhabitants as its 'population,' either. Interesting. Did you listen to the recording on the memorial to Francis Scott Key?"

"No. But it would sound different to me now."

"What do you mean? Why?"

Kayla had been wondering how to breach her findings regarding the ownership of slaves to Henry, so she figured this was as good a segue as any. "Did you know he owned slaves?" she asked.

Henry sat down next to her. "I never thought about it, but yeah, of course he must have. Everyone did back then. Well, everyone who had any money."

"I guess I just never thought about it, either. But it's kind of shocking."

Henry remained silent. Kayla pulled the picture she'd printed out from her computer. She'd continued her research all day yesterday.

"Whoa, where'd you get that? Is it the same as …?"

"Yeah. The very same. Guess what?" Again silence. "The black woman is a fifteen-year-old girl named Laura. A slave. She was a *gift* to Nannie Page, William Tyler Page's mother, from her father, Dr. William B. Tyler, when the girl was around eight. He owned four slaves. And get this: Laura's father worked for Dr. Tyler as a driver. He was a free man. He was manumitted. That's the word they used: 'manumitted,' meaning freed from his slavery. But the law in Maryland at the time stipulated that if the mother was a slave, then her children were to be slaves as well. So he asked to work for Dr. Tyler because his wife Milly was not free, and their children were not free." Kayla trembled as she stood up, her indignation palatable. "Can you believe this?"

Henry took the paper with the photograph from her. He read the description beneath it. "It doesn't say she's a slave. It says she lived with them."

Kayla tossed a file folder filled with sheaths of paper. "It's all in there. I visited the Fairview Cemetery, where she is buried."

Henry flipped through the papers, reading sections here and there. "Well, I guess maybe there's a reason for some paranormal activity to be occurring here, then," he said, motioning toward the house. "Yeah, maybe some ill will, you think?"

"Yes, of course that's a possibility. But the question we have to ask over and over again is, why now?"

Henry shook his head. "Not sure. But we have to figure it out."

"Yeah, we sure do. So what did you have the team set up?"

"Powder on the floor by the window and bedroom, and in the closet. Video cameras and recorders in the same area."

Just then, Mathew and Danielle drove up. They parked in the back but walked around front to meet Kayla and Henry.

"So are we ready to go in?" Henry asked.

"Of course." Danielle looked a bit apprehensive, but Mathew seemed bored, Kayla thought. Danielle opened the front door and walked in. Everyone waited in the large foyer for Henry to lead the way.

"Let's check out the apartment first," Henry suggested. They walked up the stairs. When they reached the bedroom, he opened the door. "Lots of activity here," he said, pointing to the footprints.

Jeez, Kayla thought, *you do this for so long, and there are hardly any signs, and now there are signs everywhere when it comes to these buildings.* She started snapping photos.

"Looks like a lot of movement but only one spirit," she said.

Henry nodded. "The indentations are rather small," he commented, standing on the other side of the bed, where the floor had been scored.

Kayla had been so busy that she had not paid any attention to the hosts. Danielle stood frozen at the entrance, and Mathew looked as though he might be beginning to believe. Kayla walked gingerly to the opposite side of the bed to see what Henry was referring to. Yes, the powder was disturbed in a way that suggested something had been moving back and forth.

"Hey … look at that," Kayla said, pointing to the bed. Henry nodded as she took photos. An obvious indentation could be seen on the cover, as though someone had been sitting on it, not lying. Kayla heard Mathew swear softly.

She took the tapes, and Henry moved to the closet where the trompe l'oeil had been.

"Still there," he said. "Nothing new. Okay, let's go to the window in the study."

Here, they found lots of different footprints, mostly bare feet. Most of them were smeared, as though the spirits had been walking on top of each other. The piece of wood was on the floor, and the window stood wide open. Henry took the recording from the corner of the ceiling, while Kayla snapped photos of the disturbed powder. Both Danielle and Mathew appeared pretty somber by this point. Kayla couldn't tell if they were frightened or resigned or a little of both.

"Let's go downstairs and talk for a while," she said as she turned to go. Everyone followed.

Once they were seated, Henry started, "We'll review the material and get back to you about any findings, probably within a day or two."

"In the meantime," Kayla said, "I have discovered some interesting history. The original homeowners, the Pages, had slaves." Mathew and Danielle looked at each other. "Did you know?"

"We knew," Danielle said. "To be frank, I never wanted to know who or when, so we agreed to let that part of the house's history remain in the past."

"Do you want to know more now?" Kayla asked politely. She did not want to reveal unwanted information.

"Yes, of course," Mathew replied. Danielle nodded.

"I discovered your photo while researching All Saints Church,"

Kayla explained, pulling out the photo she had previously shown to Henry. She then went on to describe what she'd learned.

"So that's why we're having all of this paranormal activity?" Danielle asked, sounding skeptical.

"Well, yes and no. It's just another of many clues as far as we know. It's not clear why all of the activity would occur now."

"Exactly," Mathew replied impatiently. "What's next? We need to have a séance or something?" Silence ensued. "Well?"

Kayla finally spoke: "As you know, we're involved with similar cases in two other buildings in Frederick."

"No, we didn't know that," Mathew said, looking at Danielle.

Uh-oh. Kayla decided not to beat around the bush. "There are two other historical buildings that have begun to experience similar paranormal activity out of the blue. So at this point, we're looking for motivation. We need to find the motivation, and then we'll most likely be able to find a resolution to the activity."

"What do you mean by 'resolution'?" Mathew asked.

Henry replied, "To understand what's needed to end it. Paranormal activity represents a high level of energy. It seeks resolution because it's disturbed. Let's see what the tapes show, if anything, and then we'll look at our next steps. The messages can be fear, despair, anger, any number of emotions, or a combination of them. Knowing that there was at least one slave in this house is certainly a clue, but just part of the puzzle," Henry added as he stood. "We'll let you know our findings shortly."

Mathew and Danielle nodded, rather reluctantly, Kayla thought.

"Okay, thank you," Danielle said, walking them to the door.

Chapter

56

Nick decided to go back to the office and do a little research on the superstore warehouse. First of all, where was it located? Who managed it? How many employees worked there? He wanted to be well-informed before he started to ask questions from managers and employees at the site.

While he had good intentions, he could not ignore the fax that was waiting for him on his desk. It was from the Toronto Police. *Good. About time,* he thought to himself. He had made an inquiry to the Toronto Police Marine Unit over three days ago, asking about Port A. On a hunch, he had also asked whether Tommy Mitka worked there. He had forwarded a photo that he'd taken from the Mitka house with the request for information.

Nick was not prepared for what he read:

FAX

TO: Detective Nucci

FROM: Port of Toronto

DATE: November 3

RE: Tommy Mitka, Port Use

No one by the name of Tommy Mitka working at Ports Toronto.

Port of Toronto is used primarily for container shipments arriving and departing from Eurasia. Containers are for both private and commercial use. Transportation services to and from Port include marine, railroad, and highways. Male body discovered in the Western Channel after serious storm five days ago. Badly decomposed. Able to determine white Caucasian. Neck slit. Currently residing in morgue. May be your inquiry. Please advise.

Sincerely:

Eric Blake

Toronto Police Marine Unit

Please advise? "Well, I need his DNA, of course," Nick said aloud, as he reached for the phone. *I need the DNA. I can't believe this*, he thought to himself, all the while knowing he didn't have any idea what it might mean if the body was Tommy Mitka's and, if so, whether it was related to Lily's death. "I need those contact numbers from Sam," he muttered, speaking aloud once again.

Nick hung up the phone. Eric Blake from the Toronto Marine Police Department had been quite cooperative. He said he'd have the medical examiner take a DNA sample and send it over. In the meantime, Nick decided to go straight to the top. This was too important. He identified the person he felt he needed: the harbormaster and chief of security. His name was Wilson Tremblay. Nick called, introduced himself, and said he needed to speak to Mr. Tremblay as soon as possible. It concerned the body of the murdered man who had recently been discovered in the harbor.

The person on the other end of the phone was quite polite, similar to Nick's previous conversation. He told Nick that Mr. Tremblay would get back to him within the day. Internally, Nick sighed. He'd become impatient. "Thank you very much. I appreciate it." It was all he could do for now.

Not twenty minutes later, Nick's phone rang. "Hello?"

"Hello. Detective Nick Nucci?"

"Yes."

"Wilson here. Wilson Tremblay."

"Hello," Nick said again, surprised and pleased that the man had gotten in touch with him so quickly. "Thank you for returning my call."

"My pleasure. I understand you have questions regarding the John Doe that washed up in the harbor. The murdered man, eh?"

"Yes. First, I want to say that I have requested DNA from the body. We may be able to help you identify him, based on a lead here," Nick started.

"Well, good. That's encouraging."

"And I believe I have a question specific to your area," Nick continued.

"Go ahead."

"Has anything occurred recently in the harbor, I mean other than finding a body? Any security breaches, anything strange that occurred?"

"Yes, indeed. It's been in all of the media, but I suppose you may not have heard about it down where you are, eh?"

"No. I'm afraid not."

"Well, I will make a long story short."

Actually, please don't, Nick thought.

"I'm afraid to admit it, but an incoming container ship has gone missing."

"Really? Did this occur before the discovery of the body?"

"Yes."

"Where did the ship come from? I mean, how did you lose it?"

"It came from St. Petersburg, Russia. Just before approaching harbor control, it did a 180 and then went silent."

"You mean it turned around once it reached the harbor?"

"Bingo. Never heard of something like that occurring. It's extremely expensive to do so. A lot of money and time wasted to make the trip, then undo it. Unheard of. And no further report from it."

"What was in the cargo?"

"The contents were simply labelled 'Time-Sensitive Trade Goods.'"

There was an uncomfortable silence.

Finally, Nick asked the inevitable: "You think it may have sunk?"

"It could have. The manifest showed just a small crew, the minimum required. Nonetheless, I hate to think what may have happened to them. And the number of containers shown on the manifest is the smallest I've ever seen as well. Ships rarely leave their port of origin without loading on as much as possible. We have, of course, been in constant contact with the port in St. Petersburg. The ship has not returned or reported in. Believe me—I am not happy about this. It's embarrassing, to say the least, not to mention a potential loss of life, but we have tried to search for it for days now, eh?"

"What do you mean, tried?" Nick asked. "I mean, is something impeding your search?"

"It's the weather, man. It's been hell up here these past few days, to say the least," Tremblay exclaimed, sounding a bit exasperated. "Again, I realize you don't know what is going on in your neighbor's backyard, but yeah, it's just been one storm after another. We would have found the body much sooner if it had not been for these storms. Visibility is nil, eh?"

"Well, yeah, sorry. I admit I never look at Toronto's weather," Nick replied. "Nonetheless, I appreciate what you are saying. I understand. Another question, if I may?"

"Yep?" Tremblay responded, sounding a bit appeased.

225

"Do you have the identity of the person initiating the shipment?"

"We have a name, Feliks Nikolaev, but I must warn you that often these people are not the ones pulling the strings, especially from certain countries. It's just a fact. The person is often a proxy, in other words, a name on paper."

"Got it."

"Now, may I ask a question?" Tremblay asked.

"Of course."

"I gather from your questions and the fact that you began this with a comment about John Doe's DNA that you think there's a connection between the murder and this container ship, eh?"

"Well, now based on what you have relayed to me and since the incidents appear to be somewhat juxtaposed, then perhaps there is. What it is, I have no clear idea as yet. Do you?"

A long sigh ensued. "No … none whatsoever. It's a mystery, eh? All of it. If we can find the ship, it would certainly help to shed some light on what has transpired."

"Agreed. I'd appreciate it if you stay in touch with me about any developments. In the meantime, I'll let you know if the DNA matches."

"Sounds like a deal, my friend."

After hanging up, Nick leaned back in his office chair, hands clasped behind his head. Did Tommy Mitka have anything to do with the missing cargo ship? *Yeah. Of course he did. Did it get him killed? Yes.*

Chapter

57

Guy Hardy was sick of the smell of the bleach and the odors emanating from the pit beneath the hatch door. It was about six feet by eight feet, he estimated, and no more than five feet high. He could pull himself up without a ladder. It had taken him over an hour to blow-torch it open, and even though it was cool in the Beacon Way cellar, he was sweating profusely. "Sweating like a pig," he muttered under his breath, mostly because he was trying to hold it. "That's funny. I wonder if pigs even sweat? Wonder where that even came from?" Then he noticed the blood splatter. It was everywhere. *What the hell had happened down here?*

Guy had made several trips back to the van in order to get all of the tools and supplies for the job, including three super bright battery-operated lanterns. As he made the trips, he seethed about being Hunter Crowley's errand boy. No, that wasn't right. He was more than an errand boy. He was forced to do things against his will. He was at Hunter's beck and call.

Now the whole place smelled strongly of the astringent. His eyes were stinging, even though he wore goggles. He needed to get out for a breather. And then he would tackle the stairs.

After resting and getting his head clear, Guy dragged a very long extension ladder down to the cellar floor for later. *But what to do with the discarded stairs?* He sure as hell wasn't going to pull all of that wood topside. He decided he'd dump it in the hold beneath the hatch before he welded it shut.

Fortunately, the stairs were old. The hatchet broke into them with ease. The only sound of resistance was the splintering crack that accompanied each blow, along with the ripping sound that followed as Guy applied the crowbar to the fractured wood. He gathered the strips as he went and dumped them unceremoniously into the pit.

After he'd finished welding the hatch door shut, he climbed up the ladder to the kitchen with his lanterns, pulling the ladder up behind him. He then swung a lantern around the abyss that now existed where the stairs had once stood. Unless someone was lucky enough to see that stairs no longer existed fast enough, which was doubtful given the lack of lighting, he or she was going to be in for a world of hurt. He wondered who Hunter hoped that person would be, as he finished his Flying Dog beer. *Too bad it's not him*, Guy pondered. *It would be sweet music to my ears to hear that Hunter fell and broke his neck*, he thought as he closed the door behind him.

Chapter

58

**During the day, I don't believe in ghosts.
At night, I'm a little more open minded.**
—Unknown

Henry and Kayla each drove separately to the Dulany Team's office on East Street, tapes in hand. Parker was sitting at his desk.

"How'd it go with Otto?" Henry asked.

"Okay, okay. We went over everything that happened, including my reasons for breaking in. I meet with Nick Nucci tomorrow morning. He wants to ask me everything, too. So it was a kind of a dress rehearsal."

"That makes sense," Kayla said encouragingly.

"Yeah. Yes, it does. So anything interesting from the Page house?"

"We have the tapes here," Henry responded. "Yes, we did find a lot of paranormal activity. Footprints, lots of footprints. Also, indentations on the bed where they've been hearing muffled noises at night."

"And I found out that the Pages owned a slave. She'd been given to William Tyler Page's mother as a gift by her father. The slave, Laura, was eight years old when she was given to Nannie, the mother. That's who's in the photo," Kayla added.

"Whoa ... that's something, then," Parker commented. "Okay, let's watch the tapes."

Henry set up the one that captured the area around the bed first. For the first five minutes, all they could see was a digital clock on the nightstand. "I don't remember that being there," Henry observed.

"Me either."

"What's that?" Parker asked, jumping up and pointing.

"Look, Kayla," Henry said excitedly. "Someone is sitting on the bed."

The indentation started to appear. Kayla felt goosebumps. *No kidding.* Then the noise started, or rather noises: creak, creak, creak … changes in the indentation occurred with the creaking. Someone began sobbing. In between the cries, muttering occurred, but it was unintelligible.

"Sounds like a chant," Kayla said, listening hard.

"Uh-uh. No. It's a prayer," Henry said. "It's a prayer," he repeated.

Parker nodded. "Can you understand any of the words?" he asked, listening hard.

"Only 'Jesus.' Hear it?" Now that Henry mentioned it, Kayla could hear it too.

"What's the creaking?" Parker asked.

"I think the spirit is rocking a cradle," Kayla said, coming closer to the screen. "I think that's why we see movement on the bed, a back and forth. See it?" she asked, pointing.

Parker and Henry nodded excitedly.

"I know we need to watch the rest of this, in case there's more, but let's shift to the tape of the window in the study," Henry suggested eagerly. "I'm very curious, after seeing this, to know why this spirit is crying."

At first, per usual, nothing happened. But when they started to hear the creaking noise from the far room, shapes began to gather around the window. The wooden brace used to prevent the window from being opened was knocked to the floor by an indistinct shape, a fuzzy light. Three more apparitions appeared from nowhere and flew out the window. All in all, four apparitions disappeared out the window, as the sobbing continued.

Kayla was mesmerized. "This is hard to believe," she whispered, feeling prickles from her head to her legs.

"It would be hard for anybody to believe," Parker replied in a raspy voice. "We've never seen anything like this. We've caught the occasional shape on film, but not movement like this."

"It was an escape," Henry commented thoughtfully. "I think, given the slave history in the house, we're watching the manifestation of an escape. The watchful spirit of a child in the other room cannot leave. That's why she's crying."

"But from everything I read, Dr. Tyler and Mr. Page were not cruel slave owners," Kayla explained. "I mean, there was no history of maltreatment or misery that could still be affecting the house. The Tylers and Pages educated their slaves and treated them as household members, so that when they were freed, they were able to support themselves locally and buy property."

"Depends on what you mean by cruel," Henry said matter-of-factly. "Giving someone else's child away as a birthday gift could be construed to be cruel. And then, of course, there's the word 'slave,' which you can't leave out of the equation. The two together comprise a formula that equals cruel, certainly by today's standards. Perhaps it felt that way to the slaves then."

Kayla felt ashamed for not seeing the whole episode from this perspective. "Sorry."

"No need to apologize to me," Henry replied.

The three watched and listened to the rest of the recordings, but no other paranormal incidents occurred. They'd already seen the highlights, which were more than they'd ever seen before.

"What's next?" Kayla asked.

"What's next is trying to decipher whether this is the deception that needs to be atoned for," Parker replied, looking directly at Kayla.

She was surprised. "I didn't think you thought much of that theory," she said.

"I didn't, until this. Maybe there's some kind of reparation Frederick needs to consider, on behalf of its, um, distinguished forefathers," Parker explained.

"That will never fly," Henry stated. "No one ever wants to admit wrongdoing, and history is history."

"Yeah, even at the masquerade party, Grant and Lee almost got into a fistfight, and they were just in costume," Kayla commented.

"I suppose you're right. Then an alternative might be a memorial that could be erected to sit opposite Taney's plaque by City Hall, for all those who suffered." Parker was referring to Supreme Court Justice Taney, who delivered the majority opinion in the Dred Scott case. Scott had sued for his freedom based on the fact that his owners had moved to Wisconsin, a territory that did not allow slaves. Taney doubled down, to use today's colloquial, and the court further ruled that territories could not ban slaves because they were property. "That might be the needed appeasement," he suggested.

Henry jumped in. "I think that's a good idea any time. But is this what we're dealing with for sure? The ghosts of the past are pissed off, so they're coming out of the woodwork to alert us to a wrong that needs to be righted? I don't know. Why now?"

"Well, put that way …," Parker said, trailing off.

"You know what? I suggest we take a breather. Let's not work on it for the rest of the weekend. Let's clear our minds," Kayla suggested.

Parker sighed and clasped his hands behind his head. "Good idea, Kayla. Let's call it a day. Enjoy your weekend. We'll contact Danielle and Mike early next week."

"Yeah, the break will do them good, too. They're already a bit freaked after seeing all those footprints," Kayla acknowledged.

Chapter

59

Nick and Kayla had decided to meet for dinner at JoJo's Restaurant and Tap House. It was another restaurant within easy walking distance from Kayla's house, located on the same side of East Patrick Street as the Civil War Museum.

"I like JoJo's," Kayla started. "Thanks for suggesting it."

"Yeah. It's got a great atmosphere," Nick agreed, looking around at the original brick walls and dark wood bar and floors. "Loads of draft beers … and wines," he added, knowing that's what Kayla favored.

"This is where it all began for me."

"Began? What do you mean?"

"It's where I first met the Dulany Paranormal Team, well, where I met Parker and Henry."

"Really? I wondered what happened that allowed you to find the perfect job. You seem so engaged and happy with the work. Tell me about it."

"I do love it. Before this, I was doing commercial photography, which was not compelling at all. I wanted to get out of the Beltway, so I decided to try freelance and found a house here in Frederick that I could easily afford after selling mine in Fairfax. I was sitting right over there," Kayla continued, pointing to a high top against the wall, "waiting for a friend when I overheard Parker telling Henry that they needed a regular camera because people were skeptical of digital photography. I thought I recognized Parker from TV, but I had no idea what they were referring to.

"Then they got into a discussion about how you could Photoshop any picture, even if it was produced in a darkroom, which is one of the ways I develop photos. The catch, according to Parker, and he was exactly right, is the existence of the negative.

"So I approached them, and they invited me to sit down. Once I realized they owned a paranormal agency, I wasn't as eager, but they convinced me to give it a try. The rest is history," Kayla said with a huge smile.

"And why did you want to get into that rather arcane type of photography?" Nick asked.

"Dorothea Lange."

"Who?"

Kayla told Nick all about her fascination with the woman and what Lange had accomplished during her lifetime. "I've always wanted to emulate her," she concluded humbly.

"Well, you learn something every day," Nick said, smiling.

Just then, the waitress appeared and asked if they had decided what they wanted for dinner. Kayla ordered a spinach Cobb salad, and Nick ordered the cedar plank Atlantic salmon.

"How are things going with the paranormal investigation?" he continued.

"Um. Good. Still very busy," she replied. Then she told him about the William Tyler Page house.

"You're kidding."

"You can't make this stuff up. Well, you can, but we've got the tapes," Kayla said, laughing. "Oh, I forgot a significant historical point: William Tyler Page was cared for by a slave, Laura Frazier, who had been given to his mother, Nannie, by her father, Dr. Tyler."

Nick shook his head in disbelief. "Any idea if that's what all of the … activity is about?"

"We're trying to figure that out, but nothing definitive has come up. The big question is, why now? So we decided to take a break, a breather, if you will."

"Sounds like it's needed. "

"Oh, and there's another possible piece of the puzzle I've never mentioned," Kayla added. "I've been meaning to tell you about it."

"I'm all ears," he responded.

"I found a chain in my front yard a while back, after a big storm."

"A chain?"

"Yeah. Well, not just any old chain," Kayla replied. Then she proceeded to tell him what Cory told her about the shackle. "I have a confession to make," she added.

"Please. Go ahead."

Kayla continued to tell Nick what she thought she had seen in her yard during the frightful storm.

Nick looked at her thoughtfully. Without commenting on the scene Kayla had just described, he simply asked, "Did Cory return it?"

"Not yet. I've been meaning to pick it up."

"Well, I'd like to take a look at it."

"Really? What for?"

"I just would," he said. "I doubt there's anything on it, but it would be good to have it analyzed from a different perspective. See if there's anything microscopic to be detected."

"Yeah, I could see that," Kayla said, nodding. "I'll pick it up as soon as I can and bring it to your office."

"Okay, thanks."

"Anyway, I've been talking too much," Kayla continued, changing the subject. "How is your work going? Have you found a match for the fingerprints?"

Nick winced a little. "Not yet. But we've just started. It can take a while to get through the different databases."

"Yeah, understood. What about that poor Nepali girl's murder? Any news?"

"Actually, there has been some circumstantial information that I've gathered," Nick said, describing his interaction with the manager and

Rosa. He went on to talk about the warehouse, though he had not yet gone there to make inquiries.

"Which store was this, Nick?"

"The newest one."

"No kidding?" She hesitated for only a second and added, "I had a strange experience there myself." She proceeded to tell Nick that she thought she saw a sales clerk mouthing, "Help me."

"Well, that's certainly disconcerting."

"I know. I keep second-guessing myself as to whether I actually saw him say that, but instead of fading over time, it's been sticking. I mean, a day doesn't go by that I don't think about it."

"How old was he?"

"Young. Late teens."

"Maybe he's being abused at home. Young people will often reach out to other adults if they look better than what they've got for parents."

Kayla shook her head. "I honestly don't know."

Chapter

60

Ghosts are images for what we dread.
—Sally Davenport

Amanda Borst found herself surrounded by people. They were all moving in the same direction. A light snow was falling. She could see everything and everyone perfectly clearly. And she was not afraid. "We have to do this together in order to learn from one another," one boy said to her, smiling. "We have to learn from those who have already passed."

"We have come a long way," an older woman said. "We do not want to go back. We will not continue to go back."

Amanda didn't understand. The woman was dead. That she could tell. But again, Amanda was not scared. There was a sense of calmness, a peace of mind that Amanda was experiencing for the first time in a very long while. As they moved along the streets of Frederick, the people seemed to be a cohesive band, even though some were dead and some alive. Amanda noticed that they were people of all colors: brown and black and white. They were poor and wore tattered clothes. Some were shoeless. She moved with them through the alley. They now walked along Church Street, toward Market Street. They held torches. Amanda carried one, too. Suddenly, bells began to toll. Bells from the

City of Clustered Spires were ringing all over in unison. The people began to sing the words from a post-Civil War song:

Oh freedom, oh freedom, oh freedom over me
And before I'd be a slave I'll be buried in my grave
And go home to my Lord and be free.

Amanda sang along. She felt happy. Free from dread. The people began to quicken their pace. They crossed Market Street and then moved to follow the creek. Carroll Creek. They approached the Community Bridge, filled with trompe l'oeils. Now there were more people congregating. They came from all directions. Dead and alive. All ages, all colors. All chanting. The bells continued to toll.

Suddenly, Amanda found herself standing on top of the Community Bridge, alone. The bells began to subside. She looked down at the empty, snow-laced terrain below. As all the footprints began to disappear, she felt herself floating, higher and higher, until she had a bird's-eye view of Frederick. It had been liberated, too.

Amanda awakened with a slow stretch. She felt so good. And then she remembered the dream. *How strange.* She jumped up to look outside. No snow. She could still smell it, though.

Chapter

61

Nick Nucci was back in Tommy and Lily Mitka's house. According to Eric Blake, the Toronto policeman, the DNA samples from the deceased were on their way to Frederick. Now Nick needed to gather a sample of Tommy's DNA. If he couldn't find anything obvious, he would have to ask Carmen, but he didn't want to bother her if he didn't have to, especially since he didn't have any information to relay … yet. After looking at the photos Blake had sent, Nick was pretty sure the deceased was Tommy Mitka. But he needed proof.

Except for the dishes in the sink, the kitchen was spic and span. He moved to the bathroom. This is where hoped to find something. There was only one toothbrush, but there were two combs, no hairs on them. Nevertheless, Nick picked each of them up with tweezers and deposited them in two separate baggies. *Long shot,* he thought to himself and started to rummage through the bathroom drawers, feeling very uncomfortable doing so. It was obvious that Lily and Tommy had had their own drawers, so that was good. Tommy's drawer was a mess. But that was good too. Nick began pulling hairs from the bottom of the top drawer. He also found nail clippers and scissors. He was pretty sure the hair samples would be sufficient for the test, but he continued to look through the whole house again, just to make sure he didn't miss anything. He saw nothing of the sort, so he headed back to the station.

Just then, Sam the IT specialist called him. "You got a minute?" he asked.

"Yeah, go ahead."

"The person calling your contact in Toronto sent the number through another number in Moscow. It bounced back and rang his phone."

"What's the number?"

"I'll give it to you, but it won't help. You can't call it directly; I already tried."

"What kind of person sets up a system like that?"

"Someone who doesn't want their phone traced. And I can tell you this, just to add to the mystery: Based on the satellite information we have, the phone call originated from Frederick."

Something strange was going on, Nick thought. Was it a coincidence that the missing container ship had come from St. Petersburg and now this phone number was sent through Moscow, or was there a connection? Too early to tell. But …

Chapter

62

For the first time in a long time, Kayla awoke relaxed. She figured it was kind of a clean-up day, including going to her basement and looking around. After her jog in the cemetery, she decided to develop her photos from the William Tyler Page house, the ones she took when they had returned after setting up their equipment. She couldn't imagine what she might find that they had not seen on the videos. But try she would. She suddenly had an idea. When she'd returned home last night from JoJo's, Fritchie was once again lying in the darkroom, even though Kayla had left her in the house. She realized she could set up a video camera in her own home and the darkroom to see how the cat was getting from one building to the other. She'd get the cameras from East Street later today. But first, she was going to fix a hearty breakfast and read the paper.

And so it was that Kayla happened to come across an article announcing that yet another superstore was headed for Frederick. *I should think we have enough*, she thought as she continued reading:

> "Tayden Moore (47), entrepreneur and philanthropist, persuaded Planning Commission members and the County Executive that western Frederick needed another big-box store. Construction will begin next spring."

Well, that's great. I wonder how that's going to affect the traffic? Kayla thought cynically. She had reservations about the whole decision. *I doubt I'll know anyone who gets a job there*, Kayla presumed as she put her dishes in the sink. She'd lost her appetite.

"Come on, Fritchie, let's go get some work done," she cooed as she headed to her darkroom, backpack and cameras in hand.

Two hours later, she was resigned to admit that her photos from the Page house did not reveal anything different from what the videos had so well captured. At one point, she thought she saw shadows looming, but then she had to laugh. It was in fact a shadow created by herself, Henry, Danielle, and Mathew. Yep, the four of them were looming against the wall in the guest bedroom.

"Well, that's that. Nothing new found. Okay, sweetie," she said to her feline friend, gathering her purse. "I'm going to go get some cameras so I can spy on you. I'll be back soon. I'll leave you here. You apparently can go back to the house whenever you want, anyway."

Kayla drove to the office. No one was there. She went into the equipment room and gathered six video cameras, so she could focus on different angles. *That should do it.*

As she headed back home, she decided to swing by the museum to pick up the chain (or rather the shackle, as Cory had described it). She had been meaning to do so for quite some time but just hadn't found the time. Now that Nick thought it might be interesting to examine as well, she wanted it back. Hopefully, Cory would be in.

The young man at the reception desk recognized Kayla. He confirmed that Cory was there and got into the elevator with Kayla to take her to the third floor. Again, she noticed how much colder the elevator was.

Cory was seated at his large desk. "Come in, Kayla," he said. "Nice to see you. How is the investigation going?"

"Good," she replied. "Wish we had definitive answers for the phenomena, but we're starting to triangulate some of the findings."

"Well, good."

"Anything new here?"

"No, not really. We're happy to have Amanda back."

"Oh? Good. How is she doing?"

"Well. Very well, I think. She's here today, if you want to stop by to say hi."

"Okay, great. I will. I was wondering if I could get that chain from you."

"Chain? Oh, the shackle. Yes, of course," Cory answered, sounding a little sheepish, Kayla thought.

"Is there a problem?"

"Uh, no. I'll get it," Cory said, rather reluctantly. Then he paused. "Actually, Kayla, we, meaning me and the staff, were wondering if you would donate it to the museum."

"Really?"

"Yes. We want to put it on display as an artifact from the Civil War era. We know, a terrible artifact, but people should know. The public should see what kind of abuse people were forced to endure for decades in this country, abuse not only to their physical well-being, but to their emotional and mental health, their dignity, their souls."

Kayla was moved. "You're right, Cory. Of course you're right. But …"

"What?"

"I'd just like to borrow it before I turn it over to you. I'd like to show it to a friend who has an interest in these kinds of items," Kayla explained. She didn't want to mention that there was a detective involved in the Dulany Team's investigation.

"Of course. Thank you, Kayla. We'll take it back whenever you're done with it. And we'll give you full credit, of course, I mean for the donation."

"You don't have to do that. I just found it."

"Nonetheless. We're grateful," Cory said, handing her the chain, which now lay in a cloth tote bag.

"You're welcome," Kayla said, taking the bag. "I'll go see Amanda now."

"Okay. Good."

Kayla rounded the corner and practically ran into Amanda. The woman's visage shocked her. "Amanda … h-h-how are you?" she stammered.

"Hi, Kayla. It's nice to see you. I'm doing great."

Yes, you are, Kayla thought, noting her radiantly white aura. "I'm so happy for you," she finally replied, realizing that she had remained speechless for a few seconds, staring.

"Yeah. Actually, I almost called you yesterday. I had the most incredible dream the other night. It was liberating. It truly liberated me from my malaise."

"And the spirits here in the museum? Are they still about? I mean, the hovering sensation and such?"

Amanda looked around, as if she suddenly realized something or someone was missing. "It's here, but it's soothing, not ominous. We've communicated somehow."

"Communicated?" Kayla was intrigued.

"Come, let's go to my office. I'll tell you all about my dream."

Amanda gestured to one of the chairs surrounding a small coffee table. "Would you like anything? Tea? A coffee? Water?"

"No, thanks. I'm fine. So you had a dream? Not a nightmare?"

"No, not this time. It was wonderful," Amanda exclaimed. "Just wonderful."

As Amanda relayed her dream in great detail, hairs rose on Kayla's neck. *This is quite remarkable,* she reflected. In fact, it was unbelievably eerie, she had to admit. All of it. The facts coincided with much of what was being exposed from their investigations. The Community Bridge was the center of the trompe l'oeils in Frederick. But something bothered her.

"Amanda, are you sure people in your dream were alive?"

"Oh, yes. Not all of them, though. Some were dead."

"But how could you tell? Who were these people?"

"I have no idea. But I could tell some were dead, and some were alive. But they were all friendly. No, let me reword that: They befriended me. That's why I'm so relieved. They want to be liberated. They marched for liberty, and they liberated me from my fears."

"Did the dead people speak?"

"Yes … yes. So did the people who were alive. There was a difference. They were all poor by the looks of their tattered clothes, but the dead people looked like they came from someplace else."

"You mean other than Frederick?"

"No. I'm sorry, Kayla. I misspoke. Not some other place, rather some other time. They came from another century."

Chapter

63

While Kayla was listening to the very real yet unfathomable dream Amanda was relaying, Hunter Crowley and Irakli Guramishivili were sitting in Cryin' Johnnies in Mt. Airy, a small town not far from Frederick.

"What is a foot-long hot dog?" Irakli asked after looking at the menu and taking a gulp from his beer.

"It's a foot-long hot dog," Hunter replied impatiently, obviously no longer pleased with the relationship. The last time the two had spoken, it had not gone well. But, well, this was a chance to make amends, he supposed. They needed to resolve the details on the latest package delivery. "Is everything under control?"

"You know it is."

The waiter took their orders. Irakli wanted the foot-long hot dog. Hunter ordered a cheeseburger. "This is the first time we've used the Port of Savannah," Hunter said softly, though no one was sitting near them.

"And ...?"

"Well, have you scoped it out sufficiently?"

"Do you want to do it?"

"No, that's why I hired you."

"Then let me do my job."

"Okay, fair enough." Hunter was suddenly worried that he might be forced to do it by default, and he didn't like to get his hands dirty. "I do have some new details that I need to convey," he continued.

"I am listening." Just then the meal arrived. Two more beers were ordered.

"The pick-up is at midnight."

"Really? Isn't that bad planning?"

"Yes, but that's when the ship will finally reach the port."

"Okay. Yeah, okay."

"How do you like your foot-long?"

"Tastes like a hot dog."

"Yeah, well, and there will be two people to hand over the package instead of one," Hunter continued.

"Why?"

"Don't know. Those are the directions."

"I do not like that. I am outnumbered."

I doubt that, Hunter thought, looking at the man's physique. "Any idiot with a gun could theoretically outnumber you. It's not going to be a problem."

"Yeah, okay. Anything else?"

"No. The rest is in the gym bag, as usual. You've already been briefed."

"Okay." Irakli tossed his napkin on his plate, guzzled down the rest of his second beer, grabbed the gym bag, and left, leaving Hunter with the tab.

What a jackass, he thought.

Chapter

64

"**W**ell, that didn't go so well," Kayla said as they were leaving the Page house. The three had just debriefed the concerned couple regarding the findings on the videos.

"That's an understatement if I ever heard one," Henry replied. "Mathew is ready to brick up the window. Said he knew someone who could do it pronto."

"Yeah. He acted like there'd been an intruder," Kayla remarked.

"Well, there has been, several of them, in fact, but they left," Henry said, chuckling slightly at his joke.

"I don't think it's funny. They're frightened," Kayla said.

"I am glad you explained that the spirits would most likely just switch to another exit," Parker commented.

"I wonder if the two will stay there tonight," Kayla said.

"Yeah, they're going to stay. The last look I saw, from both of them, was one of defiance," Parker said. Just then, his phone rang. "Detective Nucci. What? Okay, we're on our way.

"Seems that Detective Nucci's office has identified the prints."

"No kidding! I didn't think that was possible," Kayla said.

"We're meeting him at Beacon's Way. The detective is ready to open the hatch door. Do you have the key on you?" Parker asked Kayla.

"You bet."

Get in," Henry said, opening the van's door for her.

Kayla had walked to the Page house so she wouldn't have to worry about parking on the street. On the way to Beacon's Way, she described Amanda's description of her dream to Parker and Henry.

"So we're back to the trompe l'oeils," Parker commented. "Which means ...?"

"Back to deception," she replied, nodding her head.

"You know, Kayla, the dream that Amanda relayed to you is ten times more spooky than the Page house goings-on," Henry said, smiling. "At least I think so. I mean, who walks with the dead?"

Kayla smiled and looked at Henry. "Ya think?"

———— • ————

"Wow, talk about overkill. How many folks did the detective bring?" Henry asked as he pulled up curbside. "I guess that refurbished Mustang is Nick's, but why the two cop cars?"

"Don't ask me," Kayla said as she got out.

For some reason, her heart was racing. She didn't know why. The police and Nick were all standing at the door, chatting casually while they waited. Two of the cops held the equipment for opening the hatch door.

Nick started, "Kayla, Henry, Parker, thanks for getting here so quickly. This is Lieutenant Konarski and Sergeants Mills, O'Brien, and Richter." They all shook hands. Sergeant Richter was the only female, Kayla noted. And for some reason, they were dressed in heavy body armor. *Definitely overkill from that perspective*, Kayla thought, hoping Nick didn't have anything to do with determining their dress code.

Kayla pulled out the key. "I think I should let you all in through the kitchen, if you don't mind," she suggested, looking at their boots and thinking about the wood floors.

"That's a good idea," Parker agreed. "We don't want to scuff anything up. The foundation would not be pleased in the least."

Kayla let herself in and walked through to the kitchen. She immediately felt that something was wrong.

As the group filed through, she said, "Something seems strange. I don't know what it is." Looking at Parker and Henry specifically, she continued, "Does the house smell different to you?"

Parker put his nose in the air. "Antiseptic."

"Yeah," Henry said, nodding.

Kayla marched over and opened the refrigerator. Only one Flying Dog beer remained.

"Someone has been here," she said, turning to look at Nick. "There were two bottles of beer. One's gone."

He frowned. "Okay. Let's proceed cautiously."

Lieutenant Konarski stepped forward. "I'll handle this."

He turned on one of the lanterns and opened the door to the basement, moving forward at the same time. The group watched him disappear from their sight. There was a shout and then a crash.

"Oh, my God," Kayla yelled, rushing forward.

"Stop!" Nick ordered as he grabbed another lantern. He reached the opening and waved the light. "The damn stairs are missing. Richard?" A slight moan could be heard. Sergeant Richter quickly contacted the police switch board.

"Ambulance is on its way. I told them to bring an extension ladder and some way to hoist him up," she said.

Sergeant Mills had lowered himself down from the ledge and was now hanging by his hands. Then he dropped. Parker and Nick were leaning over with their lights. Mills had a flashlight as well.

"Richard's semi-conscious," he called up. "Looks like he has a broken leg. Not sure about anything internal. Thank God he was wearing all of this padding."

Sirens could be heard approaching in the background. Kayla went outside to direct them. She found herself shaking … because she was scared, but even more because she was mad. *Who the hell had done this? Any one of them could have fallen. This was a deliberate act of violence.*

Hunter Crowley happened to be home when Kayla entered Beacon's

Way. When he heard the buzzer, he slipped into his viewing room to watch in real time. He had hoped the detective would have been the one who fell. He wanted to back him off. Now Hunter realized he had made matters worse. The detective had even more motive to investigate. Hunter needed a Plan B.

Chapter

65

Everything is bad if you think you are being watched.
—Martha Alford

The EMTs were able to examine Richard Konarski in the cellar and stabilize his leg. He did not appear to have internal trauma, but they needed to get him to the hospital quickly to have him examined more thoroughly. They hoisted him up on a gurney with a mobile winch from above. He was conscious when they drove off. A colleague was waiting for him at the hospital, so Nick's team continued with their work. When they reached the third room in the cellar, they knew they had been foiled more than once.

"Smells like someone's already bleached away any evidence," Nick commented.

"Yep," Parker agreed. "Let's open it anyway, if we can." While the police were working to open the door, Nick described the results of the fingerprint investigation.

"We didn't think we'd find anything. It was a long shot. We started at the top and worked our way down. Lo and behold, the criminal, and I say that with a grain of salt, was local. That's to say, his first and only booking occurred right here in Frederick."

"No kidding. But I don't understand; why did you start at the top?" Henry asked, wanting to learn.

"Starting with national comprehensive databases is a tactic we chose. It covers a larger swath of potential candidates. Our own database is tiny by comparison. Nonetheless, we did eventually identify the person."

"Who is he?" Henry asked.

"Well, I must admit that the way he filled out the intake form does not reveal a whole lot. Apparently, the young man could not read or write in English very well. As far as I can tell, while the department was identifying a translator to work with the young man, someone bailed him out. What we got was a first name, Lucas Cardozo, age nineteen; he works at the new superstore. That's all that's on the form. He didn't show up for his hearing."

"What did he do wrong?" Kayla asked.

"That's kind of sad," Nick replied. "He tried to steal some food from a mini market."

"So … what does all of this mean to you?" Parker asked. "I mean, the fact that he was down here."

"It means that something nefarious occurred here. Based on the photo, Lucas was scared and hiding. From what, we still don't know. But far more worrisome than that is the fact that someone has access to this house. I mean, someone was inside when you broke in, Parker, and now this. The only reason you use bleach is to eliminate bloodstains."

"So what are we talking about?" Henry asked. "I mean, is there some kind of satanical gathering that occurs down here and includes sacrifices maybe?"

Kayla stared, as did Nick and Parker. *It was just like Henry to think up the most gruesome explanation for the blood,* she thought. *Well, his grandmother was the juju expert, so what else is new?* No one responded.

Just then, the officers finished removing the metal door, and they all stood around it. The smell of bleach was even more powerful now. At first, it was unclear what the material was laying in the hole.

"Oh, it's the stairs," Kayla remarked, having squatted to examine it more closely.

Everyone nodded in agreement.

"Someone knew that we wanted to get into the catch here," Nick said. "Have you talked to anyone about it?"

"That's not our practice," Parker said, shaking his head. "We've talked about this feeling that we are being observed here before," he added, looking at Kayla and Henry. "We've wondered if someone has a way to find out what our plans are, what we want to do next. I mean, one of the first signs that something wasn't on the up-and-up is that I couldn't get the electricity to work down here."

Nick started looking around. He went over to the hooks on the wall. "What are these for?"

"We don't know," Henry replied. "There are some in each of the rooms down here. Polly, the first representative from the foundation that we spoke with about the house, said they could have been used to hold tools way back when. I told her they were new, not originals, and she just believed that they were installed for the purpose of demonstrating what used to be."

Nick walked up to take a closer look.

<hr>

"Uh-oh," Hunter Crowley said out loud from his viewing room. "Damn that detective."

Chapter
66

The Dulany Team was now sitting in Nick Nucci's office. Several cameras with built-in mics sat on the detective's desk. "Well, at least one mystery has been solved," Parker said, sighing.

"Yeah. But it will be difficult to find out who installed them and, more importantly, why," Nick replied. "At the same time, we can be assured that someone, someone alive," he clarified, "was using this house before you all entered the picture."

"I could kick myself for not following up with those hooks," Parker said.

"There would be no reason to suspect anything like this," Nick remarked. "Their existence will help me fight to get you off without a citation. I mean, photographing you breaking in was a set-up of sorts. It was done to impede the opening of the hatch door, which it did until recently. Once I said I would get it opened, there was no other choice but to clean it out."

"But whoever did it also took out the stairs. They wanted someone to get hurt," Parker said.

"Agreed."

"Changing the subject a bit," Kayla said, "I was wondering why the police were wearing so much body armor?"

"I noticed that, too," Nick replied. "I guess they didn't know what they might be getting into, so they decided better safe than sorry. In this case, it might have been the right decision, given that Richard's injuries could have been a lot worse."

Just then, Nick's phone rang. "Speak of the devil," he said. "It's the hospital. Thanks much for the report, Doctor. Appreciate it. No internal injuries. A broken leg and some bruised ribs," Nick reported, looking at the Dulany Team.

"Well, we can all be thankful for that," Parker replied.

After the Dulany Team departed Nick's office, he called two of the sergeants who had been at Beacon's Way to accompany him to the Frederick County Landmarks Foundation office. He wanted the folks there to know that he was taking the events today seriously and that someone would indeed be held accountable.

Nick was already familiar with Helga Dorschner, given that he had intervened on behalf of Parker's mistaken break-in. He knew she was acting for Polly Rutledge, as well, who had taken a leave of absence due to the threats she had received. Helga was quite cordial. She offered the three of them a seat and ordered coffee. Her office was spotless, he noted. Absolutely nothing on her large desk, or rather Polly's desk.

"What can I do for you?" she asked politely.

"As you know," Nick began, "we secured a warrant to examine Beacon's Way. It appears there has been more vandalism." A shadow crossed Helga's face when she heard this comment. "Additionally, someone had installed video cameras and mics."

"Really?" Helga was visibly stunned.

"Yes. We would like for you to think about anyone who might be able to access the house, anyone at all. I realize it might take time, but someone familiar with the house has been able to get in and make some ... changes."

"What kind of changes?"

Nick informed her of everything that had taken place, including the injured officer. Helga looked obviously troubled.

"Perhaps whoever makes repairs can install new stairs. It should be pretty straightforward," Nick said. And then suddenly he had an idea. "Who is in charge of the repairs there?"

"I'm … not really sure," Helga replied, a bit embarrassed. "As you know, I'm just taking care of these issues until Polly returns."

"Of course," Nick said sympathetically.

"But I will find out as soon as possible and get back to you. This is very unsettling."

"Great," Nick replied, looking at the two sergeants. They nodded, and the three of them stood up. "We look forward to hearing from you. The sooner the better, of course. This is now a criminal investigation, since one of our officers was injured."

"Yes. I will do so," Helga said, standing. "I understand."

Guy Harding was standing near the garden at the other end of the house when he saw the detective leaving with the two uniform officers. *If I haven't been made yet, it's only a matter of time,* he thought grimly. *I've got to save myself.*

Chapter

67

Henry dropped Kayla off on East Street. "I'm going to get something at Pistaro's," she'd explained. "I'll walk from there."

"Okay. See you tomorrow." The three had decided to meet the next day and go over everything that had occurred to determine if there were any more clues.

Nick was going to go back to search the superstores to see if anyone knew of a Lucas. He had a mugshot of him, but as everyone knows, he thought, *mugshots do not necessarily reflect the best likeness.*

When Kayla entered the Italian restaurant, she caught a familiar face. "Eleanor? Eleanor, is that you?" she asked, somewhat alarmed that the woman was literally crying into her wine glass. The half-empty bottle was nearby.

Upon hearing her name, Eleanor quickly dried her tears and looked up. "Oh, hi, Kayla."

"May I sit down?"

Eleanor looked around and then nodded.

"Are you okay?" Kayla asked, knowing that the question sounded stupid. "Of course you're not. Do you want to talk about it?"

"Have a glass of wine with me?" Eleanor asked, although it sounded more like a plea.

"Of course. I'll get a glass." Kayla quickly returned so as not to lose the opportunity to find out what was wrong. The two were by no means close. She only knew Eleanor socially, but she looked dreadful, and Kayla wanted to help if she could.

"Nice choice of wine," Kayla began.

"Yeah, that's something I know how to do well. Selecting husbands is not."

"Oh, no, you and …," Kayla had to think of his name, "Irakli had a fight?"

"I wish."

"What?"

Eleanor started to cry again. "Kayla, something is wrong, but I don't know what."

"Just describe what's wrong."

"It started almost right after the wedding. I mean, maybe I should have checked into Irakli more than I did. But, well, you've seen him … I was head over heels in love with the man the minute I spoke with him and saw him: handsome, big, fun, smart, what more could a girl ask for?" Eleanor asked.

"What started?" Kayla asked gingerly.

Eleanor took a gulp of wine and then continued, "He told me he was in sales. I mean, that could mean almost anything, so I figured yeah, sales are good. But then he started to go on trips. Short trips, but the strange thing was I never knew where he was going, and he wouldn't tell me. All he'd say is that he'd be back in a few days and not to try to contact him, he could not be reached. I didn't like it at all and told him how I felt. He just blew me off, said I would get used to it. It was his job."

"Well, that doesn't sound so bad. I mean, so he's gone once in a while for a few days."

"Yeah, I suppose," Eleanor said, sniffling. "But then I started overhearing him talking on the phone."

"What was he saying?"

"I couldn't tell. He was speaking Russian. Mind you, he's Georgian, but he was talking Russian. I can hear the difference between Georgian and Russian. He's speaking Russian."

"Well," Kayla said, trying to think quickly, "I imagine a lot of Georgians speak Russian. Wasn't Georgia part of the USSR?"

"Yes, but the conversations sound so important. I don't know how to describe it." Eleanor poured herself more wine. The bottle was empty now. "So you know what I did?"

"Confronted him?"

"No. When he was away for one of his 'work trips,'" Eleanor said, putting air quotes around the phrase, "I went through everything I could, searching for any clues. Know what I found?"

Kayla shook her head no.

"Passports. Yep. Different passports, with different names for different countries."

Kayla was shocked. "Which countries?"

"The Republic of Georgia, of course, Mexico, Canada, Saudi Arabia, Russia; I don't know, I can't remember them all."

"Well, that is a revelation," Kayla said, again knowing she sounded shallow.

"Yeah?" she challenged. "What does it mean?"

"Well, I just mean that it's quite a find. Did you ask him about them?"

"No. To be quite honest, Kayla, I'm afraid of him now."

"Why? Has he done anything to you?" Kayla asked, sounding alarmed.

"No … nothing like that. Just that his persona is not what I knew it to be."

"Yeah, he sounds different now."

"But the worse thing happened yesterday. It's what set me off."

"What happened?"

"I followed him after he left the house."

Of course you did.

"He said he had to go out for work and would be back the same afternoon. So I was curious to see what he was up to. He went to Mt. Airy, to a restaurant called Cryin' Johnnies. Have you ever heard of it?"

Kayla shook her head no.

"Well, me neither. Anyway. Guess who he met there?"

"Don't know."

"Hunter Crowley."

For some reason, when Eleanor said the name, it sent shivers down Kayla's spine. She didn't know why.

"Here's the thing, Kayla," Eleanor said, starting to cry again. "It was Hunter who suggested I try to find someone through the Internet. Did you know that's how Irakli and I met?"

"No," Kayla lied; she didn't want Eleanor to know that people gossiped about her.

"Yeah. Hunter helped me write my profile and helped me find a site to connect to. Irakli showed up in no time with similar interests. Now, here I see the two of them together. Why would that be? Is it coincidence, or did Hunter know Irakli already? Why would he set me up?"

"Does Irakli have a green card?" Kayla asked.

"He does now. He got it super-fast, as far as I know. I thought it could take years."

"Yeah, me too. How long did Hunter and Irakli meet for?"

"Half hour, maybe forty-five minutes. They were drinking beer and eating hot dogs and burgers."

"How'd you get so close?" Kayla asked, impressed.

"I sat on one of the hi-tops outside the window."

"Do you think they could have seen you?"

"Kayla, I may be emotionally high strung, but I'm not stupid. I wore a wig, big sunglasses, Jackie O-style, and baggy jogging clothes. Neither of them gave me a second glance. I left after ten minutes."

Frankly, Kayla was surprised at how calm Eleanor was. "What were they doing besides drinking beer?"

"Talk, talk, talk. It actually did not appear that it was a 'happy meal,' either," Eleanor said, chuckling a bit. "No, they did not look happy, but it seemed like they knew each other. They were up to something."

Just then, Kayla saw the waitress approach the glass doors from inside the restaurant. She motioned no to her before she came outside.

She didn't want Eleanor to go home to Irakli drunk. "So what are you going to do now?" Kayla asked, curious and at the same time nervous for the woman.

"I don't know. He's leaving in a couple of days for his so-called work. Maybe I'll try to see where he's going."

"You mean follow him again?"

"Maybe."

"I think I'd be worried about being seen, regardless of how you disguise yourself. You better have a good excuse if he recognizes you."

"Yeah, I know," Eleanor said sniffling. "But hey, what would you do?"

Follow him, she thought. "I don't know," she said aloud.

"Yeah, right. You'd follow him. I know you would," Eleanor replied, smiling.

———◦———

As Kayla walked home, she thought about Irakli and Hunter, together. *What the hell are they in cahoots about? Poor Eleanor. First she ends up losing Buzz, and now this. Some people just have bad luck choosing a mate*, she figured. *But seriously, what could this mean?* Deep down, she felt sure that Hunter had set Eleanor up. He'd exploited a vulnerable woman, a pretty woman, who could help his friend, Irakli. *And what was Irakli's business? Why did he travel incognito to boot? Was it related to Hunter's business, whatever that is?*

As she reached Market Street, Kayla realized she'd totally forgotten to get her meal at Pistaro's. She headed to Orchid's and ordered a Thai stir fry for takeaway. She was still musing about her discussion with Eleanor. *Was there something bad going on between Irakli and Hunter? It was definitely secretive; so therefore, was it bad?*

Chapter

Nick Nucci was heading home when his phone rang. "Hello?" he answered.

"Wilson Tremblay here."

"Hello, Wilson. How are you?"

"Not so good."

"Why? What's happened?"

"We found the crew from the container ship, floating in a lifeboat off the coast. The men were almost dead. They're going to make it, but it was close, eh?"

"So, well, that's good news, isn't it?"

"Yeah. They're seeking asylum."

"Asylum? Why in the world?"

"Afraid to return to Russia empty-handed. They claim that there are both criminal and political elements that will endanger them."

"What's that mean? What were they delivering?"

"I don't know. That's what we're trying to figure out. We're still looking for the container ship. They get all nervous when we ask what's on the ship, what they abandoned. Weather's calmed down. If we can find it, maybe it'll shed light on why they look scared to death, eh?"

"Um, yeah. Can you at least find out what happened? What made them change their course?"

"They're saying they were commanded to turn around. To abort their mission."

"But who told them that?"

"They say they've never known who their boss is, but they're afraid of him, whoever he is. Oh, wait a second. I've just received a radio communication. A rudderless container ship has been identified by our coast guard. I'll let you know what we find. It may be related to the murder of man in the harbor, though I'm not sure if we could ever establish a connection."

My thoughts exactly. "Okay, please keep me posted, Wilson. And thanks."

"You bet, eh?"

Chapter

69

What a day, Kayla thought, exhausted. With her Thai meal in hand, she just wanted to put her feet up and go numb in front of the TV. Nonetheless, she couldn't help but be curious about whether her cameras had caught Fritchie coming or going, or maybe both. So after feeding her friend, she lined up the labeled tapes, poured herself a glass of wine, and grabbed her heated meal from the microwave. She then sat down in front of the screen and hit the Play button. Fritchie was lying comfortably on the back of the couch now, with an ever-watchful eye on Kayla.

"Ready to see yourself on the big screen?" she asked. The cat simply continued to purr.

Within a few minutes, Kayla jumped up and ran to the screen. *Am I seeing what I think I'm seeing?* Was Fritchie truly entering the side of the built-in wardrobe? *Yes indeed.* She quickly switched the tapes to play the one from the darkroom. As Kayla watched, Fritchie suddenly appeared. She hadn't seen her come out from the tiny wardrobe that had been in the room for who knows how long, but what else? Kayla tried to lighten the background and then rewound the tape. She was squinting so hard she was getting a headache. Then she saw Fritchie, or at least her form, come through the side of the wardrobe. But something was wrong.

That's when it dawned on her that Fritchie looked differently on the video. Now aside from knowing that the cat moved through the buildings from one built-in to another, Kayla was faced with a very strange phenomenon: Fritchie's image looked surreal. *Maybe it's an aura?* Kayla glanced over at the cat but could not discern anything similar to what she was seeing on the film. Fritchie looked as normal as ever in real time. She got her camera out and took a few snapshots of the cat that she would develop later. For now, however, she wanted to check out the wardrobe.

Kayla walked to the back of the house and went into the spare bedroom; after examining the wardrobe, she pushed in its side panel. Sure enough, it gave slightly, enough for even a fat cat to slip inside. Kayla opened the doors and squatted. Again, unbeknownst to her, a small area behind the wardrobe had apparently rotted away over the years. She could feel the coolness of the earth.

She went to get a lantern. Actually, the hole was much larger than she originally had thought, so she went to find a flashlight. Though Kayla was not a tiny person, she was able to crawl all the way into the wardrobe and get her light into the hole. What she saw amazed her: The shining light went on and on. *Hmmm*, she thought; *it's a tunnel.* When or why was it dug? Kayla had no idea. The area was small but could easily accommodate a person squirming through it, if he or she really wanted to (something Kayla had no desire to do).

Perhaps it had been a hiding area, a cache? she wondered and then smiled to herself. Most likely, she thought, it was used for storage; maybe in the summer, to keep perishable things cold and the same from the other side. It could probably have been used to transport goods, too, perhaps in inclement weather, if the carriage gatekeeper needed supplies from the owners. Kayla doubted she would ever find out, but at least she now knew Fritchie's secret.

Kayla had one of her worst sleeps ever. It even started out badly. She realized that she was just lying in the bed, thoughts racing and her body unable to relax. She decided to read for a while, but that didn't work, either. Finally, she went to the kitchen and warmed up some milk (something she had never done in her life but heard that it was helpful for insomnia). *Ugh. That's just nasty,* she thought as she tossed the remains down the sink.

She walked to the front of the house and peered out the window. Someone was walking their dog. *At this hour? Couldn't sleep either, huh, buddy?* Fritchie had followed Kayla downstairs and now sat on the window sill. She observed her watching the man and dog; she thought about going for a walk as well, but then her early morning run in Baker Park came to mind, and she quickly decided no. *That poor girl. Her whole life in front of her, and someone just snuffed it out. And no one's looking for her. So sad.* Suddenly, Kayla's body felt very heavy. Maybe the milk was working; she needed to lie down. She returned to her bed and fell fast asleep.

Some two hours later, Kayla awoke again. She sighed loudly. *Need to jog, regardless of the time.* She fed Fritchie and took off toward the cemetery. It was dark when she left, but the sun had started to come up as she approached Mt. Olivet. As she jogged, her mind wandered aimlessly. No thoughts in particular came to mind until, suddenly, she stopped. *What were the titles of the books that were knocked off the shelf in the museum?* Why had the team never even thought to ask that of Amanda? *This might be important,* Kayla thought, her heart racing. The first thing on her agenda today was to call Amanda Borst.

Chapter

~❈ 70 ❈~

While Kayla couldn't rest, Hunter was sleeping like a baby. He'd reviewed his offshore accounts, all of them across the world, before going to bed. It was his routine, no matter how many drinks he had had. It always made him happy to see the daily growth, and the accumulating aggregate wealth. Tonight had been no different. So it was in a groggy stupor that he was trying to understand what someone with a foreign accent was shouting at him over the secured phone line he had awakened to answer.

"You numbskull! Are you listening? I was double-crossed. Double-crossed! You better not have had anything to do with this. I still have the package and am bringing it to Frederick. To our backwater site. No choice."

"What?" The fog was lifting. Out of a sleepy stupor, Hunter suddenly became coherent and focused. "Irakli?"

"No, Putin. Of course it's Irakli. I'm headed your way."

"No! In no way are you to come to Frederick. You know the rules. The area is too saturated. No more."

"Yeah? Well, do *you* know the rules? No double-crosses. I was almost killed."

Irakli had Hunter's undivided attention. "Uh … Where are those guys? What happened?"

"Two goons tried to keep the package after they got the money."

"How?"

"By killing me, you idiot. That's how."

"I repeat, where are they?"

"One's in the trunk of an expensive Volvo, and the other is in the front seat of said Volvo, as though he's ready to start the engine and take off. It's their own car." Irakli chuckled. "No ID on them."

"Jesus," Hunter whispered under his breath.

"No. He's not going to help," Irakli said matter-of-factly. "See you soon."

"No. Wait!"

The line went dead. Hunter tried calling back. No answer.

Chapter

The Dulany Team was sitting in the conference room on the third floor of the National Museum of Civil War Medicine following Kayla's suggestion that they go talk with Amanda. What she had told Kayla by phone was extremely important she explained to Parker and Henry. "Thanks for seeing us on such short notice," Parker said to Amanda. "We are so pleased to know you're feeling better," he added.

That's an understatement, Kayla thought, noting the radiant white aura surrounding the kind woman.

"Oh, my pleasure. When Kayla called to ask about the books that are always falling, I was surprised myself that we had not discussed them. I guess since I knew which books are on those shelves, I never thought to mention them either. But as I said to Kayla, they're all about the Underground Railroad. Not just here in Frederick but up the East Coast and over into the Midwest."

"I didn't know the Railroad extended into the Midwest," Henry commented.

"A lot of people don't realize that," Amanda replied, "but it's quite true. There were stops all throughout Indiana and Kentucky and Ohio, all in an effort to get the slaves to Canada. For an example, Rev. John and Jean Rankin, who were white, assisted the Railroad from Ripley, Ohio. It's estimated that between the two of them and their thirteen children, they sheltered more than two thousand slaves. A former slave named John Parker also worked tirelessly from Ripley."

Reaching for a book on the shelf, she continued, "Robert Smalls is famous, in part, because of the way he escaped. One night, he stole a Confederate ship loaded with ammunition and sailed from Charleston, South Carolina, past Fort Sumter to the Union side, while hoisting up a white flag to keep the Union soldiers from shooting at them. Along the way, he picked up other slaves, including his wife and four children, at a nearby wharf. After he became free, he continued to help as an abolitionist. Later, Smalls was elected to the South Carolina state legislature and afterward to the US House of Representatives."

Parker shook his head. "I just had no idea."

"I didn't either," Kayla said. Henry nodded, too.

"When we talked by phone, you mentioned a man named Henry 'Box' Brown," Kayla interjected. "Tell us about him."

"Oh, yes," Amanda said, rising to grab another book. "This is the biography of Henry 'Box' Brown."

"That was his middle name?" Parker asked, somewhat incredulously.

"No. That's part of his story," Amanda said, smiling. "He shipped himself from Richmond to Pennsylvania, or rather had two people from his church ship him in a wooden crate to the Philadelphia Anti-Slavery Society. The box was labeled 'Dry Goods' and had a small hole in the top for him to breathe. It took twenty-seven hours."

"You're kidding," Parker exclaimed, incredulous for the second time in as many minutes.

"Too important to joke," Amanda replied seriously. "He was able to capitalize on his story and turn it into a stage show, while at the same time educating folks on how to escape their tyranny. That's how he made a living for most of his life. I often wonder if the shipping route went through Frederick. I'd like to think we had something to do with his escape, even though no one would know."

With those words, Kayla had a very sickening thought. *No. Please no*, she thought to herself. "Amanda, I mentioned your dream to Henry, but could you describe it again? It's better first hand."

"Of course. It's still very real. I don't think I'll ever forget it, nor the smell of snow." And so Amanda repeated her story.

"You said the spirits spoke to you?" Kayla asked, which is the real reason she wanted to hear the story again.

"As a matter of fact, yes. A little boy said, 'We have to learn from those that have already passed.' And an older woman said, 'We have come a long way. We do not want to go back. We will not continue to go back.' She was dead, but her words were clear."

Parker raised an eyebrow.

Kayla indeed felt sick. She had a theory, but she was too nervous, too unsure of herself and her idea to mention it right now. If she was right, a horrific injustice was occurring in Frederick, right under their noses.

Chapter

72

Nick Nucci barely made it to Toronto before another storm kicked in and the airlines were diverting traffic. But it had calmed down long enough for his plane to land. He contacted Wilson Tremblay on his way to the port.

"Good timing," Wilson said. "I went out with the team to secure her. She's just being towed in now. But ..."

"Yes?" Nick could hear a worried tone.

"I've got a bad feeling about this one."

"Why, what's happened?"

"I smell death."

Nick got out of the taxi and headed to the Toronto Ports Security Office, where Tremblay said he would meet him. His raincoat kicked wildly in the wind as he made his way the hundred yards or so. When he entered the office, an agent with a name tag indicating FELIX looked up inquiringly, noting Nick's mid-calf raincoat. "You must be Detective Nick Nucci," he said.

"Yes, I am. How did you know?"

"You look landlocked." Nick was taken aback. "Nah, just joking; we've been expecting you. Let me show you to the chief's office, eh?"

Nick followed Felix to the end of the corridor; Felix knocked, and Nick recognized Wilson's booming voice call out, "Come on in."

"Detective Nucci is here," Felix said by way of introduction.

"Okay, great," Wilson said, getting up from his desk to shake hands. "Glad you could make it."

He was as Nick had imagined: big, with broad shoulders and a pot belly. His hair was in a ponytail, something Nick had not expected, but he figured if you're the chief of security, you can do what you want. The spacious office was probably bright when the sun was shining. Nautical pictures, photos, and framed memorabilia checkered the walls, in between the windows.

"Have a seat. Want coffee or anything?"

"No thanks."

"She's coming in right now. See her with the tug?" Tremblay asked, pointing out a window. Nick nodded. The ship was just entering a docking bay. "It's wicked out there, as I imagine you now know," Tremblay continued. "We're lucky we were able to secure her when we did."

"So you were on the ship, you said?"

"Yeah. Just wanting to make sure everything was on the up-and-up. There are only ten containers on her. Very strange. Lots of spare space. It's not economical to do that, eh?"

"What did the men say about that?"

"That they just follow orders, they don't ask questions."

"Where are they now?"

"In a detention center until we can figure what the hell's going on. Come on, let's get over to her," Tremblay said, glancing out the window and grabbing a parka at the same time. He tossed a second one to Nick. "Wear this instead. Your raincoat will be shredded in no time."

The two men walked for several minutes to reach the ship. The wind was stiffer than anything Nick had ever experienced. As they climbed the iron ladder onto the deck, Nick noted there was even more wind up high. Tremblay hadn't been kidding about the storms. They were lucky to get the ship in.

"This red container concerns me," Tremblay shouted above the wind. "Come."

They walked across the deck to reach the container Tremblay had pointed to. Nick knew the man was right. There was a foul odor emanating from it.

Speaking directly into Nick's ear, Tremblay said "I've asked the crew to bring a tool called 'the original persuader', so we can open it as fast as possible. I should have thought to do so when I went to check the ship out when she was still at sea, but it never occurred to me that there might be something untoward in any of these containers," Tremblay explained.

Nick nodded.

"Okay, let's do this," Tremblay shouted, motioning to one of the deck hands. The man immediately began to undo the locks with the tool Tremblay had mentioned. Two minutes later, the doors swung open.

"Chief, you gotta see this," the young man said, just before he turned to throw up.

Chapter

73

Kayla left the museum, courting the unhappy feeling she had developed while listening to Amanda. She'd told Henry and Parker that she needed to run errands, but what she really needed were facts. They had agreed to meet later to review their findings to date and to consider if Amanda's revelations shed light on what was going on. Kayla felt that if her instincts were right, this would indeed be the outcome of their discussion.

It was the story of Henry 'Box' Brown that had planted the kernel of a possibility in Kayla, followed by the comments from the people, dead and alive, in Amanda's dream. The comment from the dead woman, "We have come a long way. We do not want to go back. We will not continue to go back," sent a shiver down Kayla's spine as she walked towards her house. The statements were not meant to be fantasy, she was sure of that. They had meaning, Kayla believed as she sat down in front of her computer to comb the Internet, committed to a very fast if brief research exercise.

Kayla searched for the most recent data and found a presidential proclamation in January 2016, declaring Slavery and Human Trafficking Prevention Month. The article went on to state that human slavery and trafficking did not just occur in other countries; it was a serious problem in the United States as well, with over seventeen thousand slaves being brought into America every year. The purposes were usually labor- or sexual-oriented, with a much higher percentage pertaining to the latter. Kayla started biting her lip. She looked up and saw Fritchie staring at her. The cat's expression was unusual; she appeared sanguine, almost sage. Kayla continued to search and read. She saw that there was a distinction between trafficking and smuggling. Smuggling referred to transportation, to moving people. Trafficking was exploitation. Kayla's antenna grew taller. Trafficking was a multibillion-dollar business that was expanding.

Kayla began to feel ill. She felt sure enough now that her hunch was right. She looked at her watch and realized it was time to meet up with Parker and Henry. She wanted their feedback, but whether they thought she was on to something or not, she was going to contact Nick to describe her findings.

Parker and Henry were already at the office when Kayla arrived. "Am I late?" she asked.

"No, we both just got here," Henry said, looking glum.

"What's wrong?"

"Nothing, really," Parker replied as he stood and started to pace. "We're both just sitting here trying to figure out what the hell is going on in Frederick. I mean, what Amanda revealed may or may not be relevant. It's just added another layer to the mystery."

"Well, unfortunately, I think I might have a clue as to what's going on. I haven't tied everything together, mind you."

"Anything would be of help," Henry said encouragingly.

"On top of that, it's not pretty."

"Jesus, Kayla. Just spit it out," Parker said, his frustration showing in his already gloomy countenance.

She took a deep breath. "I think there's a smuggling ring in action here in Frederick."

"A smuggling ring? What's being smuggled?" Parker asked, as Henry's eyes lit up.

"People."

Parker looked like he had been hit with a brick. "People?" he echoed.

Henry was staring at the table. Then he looked up at Kayla as though things were starting to click in his head.

"Yeah, think about it," Kayla said noting Henry's changed expression. "Just think. Think what Amanda described to us. You, too, Parker."

"You're referring to human trafficking?" Parker asked, somewhat rhetorically.

Chapter

74

Detective Nick Nucci and Chief Wilson Tremblay were straining to peer into the container on the now-anchored ship. The odor was unbearable. Both men had immediately pulled out their flashlights to examine the terrible contents. Nick stepped away, coughing while tightening the handkerchief around his nose. The chief had stumbled backwards slightly but was able to catch himself before falling down. Even in that split-second, as the wind continued to lash and dark clouds continued to gather, they realized what had occurred in the container; it dawned on them that it was simply unthinkable. The look of despair on the faces of the dead men, women, and children would be etched forever in their minds.

"Get forensics and the coroner here," Tremblay shouted over the wind to no one in particular. A deputy immediately pulled out his radio to comply. "Tell him to come prepared to unload and transport dozens of corpses. And get started opening the other containers."

Tremblay motioned to Nick, and all he could do was follow. He thought he might actually be in shock.

As they entered Tremblay's office, the chief closed the blinds to his windows. Then he walked over to his desk and dropped to his office chair. He motioned for Nick to have a seat in front of him. Tremblay reached into his lower desk drawer and pulled out a bottle of Canadian whiskey and two glasses. He didn't need to ask as he poured them each a healthy serving and then refilled them. Nick didn't drink the second one as fast as the first. He was starting to feel his extremities again and no longer felt the spinning sensation. He noticed that some color had returned to Tremblay's cheeks, as well.

"What the hell …?" Nick asked.

Tremblay just shook his head in response, staring at his desk with his two hands surrounding his glass. Finally, he said, "Some things make sense now. Not why those people, those poor people, were abandoned in a container ship, even more importantly why the hell they were trapped there to begin with, but yeah, one thing makes sense. Mostly, why the Russian sailors are so afraid."

Nick nodded, understanding and agreeing.

"I also think I saw some evidence of cannibalism."

Nick sat back upon hearing this. "Well, it could make sense, I guess. The thing that startled me was the diversity. Black, brown, white, men, women, and children. People from all over the place. I've never seen anything like it. The whole scene took a minute to take in. The human brain isn't prepared to grasp something like that."

"What? Genocide?"

"Actually, I think it's more than just genocide," Nick replied, taking another drink.

"What could be worse?"

"Those people were chained together. Around their waists."

"You're saying the ship was carrying trapped people? Are we looking at human trafficking then?"

"Yes," Nick said, nodding. "I believe so. With all of the refugees trying to escape into different countries, I would imagine there's ample opportunity to offer people all kinds of incentives, even if they are lies. Once desperate people agree, they're treated like prisoners and transported away from where they were, and no one, no family member, no one else can find them, and they cannot go to the authorities. There's opportunity for all kinds of exploitation. In this case, however, I don't know why the ship was told to turn around. It doesn't make sense."

"Does it say anything about your fellow, Johnny Mitka?"

"Only that if he was involved, he must have been considered a liability. On the other hand, why would he be here?"

"To help with the delivery?"

Bingo! Nick suddenly remembered the calendar he had seen on Lily and Johnny's refrigerator, secured by a magnet from some place ... Disney World, that was it. The calendar seemed innocuous at the time, but now Nick saw it in a different light. The dates on the calendar were highlighted across time: green, red, and yellow. There was also the usual doctor or dentist appointment, but the unusual highlighting had caught his eye.

"Well, the forensics team is topnotch, so if anything can be found, they'll find it. I don't know where it will lead us, but at least we can conduct a thorough investigation, eh?"

Chapter

75

Yesterday upon the stair
I met a man who wasn't there.
He wasn't there again today.
I wish, I wish he'd go away.
—William Hughes Mearns

Kayla was exhausted when she arrived home. The hours-long brainstorming effort the three of them had engaged in had taken an emotional toll, in part because of how horrific it was if they were right (which Kayla was sure they were). Suddenly, Kayla had an even more morbid thought. She looked at her watch and decided to call Nick. There was no answer. She looked up the office number and dialed it. A woman answered, "Detective Nucci's office, may I help you?"

"This is Kayla Dunn."

"Yes. What can I do for you?"

"I need to reach Nick, I mean Detective Nucci, regarding a case that he is working on; it's urgent, but he's not answering his phone. Can you get through to him for me or take a message?"

"Detective Nucci is in Toronto at the moment. I understand the weather is really bad there right now," the officer continued, "which may

282

be affecting the signals. I suggest you keep trying. In the meantime, if I hear from him, I'll have him give you a call."

Kayla's heart began to race after hearing this news.

"Oh. Do you know when he'll be returning?"

"No. He may be there a while."

"Yes … okay … thank you," Kayla said reluctantly as she hung up.

Kayla fed Fritchie and then warmed up some leftover stir-fry. While doing so, she thought about the events of the day and her need to talk with Nick. She tried his phone again, but no luck.

She sat at the kitchen table, which had been rare of late, and munched on her dinner without really tasting it. While she did so, she stared at Fritchie eating her dinner, which she finished in no time and then sauntered over and wrapped herself several times back and forth around Kayla's ankles. The cat then went to a window sill and jumped up on it, looking out as though waiting for someone to arrive.

No matter how she tried, Kayla could not shake her sense of malaise. She pushed her dinner away and poured herself another glass of wine. She knew she was drinking too much this evening but didn't care. She wanted to be numbed. She didn't know what time, but eventually she went upstairs for bed. Fritchie followed but instead of curling up in her own bed or even starting out in Kayla's bed, she jumped onto another window sill. *That's strange*, Kayla thought, though she didn't dwell on it. She knew she'd have a headache in the morning.

"Fritchie, move over," Kayla mumbled, awakening after feeling the cat on the bed.

"Fritchie's not with us anymore," a hoarse voice whispered.

Kayla's eyes popped wide open. She froze.

"Please do not be afraid," the voice continued. "Do not be afraid. I am here with a message only. You know in your heart you are right. Do what your head tells you. End the deception. Expose the murderous bastard. He is not to be trusted."

Kayla felt the weight on the bed vanish. With a trembling hand, she eventually turned on the nightstand light.

Nothing.

The event in her bedroom had truly frightened Kayla. The message had been even worse. She tried calling Nick again with no luck and then she decided to try texting, too:

Nick. Please call me. We think there may be smuggling and human trafficking occurring here in Frederick. And Eleanor told me that she suspects that Irakli, her new Georgian husband, is working with Hunter. Says it's fishy, maybe illegal. Says he speaks Russian on the phone. I think these two issues are related. Please call.

Chapter

Nick stared without comprehension at the message from Kayla. *Hunter Crowley? Irakli? Meeting together? And, human trafficking in Frederick?* He shook his head as though trying to literally shake away some impediment to his cogent abilities. He had wanted to wait around for the initial autopsy results, but he knew this was going to take some time. With this news from Kayla, he needed to get back to Frederick. He looked at his watch as he called the airlines for the next flight out. It was 1:30 a.m. In the meantime, he'd try to reach Kayla. The weather had become so iffy, he just didn't know when he'd get through. The sooner the better, obviously.

Nick did not as yet have a plan. Kayla's message raised several questions, such as determining if Hunter Crowley was involved in some unscrupulous activity. He'd have to observe the man closely. Once through to the airport, he was told flights were not operating, period, due to the weather, and it was not clear when the airport would open again. The kind woman said that it could be one hour or ten hours. The unpredictability of this weather event prevented any conclusive forecast, she explained. Nick needed a Plan B. No matter when the airport recovered, the back-up demand for seats would be overwhelming. He looked at his watch and called Wilson Tremblay.

"Hello?"

"Wilson, it's Nick. I'm sorry to wake you."

"You didn't, hang on a minute," Wilson said, looking over at his wife of thirty years, who could probably sleep through an earthquake. He got out of bed nonetheless, put his feet into his slippers, and pulled on his robe. It was cold. The wind was still fierce and the storm had lowered the temperature quite a bit. Wilson took the stairs to his office on the second floor. "Go ahead," he said as he sat down at his desk.

"Again, sorry to call at this hour."

"Honestly, Nick, I wasn't asleep. I can't sleep after today, eh?"

"Yeah, understood. Me too. Listen—I've received some news, could be critical, that may help us determine who or what is behind this whole godforsaken catastrophe. I think time is of the essence. I can't just sit here anymore, in other words. I know I'll receive a comprehensive autopsy report from you and your staff. But the airlines are down and …"

"You want to drive back to Frederick?"

"Bingo."

"It's nasty out there."

"I know."

"Okay, meet me at my office in an hour. I'll set you up with an official Port Authority SUV used for emergencies. You can use the emergency lights to help you get there faster and even the siren if need be, eh?"

"Thanks, I'll see you soon."

After Tremblay had demonstrated all the bells and whistles to Nick, he calculated the GPS settings and wished him luck.

Nick drove off in a torrent of wind and rain, hoping to outrun the storm, sooner than later.

Wilson watched as the vehicle's lights disappeared into the night. He shook his head. It was not in reaction to Nick behaving perhaps foolishly, however. He was heartbroken. He knew he'd never be the same man he was before today. Having worked for the Port for over thirty years, he had a nice pension coming his way. He and his wife had plans for travel now that their two children were married and had families of their own. But the image of those poor dead people had changed him. He knew that time might be of some help, but how do you erase the horrific, inhumane encounter that had been revealed today? *How? You can't. You just can't.*

———— • ————

Nick knew he was in a dangerous situation by traveling so fast and not really knowing the roads. Nonetheless, he continued. Cars tended to slow when they saw him coming. He didn't know if it was because of his speed or the flashing lights. *Probably both.* All in all, though, there were few other automobiles on the road. *Most people aren't this stupid*, he thought as he passed a Mini Cooper that looked like it might blow off the road. He noticed the rains were letting up just a bit but wasn't sure if it was a lull in the storm or if he indeed might be getting out of it. It was now 3:30 a.m. He'd already crossed the border at the Fort Erie Peace Bridge and was now headed to Harrisburg, Pennsylvania. From there, it would be a piece of cake, especially if the weather improved.

It soon seemed as if he was clear of it. The weather was indeed improving, creating pockets of better light from the intermittent full moon. So far, Nick had seen only one accident, an overturned semi. The rescue units were already there, and the debris had thankfully been removed from the road. Of course, he had slowed as he approached the mess, so no one from the police units paid any attention to him. It had been six hours since he'd left Buffalo. He figured he'd probably bested whatever driving time existed, on or off the record, for his trip from Toronto to Frederick.

And now, just as he had planned, he was sitting curbside across from Hunter Crowley's mansion, where he had a good shot of Hunter's Beemer parked on the circular driveway out front. Nick had decided to tail Hunter for a day before deciding on what kind of investigation was needed. "Who is this guy?" he wondered aloud, as he took the cap off his supersized black coffee.

Chapter

77

Whie Nick was driving like a madman through the torrential storm in the middle of the night, Hunter was also awake. He was fuming. After repeatedly trying to reach Irakli, with no luck, he finally decided to plan for the worst. Irakli was coming to Frederick. Crowley called Guy Hardy.

"Jeez, Hunter," Guy complained when he finally answered, "it's 3:30 in the morning."

"I know what time it is," Hunter snapped. "Now listen. I need you to get your butt over to a property not far out of town and play guard. You're waiting for a man named Irakli Guramishivili. He'll be arriving with cargo. Help him with whatever he needs. Don't ask questions. Don't talk, period. And call me as soon as he arrives, if I'm not already there."

"Not far out of town? Where is this place? How the hell am I supposed to know where it is?"

"It's between here and Middletown. It's on the right. The buildings are abandoned. There's a crumbling barn. You can't miss it."

"I don't know if I can find it in the dark."

"You can," Hunter barked. "Just do it!" He slapped his cellphone shut.

Fortunately for Guy, he had recently purchased a used car. He was aware that winter was soon approaching, and while he enjoyed walking and didn't mind taking public transportation, he knew that being dependent on both modes of transportation throughout winter could be a challenge. He was seething as he started the car up and pulled out onto the dark street. He did not have a life. Hunter Crowley had taken control of it months ago, when he threatened to expose Guy's felonious past. In retrospect, he should have just left town, especially now that the cops were snooping around. Frederick was not the only place he could live. He could start over anywhere. But it was too late for that option, he figured. That blackmailer was never going to let him get away. Guy had worked too long with the man, and now he knew Hunter's secrets as well as being complicit in some pretty bad actions. He was doomed. He sighed heavily, feeling like crying for the first time since he was a small child. He remembered his father had kicked him for doing so.

Guy was now on his way toward Middletown. Over thirty minutes had elapsed since Hunter had called. It was still dark, but sunrise was only an hour away. He could now see silhouettes of buildings along the two-lane highway. But which one was his?

Suddenly, Guy squinted to make sure he was seeing what he thought he was seeing: a tractor trailer was racing down the hill in front of him and began to fishtail. At that moment, the driver slowed the vehicle considerably, bringing it under control just in time to pull into a dirt driveway about two hundred feet from where Guy had pulled over. From his position, he got a good look at the driver. His demeanor and actions reflected a frantic human being who had just escaped the asylum. And the man was huge. He was unable to discern his face, however, due to the mass of dark hair that obscured it. He wondered how the man could see to drive.

By now, with a sense of dread, Guy figured this was his rendezvous contact. He inched forward in his car, trying to assess the situation. He saw that the man had apparently unhitched the trailer behind the second building, given that he was now pulling the truck around to park. Guy saw him jump out of the vehicle and head to an adjacent building, which he entered. He looked at his watch. It was five fifteen. Guy sat there for a couple more minutes, engine running. Finally, noting that Hunter had intimated that he also would be coming to this locale, Guy checked out his rearview mirror. Nothing. And with that observation, he thumped the accelerator with a sense of immense satisfaction and sped down the road past the building, leaving Frederick forever in his past.

Chapter
78

What do ghosts have to fear? They exist because the worst has already happened to them.
—Otto Kirk

Kayla was now sitting on the edge of her bed. She'd pulled the comforter around her thin tee shirt but was still shivering. She didn't know if it was because she was actually cold or because she was scared. Never had she experienced such a chilling event. Up until now, she realized, she'd been a witness to the paranormal world, observing with her eyes, her ears, her camera. Yes, the trompe l'oeil had reached out to her. That was something, huge in fact, but it had felt like a plaintive act. It had frightened her; it did not disturb her. But this visit by an ... an apparition was personal. She realized she was crying slightly and rocking back and forth. She took a deep breath, trying to calm her nerves. Then she reviewed what it had said: "Fritchie's not with us anymore." She looked around. Well, the cat was not with her, but what did she expect? The poor thing must have been frightened as well and ran down to the living room. *Then what did it say?* Kayla asked herself, taking another deep breath.

Please do not be afraid. Do not be afraid. I am here with a message only.

You know in your heart you are right. Do what your head tells you. End the deception. Expose the murderous bastard. He is not to be trusted.

Kayla knew in her heart that Hunter Crowley was the murderer. She hadn't included it in the text to Nick. But, she knew in her heart that he transported people all over the region, maybe even through tunnels like the one in her house. Maybe the people crossing her lawn were real, after all. Nick had told her his analysts had found bits of skin tissue in the shackles. The shackles from a previous century, used again today? She shook her head in disgust. She knew, too, that the boy in the superstore had reached out to her for help, literally. She could see his face, as if he were standing in front of her right now. And Amanda's dream was prescient. The dead and those alive had gone to the Community Bridge to say, "Enough is enough." The dead were ever-present with those alive. Kayla had just experienced it herself. She now believed that she was in fact never really alone. Just as Cory had commented about the museum ... what had he said? *It's hard not to think that they're all around here, all of the time.* She now knew it to be the case.

The abhorrent situation in Frederick had stimulated intense paranormal energy. In more ways than one, they, the citizens of the past and the slaves of the past, were trying to relay the message. Frederick's citizens, past and present, would not tolerate human trafficking again. Kayla knew that Parker and Henry would be surmising the same conclusions, based on the lengthy discussion the three of them had had the previous day. They had been overwhelmed by the stark, ugly realization that trafficking was indeed occurring. Then she thought of Kamala. She was a human trafficking victim, she knew now. No doubt. And that made her mad. Was Irakli Hunter's only accomplice? She doubted it. She looked around. Her clock said three fifteen. She got out of bed, put on her sweat pants, and decided to look for Fritchie. She hoped her little friend was not too traumatized.

By four thirty-five, Kayla had searched everywhere for Fritchie, in vain. The wardrobes, the tunnels … Kayla had even crawled halfway through the one in her house before becoming too claustrophobic. She'd wiggled her way backwards to get out, her heart pounding. Now she was searching for the cat's microchip report. She was going to report her to every vet and humane society east of the Cumberland. The cat must have gotten out somehow due to intense fright. She just needed to be rescued. Now Kayla could not find the folder where she had placed the report. She needed that number. She remembered looking at it and knew she could never memorize it. It was too long. Besides, she needed to show or explain which vet had inserted the chip and so on. She called Dr. Kotei, knowing it was too early but wanting to leave a message. Nothing. And there was no voicemail option. The phone just rang and rang. She changed clothes, put her cell in her pocket, and went outside, now that it was finally light enough to see. She walked in ever widening circles, calling for Fritchie, but to no avail. In between, she kept calling the vet. Still nothing. Now the ghostly entity had been totally forgotten. Kayla was in distress. Her pet was missing.

Chapter

79

Nick had just begun to doze off when he was startled by Hunter's BMW flying past. He started his car and followed the man at a good distance. There was hardly anyone else on the roads at that hour, so tailing him without being noticed would not be easy. Frederick's downtown roads simply did not lend themselves to inconspicuous movement, whether by car or on foot. They were narrow with multiple stop lights, stop signs, and one-ways. Plus, Nick was in the outsized SUV he'd borrowed from Wilson. He should have gone home to switch to his own car, but he hadn't wanted to waste time and possibly miss seeing Hunter leave.

Nick didn't need to worry. Hunter was driving like a man possessed. *I'd arrest him for speeding and reckless driving if I wasn't tailing him*, he thought to himself. Fortunately, he didn't have to run as many red lights since he was holding back while Hunter ran them head on. Most often, the light had turned green by the time Nick reached it. As Hunter headed out toward Middletown, Nick checked the gas tank. He'd filled it a couple of hours before reaching Frederick but knew that the vehicle must be a gas guzzler. He had half a tank and hoped it would be enough. *Where the hell was the man going?*

Suddenly, Hunter slowed and took a fast right. Nick slowed as well. Now he was crawling. As long as Nick could remember, the buildings in this location were empty. There was only one way in and out. The land had been part of a farm that belonged to an elderly man, Clive Watson, who resided now in a nursing home. He had no relatives. The farm had been in the family for generations. The buildings had been used for storage at one time. Watson refused to sell it. Nick could understand the sentiment, but it was definitely now an eyesore, not to mention potentially dangerous to anyone in or around it. Nick knew that there had been recent discussions of condemning the buildings, or at least the main barn. He looked around for a place to park, but there didn't seem to be anyplace that was convenient and hidden. It was just a two-lane highway. Finally, he sighted two trees that could shield the vehicle somewhat and pulled off the side of the road behind them.

Chapter

80

We awoke to find we were still in an endless nightmare.
—Justin C. Perkins

"**W**hat the hell were you thinking?" Hunter roared as he headed toward the building where Irakli was standing in the doorway, waiting for him. "What the hell?"

"What do you mean, what the hell? I am doing my job. Something you should have done."

Hunter pushed past the huge man into the dimly lit room. The windows were filthy, but through them Hunter could see the trailer parked behind the building. *Jesus Christ.* "Are they even alive?"

"Yes, they are alive. You should have heard them screaming as I was driving. The trailer did not drive straight." Even though he got the gist of the phrasing, Hunter detested the man's inability to speak English correctly.

"You mean it was fishtailing behind you, no doubt," Hunter growled, his head still throbbing from the hangover.

"Yes. Fishtailing. That is a good one," Irakli said, smirking and nodding his head as he observed the padlocked trailer, from which muffled shouts and banging against the sides of the trailer could be heard.

"How many are there in this delivery?"

"You should know. You made contract. Eighteen: fifteen men and three girls."

Hunter shook his head as he paced. "Well, genius, what's your next step. Your Plan B?"

"We need to get them food and water, and then we contact our contacts and see who needs what. No more middle men. I will drive them. That is what those deceivers were supposed to do once they collected them from me."

Hunter winced as he observed how casually Irakli was talking. The man had just killed two people.

"Have you contacted the contacts? What's your timeframe?"

Nick's blood was boiling. He'd spotted Hunter's BMW and shortly after heard the man's voice and then Irakli's. He couldn't believe what he was overhearing as he squatted beneath a window close to where the two men were arguing inside the warehouse. Images of the corpses in the container ship kept flashing across his eyes. *Thank God for Kayla's text.* But here he was, without a means to contact anyone from the station for backup without moving away from their conversation. It was dangerous to be alone, but he didn't want to miss anything, so he stayed. *In fact ...* Nick turned off his cell; the last thing he needed now was an incoming call. He could figure the criminal charges later; he needed to remain to see what would transpire and to gather as much information as possible.

"Listen, asshole. I just drove for hours and saved your damn ass by keeping these people. I could have just run away. You need to do your work."

"I told you not to bring them here."

"Yes. But you did not say where to take them. You did not provide leadership."

Hunter was starting to lose his confidence. He didn't have a Plan B but didn't want to let Irakli know how vulnerable he was. "The point is, we're now in Frederick. It's not so easy to disappear people from here."

"Ah." Irakli made a sign with his finger and turned to make instant coffee. This was a make-shift office with a microwave, a small refrigerator, and a deep freezer, which had probably been left over from the owner. There were two standup lamps with lightbulbs but no shades, along with a table and three chairs. "Disappear? Disappear? No one knows they are here. What do you mean ... disappear?"

"I mean, how are you going to transport them out of here? You think one or two or three will just get in the van with you and sit quietly? Or you going to serve them food and water in that trailer?"

"No. Of course not," Irakli said, stirring his sugared coffee. "You are going to help me tie them up and gag them first. It is going to be a very long day," he concluded, leering at Hunter.

Hunter could feel the blood drain from his face. He was the man in charge. He didn't take orders. And he had no plans whatsoever to get down and dirty with Irakli. He took care of money and accounts, not refugees. He couldn't imagine even touching one of them, much less manhandling them. He looked around. He wanted to run away. But the package had been delivered here, to Frederick.

"Do not think about leaving," Irakli said as he sipped his coffee, as though reading Hunter's mind. "You do not want to become one of them, do you?" he asked as he motioned with his head toward the trailer.

Suddenly, Hunter knew what his Plan B was. The trailer had no connection to him. None. "Of course I'm not thinking of leaving. Do you have all of the supplies here? The food? The water? The rope to bind them with? It's going to get hot in there eventually, so the sooner we get started, the better."

"I have everything. Of course." Hunter had already eyed a loose two-by-four that looked perfect. "I will have another coffee and then we will start."

When Irakli turned to put the cup in the microwave, Hunter moved for the piece of lumber. In full anticipation of betrayal, Irakli watched Hunter's reflection in the microwave door. Hunter bent for the two-by-four, but as he stood, Irakli grabbed it from him and swung it against Hunter's shoulder, knocking the hungover man to the ground. Hunter stayed down, groaning. Irakli didn't care and didn't hesitate. He raised the board above Hunter's head like a caveman preparing to attack an animal and swung.

With his last gasp, Hunter whimpered beseechingly, "Why me?"

Irakli just laughed as he swung, and then swung again, and again.

———————◆———————

Nick could hear the murder occurring but could do nothing to stop it. The sounds of the beating and breaking bones started to recede at the same time as the cries and pounding from the nearby trailer reached a crescendo. *This guy has got to be stopped!* With his gun ready, Nick edged around the building to the front door.

Chapter 81

In a panic, Kayla decided to drive to Dr. Kotei's office to get Fritchie's microchip report. Maybe he was conducting an operation and couldn't answer the phone. She didn't care. This would be the fastest way to get what she needed, anyway. Kayla ran back to her house, gathered her purse and jacket and jumped into her car. The ride wouldn't take long. It was still early so there would be very little traffic.

Kayla took a right when she reached the broken down barn, just as she had the first time she took Fritchie to the veterinarian. *Seems so long ago now.* As she pulled into the lot, she saw the BMW SUV. Kayla immediately noticed the signature vanity tag: "Jobs 4U". *Hunter Crowley? What is he doing here? Strange.*

She slowed even more but continued to drive toward Dr. Kotei's building before stopping all together. The feeling Kayla suddenly had was not just one of trepidation but an intuitive alarm for her safety. She turned the engine off and unlocked the door before removing the keys so it would not make beeping noise when she exited.

Once she was out of the vehicle, Kayla could hear riot like-noises and pounding coming from the other side of the building directly in front of her. She slowly walked toward it. That's when she saw the trailer and at the same time recognized that the noises were emanating from within it. Kayla approached it slowly. When she saw the padlock, Kayla realized that people were trapped inside. She looked around and found an iron bar to snap the lock with. Suddenly, Kayla heard a gunshot. She dropped. The people inside the trailer became silent. Her heart was racing, she had never heard a gunshot before, but she knew that is what it was. It came from the building near where Hunter's car was parked.

Kayla ran stealthily toward the building and then kneeled so she could cautiously look in a window. What she saw in a glance horrified her. Hunter Crowley was lying on the floor, covered in blood. She would not have been able to recognize him except that his car was parked nearby. Nick Nucci also lay there, apparently unconscious but alive because Irakli was tying him up on a chair. A can of gasoline lay on the floor nearby along with a pistol.

Kayla slid down the wall of the building and sat with her back to it. She bit her lip and tried to stop shaking. She had to think. Kayla now knew in her heart, without a doubt, that the people screaming in the trailer were being trafficked. She had to get them out but she knew in her head that she had to save Nick first. *How?*

Then it hit her. There was no way and no time to get Nick out first. Kayla took a deep breath. She jumped up and ran toward the trailer, grabbing the iron bar on the ground along the way. She knew she had at the most two chances to break the lock before Irakli would hear her. With her running momentum and the bar behind her like a baseball bat, Kayla swung with precision at the neck of the lock. Crack! People from the inside did the rest. They were swarming out of the trailer within seconds. Kayla simply pointed. The rage was palpable. Kayla stood still as the crowd dashed past as though she was a rock in a rushing stream. When they got to the building that Kayla had pointed to, she heard a shot. One person fell. The other people immediately dispersed and ran to the windows. The men kicked them in with their feet. More shots. Now with the multiple distractions, the people were able to enter through the door and the broken windows. Kayla ran, too. She knew she'd created the chaos, but hoped it was a good thing. She was right.

Irakli was down. People were grabbing at his jewelry as they punched and kicked the man. Nick was conscience but helpless in his tied up state. Kayla ran to his side, pulled the stuffed handkerchief out of his mouth and tried to undo his knots. It was not possible. "Grab that dinner knife," Nick said, pointing toward the microwave. The serration was minimal, but better than nothing. After Kayla sawed for 30 seconds, Nick pulled the rope apart. He took the knife and undid the ties around his feet. Jumping up, Nick attempted to weave his way into the crowd to stop the massacre.

"Stop! Stop!" Nick shouted, but could not dissuade them.

Maybe they couldn't understand him or maybe there was no desire. They didn't stop. The take down was not only effective, it was brutal. Irakli no longer moved. The crowd didn't stop there. With the jewelry already gone the people tore his clothes off and handed them out. Shoes and socks were last. After the men had stepped away, the three girls rushed forward and repeatedly kicked the bloody body as they cried. One girl reached down and clawed at Irakli's face until Nick was able to pull her away.

Chapter

All of the ambulances and several patrol cars had left. Kayla sat in her car. She was drained: emotionally, mentally, and physically. This incident had been horrible. She'd called Parker and Henry, and they were on their way. It was their case too. Though the police had cordoned off the entire area, Nick had made arrangements for the two of them to enter. As Kayla saw their van appear, she got out of her car and waved. Parker drove slowly toward her. She was relieved they were here.

She hadn't been able to explain much to Parker, in part because it was so complicated, but more importantly because it was so improbable. *How do you describe something like this?* she wondered as she observed the scene. *How?*

"What the hell?" Parker asked as he approached. "Are you sure you're okay, Kayla?"

"Yeah, well, okay as in not physically injured, but I don't know about all the rest. I'll have to wait and see."

Nick walked over too. He shook hands with Parker and Henry.

"How are the others?" Kayla asked Nick.

"Irakli managed to kill one of them. Three others are injured but not badly."

"Can someone explain what happened?" Parker asked again, shaking his head.

Nick succinctly described the entire event, including what he had found in Toronto. The team looked especially stricken when Nick described the grisly details about the "cargo" in the container ship.

"What have people become?" Parker asked.

"Actually, this type of inhumanity has been around forever, if you think about it," Nick replied. Parker nodded.

"There's a lot I still don't get," Henry remarked. It was the first time he had spoken since arriving. "What were you doing here, Kayla? Why did you come here?"

Kayla was startled. Up until now, she had totally forgotten about Fritchie. A pang of guilt struck her.

"I came to see your cousin, the veterinarian, Dr. Kotei. My cat is missing."

Henry stared at her. "I have a cousin named Kotie who lives in Baltimore. He's a Gulf War veteran, not a veterinarian."

"But I thought you said he was a veterinarian," Kayla insisted.

"Nope. Anyway, why would you think he was here?"

"Well, it must be a coincidence that a Dr. Kotei, my veterinarian, has an office in one of the buildings here," she insisted. "But never mind for now," she added, realizing deep down that in fact there was no Dr. Kotei here. *That's why the call had not been answered. The entity, the visiting spirit, had been truthful when he said that Fritchie was no longer with them. Fritchie, quite simply, had been her paranormal guide up until now. There never was a Dr. Kotei.* Kayla shivered and sat down on the ground. Parker squatted to comfort her.

"So what's next?" Parker asked, looking up at Nick.

"Well, first I need to talk with Eleanor."

"Oh, yeah," Kayla remarked. "I'm sure this is going to be a shock to her. She may need some help coping." *Or maybe she'll be relieved.*

"We have a counselor at the station," Nick added. "And I need to get into Hunter's house, to see what's going on there. Do any of you know if he had any relatives? They'll need to be informed as well."

The Dulany Team all shook their heads no.

"I'll stay in touch," Nick concluded. "Of course, I'm not sure if this …" and he looked around again, "this tragedy has anything to do with your investigation, but if it wasn't for your perseverance, we wouldn't have discovered this trafficking ring. I'll keep you informed of any findings along the way."

"Wow, what a mess," Henry remarked, watching him walk off. "He's probably going to have some sleepless nights. You too, Kayla."

"Yeah, I'm sure of that," she said, sighing.

"Are you up to a meeting, Kayla?" Parker asked. "I think we have some issues to review."

"Of course. I just need to go home first."

"Okay," Parker replied. "Why don't we meet late this afternoon?"

"That works for me," she said.

———◆———

As she drove home, Kayla reflected on the circumstances leading up to today's events. As she thought back, she realized that Fritchie had been her guide through the paranormal events, ever since she had arrived. She now had a hunch that she wanted to follow up on before talking with Parker and Henry. When she got home, she went straight to her darkroom. The emptiness saddened her. There was no Fritchie. A few days before, the cat had looked different to Kayla, somehow. So she had taken several portraits of her. Now she wanted to develop those photos.

She hung up the photos to dry and pulled out her magnifying glass. But she didn't need it. It was clearly evident that Fritchie was not alone. *These are not orbs*, Kayla thought. They were full shapes, hovering. Fritchie herself was not solid. "Translucent" was a better word for it. The hairs on Kayla's arms and neck went straight up. Her heart was pounding. *Did I just imagine Fritchie, or was she a spirit?* She looked over at the cat dishes. *No. Fritchie was real, but maybe she just was not of this world. Kind of like Amanda's dream, where the dead walked with those still alive*, she thought as she sat down, staring up at the photos. *Unbelievable.*

Chapter

83

Nick had just hung up from his conversation with Wilson Tremblay. He'd described the events since he'd left Toronto, less than forty-eight hours ago. He explained that an officer was returning the car as they spoke. There was not much news on Wilson's side. He was still waiting for results from the coroner, and the sailors still weren't speaking. The two had agreed to stay in close touch. It was obvious to both of them that the human trafficking ring in Frederick was likely related to the container ship in Toronto.

Nick's effort to reach Eleanor had been unsuccessful. He'd left two messages and provided her with his email address as well. He'd keep trying and hoped she'd get in touch. Just to be on the safe side, he'd sent a patrol car to check on her at her residence. They'd reported back that the house was locked up; no sign of Eleanor.

Nick took a short nap and then, with a large coffee in hand, drove to Hunter Crowley's house. His team had already cordoned the property off. A couple walking their dog was staring at the house from the sidewalk. Nick simply nodded at them as he stepped over the yellow tape. He wasn't in the mood for chit-chat, much less answering questions about what was going on.

When he entered the house, he thought back to the masquerade party Hunter had hosted here, not long ago. *What deception.* Hunter was conducting his nefarious work right within their midst. Today, the place looked as though it knew its owner would never return. It was dark, dank, and lifeless. Nick entered the kitchen to get a glass of water. A half-empty coffee pot sat on the stove. A piece of toast lay next to it, no plate. The trash can contained cartons from KFC and several empty beer bottles. An empty bottle of Scotch sat next to the trash can. Hunter must have had quite a hangover, Nick reflected, wondering if it had impaired his ability to deal with Irakli. *Maybe.*

He decided to first check for an office. He glanced into the master bedroom as he passed it. It was a mess. The next room's door was closed. He opened it cautiously. Bingo. Calling it an office was an understatement. It looked like Hunter had customized this room: very big with complex adornments. And, lo and behold, it came with a dog. Second Chance was lying in a huge dog bed next to the mahogany desk. His tail thumped when he saw Nick.

"Hiya, boy," he said soothingly as he approached the animal. *Who's going to take care of you now?* he wondered sadly.

Second Chance had already stood and come over to Nick, as if waiting for something. Nick looked around and saw a container of dog treats on Hunter's desk. He pulled one out and gave it to him. "You must be hungry. Bet you didn't get your breakfast this morning, huh?" he said, watching the dog gobble the treat down. He emptied the container out on the floor for him.

Then the detective sat down at Hunter's desk. He looked at everything on the surface and in the drawers. But, in fact, Hunter had very little committed to paper. Nick tried to get into the computer. He used "Second Chance" as the password, but that didn't work. He continued to try combinations until he stumbled across an easy one that used initials and dates. *Too easy.* Unfortunately, there was nothing on the computer except frivolous emails. *Where did he keep his business dealings?* He felt around underneath the desk's top and quickly came across a button. "You've got to be kidding me," he muttered as he pressed it. "Oldest ploy in the book."

Nick stood up as the wall in front of him slid open. He knew from experience that rooms like this were often booby-trapped. *Was Hunter that kind of guy? Perhaps.* Nick felt around the door frame. Nothing. He walked inside, gave a low whistle, and snapped on his phone. He hit the speed dial number for the IT department.

"Sam? I need you to get your best team over to Court Street, Crowley's house. I'll be waiting for you. First, call the Bomb Squad and have them come, too. I want them to check out the residence first. Bring all your gear; I found a very sophisticated computer and tape recording room. Any questions? Okay. Thanks."

Nick hung up. *It wouldn't be long now.*

Chapter

Kayla entered the Dulany Team's office with a sense of relief and closure. "Hi, guys," she said brightly.

"Hey, Kayla," Parker said, looking up. "Grab a glass." He and Henry had apparently just been chatting. Kayla didn't see anything on the conference table except two glasses of wine. After setting her materials down, she poured herself a glass.

"So what's new?" she asked as she sat down.

"Very funny," Henry replied. "We've been waiting to hear from you."

"Yeah, I know. I've got some explaining to do."

"Well," Parker said, "please don't keep us waiting any longer. Why was Nick there at that site? Why were you there?"

Kayla took a deep breath. Then she explained how she ran into Eleanor, who had told her about Irakli and his many passports and his calls in Russian and his meeting with Hunter. "After I got home, I decided we might want to clue Nick in our discussion about human trafficking. I tried calling him several times, but there was no answer, so I called his office," Kayla explained. "His assistant informed me that Nick was in Toronto and didn't know when he might return. ."

"Anyway, given what I'd just heard from Eleanor, it seemed even more important that I contact Nick. I sent him a text alerting him to the fact that Irakli was conducting transactions in Russian and that he and Hunter appeared to be working together. Nick must have put two and two together and followed Hunter out there to where were today. When I got there, I saw Nick being tied up by Irakli, with Hunter dead on the floor."

Parker and Henry just shook their heads.

"The fact that you just happened …," Henry started.

"No. As I told you before, I was going to my cat's veterinarian's office. She'd gone missing, and I couldn't find the microchip report. The vet wasn't answering my phone call, so I decided to drive out there to get it. But …"

"But then you saw Nick and Irakli."

"No. The 'but' is actually about my cat," Kayla started to explain, as she removed the photos from her folder. This is … was … might have been Fritchie, my cat."

"Fritchie? You named her after that woman … the one in the poem?" Henry asked, chuckling.

"Yes, I named her after Barbara Fritchie. It fit."

"But what's wrong with her?" Parker asked, ignoring the discussion about the cat's name. He was examining the photos instead.

"That's what I'm trying to get to," Kayla replied, sounding exasperated. "I'll tell you the whole story if you stop interrupting."

"Go ahead," Parker said, nodding and leaning back. "We're listening."

"This cat showed up early in the fall," she began, "about the time we started the foundation's investigation."

Kayla continued to describe the events surrounding Fritchie as they unfolded in real time, including her visit to Dr. Kotei, the veterinarian, the cat's disappearances and reappearances, finding the tunnel in her own home, and so forth. She tried not to leave out any detail.

"And then last night, I had a visitor." Parker raised an eyebrow. "He came in the middle of the night. I felt something on the bed and thought it was the cat, so I said, 'Move over, Fritchie,' but instead, I heard a voice say: 'Fritchie's not with us anymore.'"

"Jeez, Kayla," Henry exclaimed.

"I know," she replied softly. "I know. Spooky. Then he ... it ... the spirit said, and I'm quoting because I will never forget it, 'Please do not be afraid. Do not be afraid. I am here with a message only. You know in your heart you are right. Do what your head tells you. End the deception. Expose the murderous bastard. He is not to be trusted.'"

"Good Lord," Parker said. "A bedtime visitor, no less. They're common, but usually the ghost is known to the person. Did you recognize him?"

"No. I didn't even look at him. I was paralyzed. It all happened so quickly. After I pulled myself together, I realized what the spirit had said was so true. We had already figured out there was a trafficking ring. But we didn't know who. The spirit was telling me I did know who. It was Hunter. He is ... was the murderer." Parker poured more wine for all of them. "And I realized, too, that what the spirit said about Fritchie had also come to be true. My cat was nowhere to be found. So ... I decided to drive to the vet's office, as I mentioned."

"Yeah, about that vet's office, Kayla," Parker began. "There's no such building there."

"I know that now," she responded. "I know. I realized it this morning when I arrived at the site. That's one thing I simply cannot explain. Did I dream it? Maybe. But Dr. Kotei seemed so real. Anyway, that's not really the point, is it? The point is that if I had not believed that the vet's office was there, and if Fritchie had not gone missing, I wouldn't have been there and seen Hunter and Irakli meeting."

"That's true," Henry agreed nodding.

"So you had a ghost cat with you for the past three months," Parker commented. "Why didn't you ever mention her?" he asked, while examining the photos.

"I didn't think to mention her. It wasn't on purpose. We've been so busy. But I must say I did not know Fritchie was a ghost until this morning."

"My Grandma Mercy had a ghost goat for the longest time," Henry said matter-of-factly.

Not this, Kayla thought.

"She believed it was her Uncle Kofi. He showed up around the time of the man's passing. She never purchased the goat. No one in the village claimed him. He was just there one day. She told me the other goats shied away from him. She would feed him after she'd herded the rest of them into their pen."

"Ghost animals do exist," Parker said, nodding. "Sometimes, they seem to be attached to a human spirit, like your grandma's goat, and other times, they are there to make a statement, like Fritchie. It seems that indeed she had a message, more than one. Now she's moved on."

"It's sad," Kayla said. "Fritchie was really instrumental during the entire investigation, and I didn't even realize it until now. Without her, we wouldn't have known about Hunter's human trafficking ring, which I believe has been the cause of all of the paranormal activity. He deceived all of us, except the town's victims of the past, the victims of slavery." Parker and Henry nodded somberly. "And there's one more thing I believe: Kamala was a victim of the ring. Hunter may even have murdered her himself."

Chapter

When she awakened, Kayla dressed to run as usual. She decided to run in Baker Park again. It was more familiar and just made her feel better, especially with Fritchie gone. Now that Hunter was gone and the idea that Kamala was probably a victim of the trafficking ring, she felt it was safe again. It was later than usual. She didn't have any work that day to speak of. Nick had said he'd get in touch with all of the follow-up findings, but he'd be pursuing all the ties to Hunter first. She figured it would take a while.

As she began her run in the park, she saw people she didn't realize she'd been missing. There was the bird watcher, the couple with the dog and Frisbee, the other joggers, and the quarter-hour toll of the bell tower. She was back. And everyone was so friendly. Practically everyone she came across had a big smile and a wave. This reception, if she could call it that, helped her shake the gloom over her loss of Fritchie. She was feeling better already.

Near the end of her run, Kayla's phone rang. It was Henry. "Yeah, hi, Henry what's up?"

"Where are you, Kayla?"

"Where are *you*, Henry?"

"Very funny. How soon can you get to Beans and Bagels?"

"Well, I'm just finishing my run."

"Then run over here now. We'll be waiting." Click.

Kayla did just that. When she arrived, she found Henry and Parker at one of the larger tables in the back. They were sipping coffee, talking, and pointing at a newspaper.

"Hey, Kayla, have a seat," Parker offered, pulling out a chair. "Look, we're famous."

Kayla glanced down at the newspaper. "Famous by being in a tabloid?"

"Ah, forget that part. Look, the article talks about how we solved a real-life horror story," Henry said, pointing.

Kayla read the brief piece. "Well, yeah, it is good publicity, that's for sure. I hope Nick was able to get a hold of Eleanor. I would hate for her to find out about Irakli through this article."

"Good point. But contacting her was first on Nick's list," Parker commented.

"I know, just saying," she responded. Then she had a thought. "You know, it was strange when I was jogging today. I went back to Baker Park, and everyone I saw gave me a big grin and a wave. I mean, people I don't even know. You think news has traveled that fast?"

"This is Frederick," Parker and Henry said in unison.

Just then, the proprietor of the Beans and Bagels brought Kayla a cup of coffee and served the three of them a plate of hot bagels and different types of cream cheese.

"We didn't order …," Parker started.

"It's on the house," the owner said. "It's the least we can do. We're proud of you," he added, nodding at the newspaper before walking off.

"I guess you're right," Kayla said, taking a cinnamon bagel and loading it with walnut cream cheese. "But many details are still missing. We don't know the half of it. We'll have to wait until we hear from Nick to get the full story."

"That's true," Parker commented. "But for right now, I want to cherish our newfound fame."

Kayla smiled to herself. It was just a tabloid. But it was news.

Nick called as Kayla was walking home.

"How are you doing?" she asked him.

"I'm okay. Lots of work still. How are you? Did your cat show up?"

"No. But otherwise, I'm okay." Kayla contemplated telling him that Fritchie had most likely been a ghost but decided that little tidbit might be too weird, even for someone as open-minded as him. Not to mention what he might think of her. "Have you seen the *Daily Review*?"

"Yeah. Pretty light on the facts, but everyone knows Hunter and Irakli were criminals now."

"And that they're dead. Did you get in touch with Eleanor?"

"Yeah, she finally returned my call. She said she had been uneasy living with Irakli lately, so the last time he left for his work, she packed up and went home to stay with her parents. I don't know the woman, but she actually sounded relieved that he is dead."

"Well, given what he's done, and given that she didn't feel good about him anymore, I can't blame her."

"I know. She'll be coming back to Frederick tomorrow to work things out. But that's not what I want to talk about. I was wondering, Kayla, would you like Hunter's dog?"

"Second Chance?"

"Yeah. I thought since your cat is still gone, maybe you'd like some company. He's got nowhere to go. Of course, if you think you'll find your cat soon …"

"I don't think I'm going to find her, Nick. But a dog? A big dog, too."

"He's gentle."

"I know. No, I like him. Why don't we give it a try? If it doesn't work out, I'll find him a new home."

"Okay, deal. Can I drop him off now?"

"Sure thing, I'm almost home."

Later, as she and her dog sat on the stoop outside her front door, Kayla believed taking Second Chance might just be the best thing that had happened to her in a long, long time.

315

Chapter

As more people became aware of what had taken place on a virtually abandoned lot outside of Frederick, interest in the Dulany Paranormal Team grew, as did the validity of their work.

Three days after the event, Polly Rutledge called Parker. "Hello, you sweet man, how y'all doin'?" she asked. "Y'all sure did take the bull by the horns with this case."

"Polly?" he asked. "Are you back at the foundation?"

"Yes. Yes, I am. And it's good to be back too. But I'm not there right now. I'm at Beacon's Way. I was wonderin' if you and your team could join me here. I know I'm not giving y'all any notice, but I just got here myself and want to show you somethin'."

"Well, as a matter of fact, we can be over in a few minutes. Everything okay, by the way?"

"Everything is perfect. Just perfect."

Parker thought he could hear her smiling.

When they arrived at Beacon's Way, Polly was out on the porch. The three walked up to the smiling woman.

They all kissed her cheek to cheek. "Looks like the hiatus was just what you needed," Kayla said.

"Oh, darlin', it wasn't a hiatus. I was just damned scared. But I sure do feel better, you're right about that. Please, y'all come in," she said, motioning for them to enter.

As they walked into the grand room, Polly turned to face them. "So what do y'all see? Or what don't you see?"

Kayla thought she looked like a little girl in front of the class during show-and-tell.

It became apparent immediately. "The spirits are gone," Kayla stated simply.

"Yes, indeed they are," Polly said, beaming.

"No more peeling paint," Henry commented.

"Curtains look new again," Parked said, nodding.

"And wait till y'all see the cupola."

They all trudged up to the highest place in the house. As they passed the master bedroom, Polly waved at it. "No more armoire movement, either," she said.

The cupola was clear. No wet ceiling, no smell, and (sadly, Kayla thought), no trompe l'oeil.

"And the cellar?" Parker asked.

"Oh, honey, I haven't been down there. We still need to rebuild the stairs. But … I will tell you that the lights have been repaired. Hunter had turned it off somehow, but our electrician was able to find the electrical break. So let's go downstairs for some tea. I have more to tell."

The three looked at each other and obediently followed Polly down to the kitchen.

Kayla looked in the fridge. One beer left.

"Join us, sweetie," Polly said, pulling the chair out for Kayla. "So it seems the ghosts are gone, right?" The three nodded. "Well, guess what, y'all? They're gone from the Page house too. No more open window, no more creaking, and guess what else?"

"The trompe l'oeil is gone," Kayla said.

"You are correct, young lady. Danielle and Mathew are quite relieved, as you can imagine. But they say they're true believers now. It's opened up a whole new world for them, so to speak," Polly said, laughing again.

"And the museum?" Parker asked.

"Yes, the ghosts and the painting at the museum are gone, too. Well, the recent paranormal activity has stopped. Amanda said the books are no longer falling down. Cory said he's a changed man too. He told me that even when he's alone in his office or anywhere in the museum, for that matter, he now knows he's not really alone. But it doesn't bother him. He said it's almost reassuring."

Parker said, "These changes are all so sudden. I'm truly surprised that things would reconcile so quickly, so completely. We had plans to follow up with everyone after the dust had settled, but this is stunning."

"Well, I don't know about your paranormal business, but I do know that the spooky things had started rather quickly," Polly tried to explain. I mean, one day everything was fine, and the next day, things were all topsy-turvy. I mean, what I'm saying is that it ended just like it started. And now there are no ghosts."

Epilogue

A week after the meeting with Polly, Nick Nucci contacted the Dulany Team and asked them to come to his office for a debrief. In the meantime, the team's reputation had soared, after being so integral in bringing down an international human trafficking ring. They were mentioned in several national newspapers, not just tabloids. The fame was a bit unsettling. But as Kayla had remarked to Parker and Henry, at least they were not the butt of ghost jokes anymore. In fact, for a split-second, Parker had considered increasing their fees but decided against it. He concluded it would just be too greedy to capitalize on exposing something so awful.

"Well, this should be interesting," Henry remarked as they pulled up to Nick's office.

The detective was waiting for them. Kayla noticed that he had a white screen pulled down in his office. "Does anyone want a coffee or soft drink?" he asked. No one did.

"Well, thanks for coming. I'll be holding a press conference tomorrow, but I wanted to let you know what we found rather than have you hear it secondhand."

"Who else is 'we'?" Henry asked.

"Oh, sorry. Wilson Tremblay. He's the harbormaster and chief of security at the Toronto Port. He'll be presenting with me. It was a joint effort between our two countries to determine what exactly happened with this trafficking ring. We still don't have all of the answers, but we do know the roles that Hunter and Irakli played."

Kayla had never seen Nick so studious. He was all business.

"By the way, you all are invited to the press conference as well," he added.

Parker glanced at Kayla and Henry; he replied, "I'll speak for the team. We'll pass up your offer. Our presence would be a distraction. People should be focused 100 percent on the horrendous exploitation and cruelty of human trafficking."

"Well, if you think so, thank you," Nick said. "We'll give you all full credit, of course.

"About our findings now," he continued. "First of all, working backwards, Irakli murdered Hunter. I heard him do it but was unable to stop it. When I confronted him, he quickly overcame me, I'm sorry to admit, and would have killed me if not for Kayla. When she released the people in the trailer, they overpowered Irakli and beat him to death. We found another body at the site as well. Lucas Cardozo was found dead in the freezer. He was the person hiding behind the washing machine in the cellar, Kayla. He's the same person who was arrested for shoplifting. We believe he was being trafficked and was perhaps in the hold in Beacon's Way. Somehow he must have escaped. He may have remembered the house and used it as a sanctuary after he broke in. He obviously had become a liability to them."

"It seems, though not conclusively yet, that Hunter acted as CEO for the ring in the States," Nick continued. "His counterpart worked from Russia. Hunter's office at his house was equipped with a multitude of recorders, camera monitors, and phones. He had the cameras installed at Beacon's Way and recorded all activity that occurred there. He could watch and listen to you every time you entered the cellar. He also could watch and listen to the people he had stay there inside the small cache, beneath the steel hatch door, as a way station. Apparently, some of the people were injured there, which is why Hunter tried to keep you all out of the cellar by shutting off the electricity. Eventually, he had to have the place sanitized with bleach so as not to leave any traces. Lucas was a loose end who had to be quieted."

"This is so disgusting," Kayla said. Parker and Henry nodded in agreement.

"I'm sorry to say, it gets worse," Nick replied. "Hunter was moving people through cellars and tunnels all over Frederick. The people were always in transit to a particular work destination, some even here.

"The person who worked for Hunter prior to Irakli was named Tommy Mitka. We have evidence that Hunter had Tommy killed once he broached a communication protocol while he was working for Hunter in Toronto. Toronto was one of the ports where people were transported to. We have circumstantial evidence that Hunter also had that man's wife, Lily Mitka, killed. Once that Mitka breach occurred, Hunter aborted the shipment arrival and sent the container ship back to Russia, which is what Officer Tremblay and I uncovered in the port."

"Who are these people who get trafficked?" Parker asked. "Sorry, I don't mean to interrupt, but where are they coming from?"

"They're down and out people, people with no hope, family, even citizenship. Many are refugees. Enticing promises of work and education, stability, and security are made. They come of their own free will, but the outcome is of course not as promised. They are coerced into working for starvation wages. Many of the females are forced into prostitution. They have no rights. We believe, although this is again circumstantial evidence, that someone involved in the ring, either Hunter or Irakli, perhaps Tommy Mitka, killed Kamala. Hunter has a golf cart that matches the tire tracks on the bridge in Baker Park."

"Why don't more run away?" Henry asked.

"Where to? They are never given visas and are told they will be sent back to where they came from. The alternative, to remain, is better than those propositions."

"What about the people in the superstore?" Kayla asked.

"Yes, many of that labor force are trafficked persons. Not all, but many. We discovered that the local management had nothing to do with the hiring. All employee decisions came from corporate. The local managers were shocked to find out that many of their employees were working without green cards.

"The Russian container ship that Hunter aborted in Toronto," Nick continued, "held ninety-five people. All died from exposure and lack of water. The Russian sailors will receive immunity from Canada."

"But what about all the people who haven't been accounted for?" Parker asked. "If it's an international ring, what about the rest of them?"

"You're right," Nick agreed. "The tentacles are many and far-reaching. We're continuing to track them down. It's going to take some time."

Kayla, Henry, and Parker remained silent. The information was overwhelming.

"Do you have any questions?" Nick asked.

"Do you know who attacked me at Beacon's Way?" Parker asked.

"No. That has not been determined yet. Obviously, someone working for Hunter."

"And who took down the stairs?" Henry asked.

"Again, nothing conclusive, but someone who worked for Hunter, no doubt."

Silence again. "Well, as I mentioned," Nick said, "we're having our press conference tomorrow. We'll give you all full credit, but it seems that you've been accruing a lot already."

"You're right," Parker said, smiling.

"So what's next for the team?" Nick asked, looking at Kayla. "Are you all going to just take a well-deserved break?"

"Well, funny you should ask," Parker responded, removing a packet from his backpack. "All this publicity has garnered more work for us. We've received requests from all over the country. We have letters of inquiry here from as far west as California, to New Orleans, Georgia, a town in Maine, and one from Boston. The team decided to go for the one in Boston. It's most urgent."

"Boston? So ... when will you be going there?" Nick asked.

"Soon. We've got some homework to do before we leave. We hope we are as successful there as we were here," Parker said.

"Oh. Well, what's the assignment, I mean, case? What's the problem?" Nick wanted to know.

"You've heard of the Alibi by Ghost case?" Parker asked.

"Of course. Who hasn't? I think it's a first," Nick replied, looking interested. "Oh," he continued, "you've been hired by the victim's family to dispute the alleged killer's statement that a ghost caused the grisly murder, not the professor."

"Um," Parker stalled. "Actually, we've been hired by the accused."

Nick tried to hide his surprise. "Ohhh. Well, I guess you do have some homework to do."

Nick drove up to find Kayla and Second Chance sitting on her stoop. It was late afternoon. The temperature was dropping. She was wearing a light sweater and was about to go get a jacket when she saw him and waved. Nick parked the car and came to join them.

"I hope you don't mind me just dropping by," he started. "I should have called but ..."

"I'm happy to see you, Nick. How did the press conference go?"

"As good as can be expected when your whole subject matter is grim and grimmer. How are you doing?" Nick petted Second Chance as he sat down. "How's Second Chance adjusting? Actually, how are you adjusting? Maybe the better question is how is the adjustment going?"

Kayla started to laugh. "It's great. I love him. Thank you so much for thinking of me."

"My pleasure. Have you thought about naming him Third Chance?"

"You never looked at Second Chance's papers, did you?"

"Noooo ... why? Is something wrong with him?"

"No. It's just that he's not a rescue dog. Hunter paid big bucks for a purebred and apparently had him trained by a professional trainer, right before he moved to Frederick. He obviously made up the rescue dog story to ingratiate himself to us all. So, Second Chance is the correct name."

"Jeez," Nick said, shaking his head. "Everything was a deception."

"Yeah. No kidding. Good thing the ghosts were able to communicate, huh?" The two sat silently for a couple of minutes.

Then, Nick said, "You know, Kayla, I was thinking about what you said about your hero, Dorothea Lange. How much you admired the work she did and what an impact she'd had on humanity."

"Yes?" Kayla was impressed that Nick had remembered.

"Well, if you think about it, you've already had a huge impact. I mean, your photos helped to bring this human trafficking ring down."

"Everybody did that. I mean Parker, Henry, you, Eleanor."

"Don't be so modest. I'm just pointing out the obvious."

"Well, thank you. What's in the grocery tote?" Kayla asked, changing the subject, to avoid the attention.

"Oh." Nick pulled out a hockey parka. It had "BC" on the front.

"It's kind of old," Kayla said, laughing, "and huge. Oh." She stopped. "Boston College?"

"My alma mater. I played throughout college. I thought you might want to have it in case it gets cold," he added as he placed it on her shoulders.

"Wow, Nick. Thanks."

"Again, my pleasure. So, are you looking forward to going up there?"

"Well, I'm not looking forward to experiencing any blizzards, so thanks again for the parka, but yeah, the case sounds intriguing."

"You're taking Second Chance?"

"Of course. He's a member of the team now. We're driving up in the van."

"Great. Well, now that you know that I graduated from BC, I should also tell you that I have lots of friends, lots of contacts, and lots of colleagues in Boston. I visit often. Should you need any help …?"

Kayla laughed again and reached over to give him a kiss. "I'm sure we will. You can count on it."

CPSIA information can be obtained
at www.ICGtesting.com
Printed in the USA
LVOW11s0610261217
560813LV00001B/52/P